Stolen Miracles

and

Other Deeds of Dubious Intent

Stolen Miracles

and

Other Deeds of Dubious Intent

A Novel

Cheri Cramer Johnson

Jan,
Thank you for
your help.
Cheri C. Johnson

SANTA FE

Sunstone books may be purchased for educational, business, or sales promotional use. For information please write: Special Markets Department, Sunstone Press, P.O. Box 2321, Santa Fe, New Mexico 87504-2321.

Book and Cover design › Vicki Ahl
Body typeface › Book Antiqua
Printed on acid-free paper
∞
eBook 978-1-61139-251-7

Library of Congress Cataloging-in-Publication Data

Johnson, Cheri Cramer, 1945-
Stolen Miracles and Other Deeds of Dubious Intent : a novel / by Cheri Cramer Johnson.
pages cm
ISBN 978-0-86534-658-1 (softcover : alk. paper)
1. Miracles--Fiction. 2. Grief--Fiction. 3. New Mexico--Fiction. I. Title.
PS3610.O3239S76 2014
813'.6--dc23
2014003089

WWW.SUNSTONEPRESS.COM
SUNSTONE PRESS / POST OFFICE BOX 2321 / SANTA FE, NM 87504-2321 /USA
(505) 988-4418 / ORDERS ONLY (800) 243-5644 / FAX (505) 988-1025

For my family
and to women everywhere,
who change the world,
but whose deeds
go unrecognized and unsung.
My hat is off to you.

Introduction

There is a very old tradition of storytelling in New Mexico which delights in embellishing the tales of ordinary people. There is joy when listeners find they play a role in the adventure. Laughter is one of the major results, as all listen and learn how interconnected they are as the situations and predicaments unfold.

There is always time for the interruption "...remember when" or "you forgot the part about abuelo..."

These stories fill winter nights and family gatherings. The enchanted landscape of New Mexico always plays a part, and traveling long distances is accepted as natural.

For those of you who don't live in New Mexico, we remind you that the Spanish have been here for 400 years or more, and the Native Americans—well, for them you have to add at least another zero!

Some of you may conclude that this "almost true" story is, like green chile, an acquired taste.* But be warned, if you get into it and acquire the taste, you will find yourself, like me, with a lifelong addiction for folks who take life as it comes and who love and care for each other and the land they share, have shared, and expect to share in the future.

Gracías a Dios no somos un Neuvo York o un Los Angeles!

*Chile is the plant; chili is made with beans and meat; Chile is a country in South America; and chilly means you're cold!

Persons of Interest

Los Santos

Estrellita (Lita) Cordova
Benito (Ben) Cordova (grandson)
Christina (Tina) Cordova (granddaughter)
Kip Stokes (Tina's boyfriend)
Emilio Maestas (deacon/woodcarver)
Jovita Esquivel (gardener)
Virgie Torres (goats/cheese)
Fr. Mondragon
Amy Jenkins (jeweler)
Sunshine (Sunny) Jenkins (Amy's daughter)

Minor Players

Tessie (café)
Leonard (Lenny) Salazar (police)
Hugh Baughman (rancher)
Sweetie Baughman (his daughter)
Jorge Gomez (musician)
Epie Vallejo (farmer)
Kitty Gato, Glow, and Tima (pets)

Law Enforcement

Luis Fernandez
Lydia (his wife)
Jerry Lucero
Mitch Sweeny (FBI)
Nate Courtney
Carol and Rowan (agents)
Frank Quintana

Professionals in New Mexico

Ellen Hadley (nurse)
Charles Godwin (art appraiser)
Tito (garage owner)
Floyd Patrick (lawyer)

The South Valley (Albuquerque)

Manuel (Mano) Baca
Sadie Baca (his wife)
Junior Baca (his son)
Mona (Junior's wife)
Tres Baca (Mano's grandson)
Lorenzo Gurule (Mona's brother)
Mrs. Sosa (Mano's neighbor)
Mr. Skettering (Mano's lawyer)
Raul Apodaca (Al Luna's thug)
Manny Archuleta (Al Luna's thug)
Ricky Travis (cyclist)
Karla (Ricky's girlfriend)
Alex Serna (pig farmer, artist)

Santa Fe

Dolores Maldonado
Petey (her brother)
Millie Saavedra (Dolores' neighbor)
Al Luna (Mano's partner, in prison)
Prison warden
Sid Salazar (a guard)

East Coast

Ronnie DeMarco (funeral director)
Dominic DeMarco (his uncle)
The Gamboa Family
Enrico Gamboa (the Godfather)
Carlo Fierro (his negotiator)

Real People—Really!

Mary Ann Weems, Gallery Owner - Albuquerque
Ernest Thompson, Ernest Thompson Doors - Albuquerque
Sarah Blumenschein, Artist - Albuquerque
Kathy Glidden, Artist - Albuquerque
Steve Hanks, Artist - Albuquerque

Prologue

Newark, New Jersey, June

After the last of the family and friends left the viewing, Mr. Ronnie DeMarco of the DeMarco Funeral Home places a tissue over the face and lowers the lid on the casket. He puts a small wedge near the lock so the lid won't close all the way and spoil the makeup on Mrs. Bartaluchi.

It's time to go home and reply to those emails about the money he had sent to New Mexico. The money the Baca family says never arrived. He goes from room to room, checking the lights, the thermostats, the flowers.

When all is as it should be, Mr. DeMarco locks the back door and heads toward his gray Mercedes in the parking lot. He's proud of that car. He knows it is good for business. People like seeing him drive up or leave a service after paying his respects. It makes them feel important.

He beeps the locking mechanism and steps into the night, away from the building

"Not so fast," says a raspy voice from the shadows.

"Please step over here, Ronnie," says a mellow voice. When Ronnie turns, he is looking down the long barrel of a rifle. "Move, man," says the first voice.

"Take my wallet," stammers Ronnie, turning from one man to the other. His hands shake as he tries to undo his watch. "Here, take this. It's a Rolex."

"Ronnie, we're not gonna shoot ya."

Relief floods over Ronnie.

"This evening is a lesson that when ya deal in drugs, ya don't mess with the Bacas."

"But I never..."

"Callate la boca!"

"That's right, you never came up with the money."

"But I did!"

"Besa mi culo, gringo liar."

"The money left here and was dropped there on Saturday! Have we ever stiffed you? I swear, the DeMarcos don't..."

"The only thing in that hole was beans." The rifle pokes him in the back.

"No, no...it was money!"

"Shut up, cabron," snarls the guy with the gun.

The shadow man steps forward and duct tape is slapped across Ronnie's mouth. "Just stand there. We don't wanna hurt you."

Ronnie watches as his wrists are bound with the same silver tape. What are they going to do? If he tries to run, they'll shoot him. They tape his ankles and a hand reaches out to steady him.

He tries to say something, but can't understand himself. He begins to cry.

"Pick him up," says the little man with the rifle. "Put him in the middle of the parking lot. I'll get the truck. You set up the camera. Mano don't wanna miss this. Rapido!"

"Si."

The hands holding Ronnie upright let go and he drops to the ground.

As Ronnie DeMarco squirms and moans on the pavement, struggling for air, the tap-tap of receding cowboy boots on the pavement is drowned out by the rumble of a large truck backing across the lot toward him. It's about to run over him. He feels his bladder let go.

The truck pulls forward and stops. Lights flood the parking lot.

"Ahora!" yells one of the men. "Watch this, you prick!"

Ronnie's eyes bulge. He tries to scream. He can't breathe. He chokes as the bed of the truck tilts and six tons of dry, dusty pinto beans rain down on him. It only takes a few seconds for the mountain of beans to cover him, and a few more before the truck is empty.

Under the pile, Ronnie DeMarco has stopped breathing, his ribcage crushed beneath the weight.

Dust rises in the damp night air, aglow in the headlights. The parking lot shimmers in silence.

Doors slam.

The headlights move off.

Somewhere, a cicada sings.

Taos, New Mexico, the Previous October

Estrellita Maria Sofia c'de Roybal y Cordova, widow, grandmother, and heir to the Roybal Land Grant, bolted through the doors of her late husband's law office so quickly that she hadn't even buttoned her coat or pulled on her gloves. She caught her breath in the cold and moved around the corner of the entrance out of the wind, but, more importantly, out of sight. She stood on the sidewalk and leaned against the adobe building.

She felt foolish. She should have stayed inside where it was warm to wait for her grandson to pick her up, but she couldn't have stayed in that office with Ben's old law partner, Floyd Patrick, another minute.

She had waited on him to return after lunch and had caught up with the news the office manager, Silvia Piño, had about her new house.

Then she had to wait while Floyd rummaged through the papers on his desk. All the while, the eight-point buck above his head studied her with his glassy, impervious gaze as if he knew all her secrets. Lita was uncomfortable thinking the trophy was another way for Floyd to intimidate her, until she noticed his fishing license dangling from one of the prongs on the buck's right antler. She wanted to scream as Floyd reclipped and reshuffled documents. All this only to learn there was nothing to be done.

What did he mean? There was always something that could be done!

She had only wanted enough money to fix the church roof. It should be found from somewhere within the land grant account itself, or from her private account, or the insurance Ben had.

Floyd had said, "You can't commingle monies."

Floyd said she could sell "some land. Fix the church and have money left for Benito's college! The insurance was a company account."

Now if that wasn't commingling!

She dropped her book bag and briefcase at her feet and fastened her coat with thin, trembling fingers.

"Calm down, Lita," she told herself. "It won't do to have Benito see you upset."

She worked on her gloves and pulled her collar close, not knowing whether it was to keep out the icy air or keep in her anger.

Floyd was like an old dog: useless, content to lay by the stove. Where had the fire in his belly gone? She still had hers!

He could have shown more interest. She needed to know what the Bureau of Land Management was up to, and he had laughed at her concerns! He knew she always worried about the BLM!

He didn't have to worry, it wasn't his problem. His ancestors hadn't walked the land grant and pledged their lives to the land and its inhabitants for the past four hundred years.

She inhaled deeply and let out a long breath. Imagine, he suggested she get away, take a cruise, or go to Europe! What was he thinking?

He knew she had to make a home for Benito and make sure there was a place for Tina when her granddaughter grew tired of the big city.

Didn't he keep up with her problems enough to realize she would have to pay the taxes on the Esparzas' place again this year, as they'd lost their apples to a late freeze, and alfalfa to too much rain?

Inside, Floyd piled the documents for Silvia Piño to put away. He wondered if Lita would ever let go of her worries. Since Ben died, she'd lived in constant fear that something would go wrong or that her life would change. He knew one thing for sure: If Lita Cordova hadn't married that cold son of a bitch, she'd be happier.

Poor Lita didn't have a chance to have a life. She'd inherited that damned land grant and all the responsibilities that went with it. Then Ben came along and plucked her up to help further his agenda.

Knowing her, she'd be crazy by now if she hadn't hooked up

with Ben. She had always trusted her husband to take care of the land.

Floyd patted his leather vest pocket and pulled out his tobacco pouch. Yup, old Ben had a zealous hatred for the BLM that just about matched Lita's fear of them.

He used to envy them working so close like they did. Still, it was a shame that she never got to be really appreciated as a woman, as pretty and as feisty as she was.

He drew on his pipe as he held the flame over the bowl and inhaled, knowing that Ben Cordova had left his wife in the best and safest position, legally speaking, that she could wish for. He exhaled slowly.

Too bad she didn't believe it.

One thing for sure, that insurance policy that Ben had taken out on himself for the practice, which had ended up taking care of his secretary, Silvia Piño, like he had promised—that was one thing that he would never let Lita know about.

Outside, Lita took another deep breath. If Ben were still alive, he would have been on top of the situation. She would have known what was going on with the money and the taxes. The church would have been taken care of. The two of them had worked well together, talking and planning ways to keep the land grant in one piece and the government out of the picture. She pushed her hands deeper into her pockets and straightened her back. Estrellita Cordova hadn't caved in yet, and she wasn't about to start. She still had steel in her spine! She would have a smile for her grandson when he drove up. Yes, she would be just fine when she was out of Taos and on her way to Los Santos.

Owen Wills was getting a headache.

No, he'd had one for two days now. Its name was Millicent Quinn Brown.

She had descended on the library last month, straight from Boston. She was doing a dissertation on the "Reading Habits of Indigenous and Hispanic Peoples of Northern New Mexico." Thank you.

Her nasal "Baasten" accent set everyone's teeth on edge.

Millicent Q. B., better known to the staff as "Millie the Quintessential Bitch," had driven the rest of the staff to distraction and had poked her dripping nose into everyone's files.

She kept a running verbal list on how lacking the library was and what a sorry condition the books were in.

Apart from the world of her books, her life was negative. She couldn't abide chiles, red or green, and everything else caused an allergy.

"How could sane people stand living in such mean conditions? My Gawd! The buildings here are made of mud! Mud, for Christ's sake!"

Didn't anyone around here know what the word "culture" meant?

The head librarian was out with a strange flu, the East coast type, and the rest of the staff kept their distance by feigning similar symptoms.

Owen had finally been stuck with her for her last week in residence. She had spent yesterday and today with him in the tri-county bookmobile, putt-putting down the roads, putting down the stops, and the readers.

She had been unimpressed with Mora and Truchas.

Questa had been worse.

Owen didn't think she'd stopped her mantra of woe once to look at the beauty around her.

At least he'd given Emilio Maestas the heads-up last month that an albatross would be coming along today to Los Santos.

Thinking in nautical terms for a moment, he decided she could aptly be called a pain in the aft.

Winter was coming. The blue skies of morning had given way to on-and-off spits of sleet.

Owen jiggled the heater in the bookmobile and hoped his wife, Miriam, would have something hot for supper. In a perverse way, he was glad the weather had turned. It was good that the chamisas were all blown and most things looked dead. He admitted to himself that he was pleased that the low clouds hid the majestic peaks. It was as if they were conspiring to keep anything of beauty from this nasty creature. He smiled to himself, knowing she would never see the orchards in bloom or be here to smell the lilacs as they hung over the fences. Nor would she ever glimpse the eye-popping colors of the geraniums as they filled most window sills in the village.

On second thought, he could almost feel sorry for her. Millicent Q. Brown would be gone long before the faralitos were lit. She would miss the magic.

Going up and around the last bend, he called back to her, "Ah, here we are in beautiful Los Santos!" Driving by the lone gas pump at the Allsup's, he slowed down in front of the Dairy Queen. How long had that been closed? Benito Cordova waved to him as he passed. He's probably going after his grandmother. She was a strange one, Lita Cordova. No, not strange, surmised Owen, but rather out of place. Sure, she'd grown up here, but she sure didn't read like the rest of them. She checked out books that most of them had never heard of, except maybe for the mysteries. She liked those. He'd warned Millicent not to tape or question Lita if anyone else was around. He didn't want her to think he'd ever talked about her.

He turned left at the little plaza, and there they were in front of the café, his faithful readers, with a bank of clouds rolling down the mountain behind them. If they didn't hurry, it would swallow them completely.

For a moment, Owen felt like a superhero, arriving just in time, saving all humanity from being ingested by mysterious forces. He should change his fantasy fiction diet and go back to biographies.

Tessie's Café shielded the library patrons from some of the wind, but they were paying no attention to it. It was whipping bits of trash down the street as he pulled up.

Deacon Emilio Maestas was sitting on a bench with his sheepskin coat open to shield five-year-old Sunny Jenkins from the wind. The church deacon was taking his role of protecting the flock literally.

They had been sharing a bag of Fritos while they waited. Sunny had been learning a new word for the day, or for the moment. She followed Emilio around like the puppy she so desperately wanted.

In order to save himself from her incessant questions, he was entertaining both of them by directing their conversation. At least he could limit somewhat the directions her inquisitive mind would take. Some days she learned as many as five or six new words.

Often, Owen was flabbergasted by her speech. When she started school, her teachers would probably want to wring Emilio's neck.

"Look at that dirty old bum! I bet he's a child molester. Doesn't her mother worry about her?" hissed Millicent.

Owen sighed. Millicent had been eager to meet the master santero, and here he was along with their good friend, Sunshine Jenkins.

Little Sunny's mom was an artsy jeweler, a retro hippie, really, who sold her work to tourists in the summer and the odd skier in the winter. Too bad she didn't seem to pay much attention to her daughter. There was Sunshine, looking blue in faded jeans, a thin cotton sweater and her favorite pink jellies on her feet.

Personally, Owen thought Emilio looked like he needed a shave, but that didn't detract from his thoughtfulness in caring for the little girl.

His two friends had their heads together, seemingly oblivious to the bookmobile.

"Now, tell me this morning's word," he urged. "Can you spell our new word?"

Coyly, she shook her head and shrugged her bony shoulders.

"B-a-m-b-o-o-z-l-e. And what does it mean?"

"To twick, for fun or pwafit."

"Close enough, my snaggletoothed scamp. Now let's see what Mr. Wills has for us today, and don't say anything. Today you are going to have the rare opportunity of seeing a bamboozler in action."

He carefully closed the Frito bag and put it in a wide pocket. He winked at the girl as he pulled a tattered book from beneath his arm. "Let's have some amusement, mi chica."

Sunny had two books with her. She had had them for some time. She was still trying to decide whether or not to trade in *Clifford the Big Red Dog* and *Curious George* or take them home again. It wasn't as if she didn't have them memorized, but if she returned them, it would be giving up good friends. Sunny knew friends were hard to find.

Owen opened the door and let down the steps.

He nodded to Jovita Esquivel and her cousin, Virgie Torres, who were jabbering away at each other.

He grinned at Sunny and lifted her up the steps as he wondered what the women were having such an animated conversation about and how they could gesticulate with such cumbersome bags.

He'd find out soon enough, as they were usually talking business or gossiping about their neighbors and felt free to share their insights.

The two of them had started making cheese a few years back when Jovita had bought some goats. Her nephew, a county extension agent down in Doña Ana, had told her goats had a higher nitrogen content in their manure.

Jovita was a gardener, and nitrogen was what she wanted. She had started out soaking manure in water to make a "tea" out of it for her garden and the church's flower beds. She called it G.M.T. Now everyone called it "tea."

She sold gallons of the stuff. The goats had taken over her backyard and had multiplied. She decided the goats were good for more than tea and cabrito stew, which Virgie's husband hated, so Jovita and Virgie had started making cheese. For some strange reason, **Queso de Cocina** had taken off, and now their cottage industry was selling cheeses to chichi restaurants in Taos and Santa Fe.

Owen was shutting the door to keep out the cold when Benito pulled up behind to drop off his grandmother.

Lita joined her friends, and Owen noticed she was as quiet as the others were talkative. He snorted. He knew she was their silent partner in the cheese business, but really, wasn't this carrying things a bit far? She kept the books and had little else to do with the business.

Lita hadn't wanted anything to do with **Queso de Cocina**, but Virgie's mother's first father-in-law had been married to Lita's father's half-sister's cousin, and family helped family, after all.

Owen knew Lita owned a large ranch northeast of town which she leased to a rich Tejano whose daughter, Sweetie, visited on vacations and had a crush on Ben Cordova.

Some time back, when the goats were overtaking both Jovita's and Virgie's places, Lita bartered a lower meadow and sheds for the Nubians in exchange for all the extra dung Jovita didn't need for her liquid fertilizer. Hugh Baughman, the Texan, used his share to enhance his upper pastures. He fed wild game up there, some of which were exotics he shipped in for hunting parties with his rich friends. Everybody was happy. Virgie even took Hugh samples of cheeses when they were ripe. Owen mused that Lita was a one-woman department of economic development.

Virgie took a last drag from her cigarette and put the half-smoked butt into a mint tin. The butt would go into the tea. Jovita had read somewhere that tobacco juice helped keep munching bugs away from young plants, and now had everyone she knew saving butts for her.

Virgie pushed up her thick glasses and pounded on the bookmobile door.

"Mr. Wills, you want coffee? We're going inside while they do business." She nodded toward Emilio and Sunny.

"Love some; just black." He looked at Millicent. She wrinkled her nose and tapped her thermos of green tea.

"Just one," he called after them, and turned to his first customers of the day.

Inside Tessie's Café, Virgie kept up her banter. "What you gonna get, Lita?" Not waiting for a reply, she hurried on. "Jovita's got a hold on a garden book. She's bringing back her Anne Rice. Don't know how she can read that creepy trash! I'm here to bring back some bodice rippers and see what's new. Four coffees, Tessie. We'll doctor them up ourselves."

"To go," piped in Jovita. She turned to Virgie. "Remember, Emilio said we were to check out or put a hold on something really highbrow today. He's playing tricks on that woman with Mr. Wills."

Lita pulled out her who-done-its and said she hoped to find an Iris Johansen. She was fascinated by the way the main character, Eve Duncan, the forensic sculptress, was able to put the pieces of a person together from a few scraps of information. All she needed was three or four bits of bone. Lita admired the forethought that went into each decision. It was like that Gil Gresham on CSI.

Lita had the best television reception in town because of her satellite dish. Jovita and Virgie always came over on Thursday nights and they watched it together. Lita enjoyed the problem-solving and the way the actors carefully used their latex-gloved hands to work with the evidence. Jovita liked the gore, and Virgie waited each week to see if any of the characters would fall in love.

Inside the bookmobile, Millicent switched on her tape recorder. Emilio motioned for Sunny to go first.

"Well, if it isn't my favorite, Sunshine Jenkins," said Owen. "And how may I assist you today?" Sunny just grinned, showing off her empty space.

"My goodness, have you chewed on my books till you've worn away a tooth?" he teased.

She giggled and wiggled like a favorite puppy.

"I swear you wore that tooth away on my books! Tell me, my friend, when did this event take place?"

Millicent rolled her eyes.

"Lath Thaterday. It juth came out when he tied a stwing an' thlammed the door," she lisped while patting Emilio's arm. Millicent harrumphed.

"Goodness, Sunny. That is an amazing story! Perhaps it might just be possible, since I'm a lucky man and you're so brave, to persuade you to trade your books for say, *The Casual Observer*? Tina Bee is a quiet charmer who learns a great deal by watching. Or, how about..."

The conversation, interspersed with giggles and sighs, continued for some time till Millicent interrupted. "According to the records, her two books are overdue."

Sunny looked at Owen and hugged her books closer, her tongue nervously working at the empty space.

"Now, Miss Brown, we don't want to deprive anyone of their good friends, do we?"

There; that seemed to shut the harpy up.

"Tell you what, Miss Jenkins, why don't you take this book, too," he said, stamping *The Casual Observer* card and handing the small book over.

Then he let her wheedle a copy of *Molly Mullet* from him. *Molly Mullet* was a keeper. He knew she would love Molly, who could do things no man could. Molly could slay dragons! He'd picked it out of the discard bin at the main branch. He made a habit of going through the worn-out, dated, or politically incorrect books to give to kids on his route. Sunshine had received more than one such keeper.

Millicent, bless her blundering, tried to make amends with the child. "Honey, did it hurt when you lost your tooth?" she asked with a simper.

Sunny looked her straight in the eye and said, "My lachrymose glands didn't drip."

Emilio was next. As he stood up to the counter, an abashed Miss Brown asked, "Your name?"

Emilio turned and gave Owen a wink. "Rudolpho Mendoza Pendejo."

He turned back to Owen. "I got this here book last summer," he said with a thick accent. "I got it for my boy over in Truchas." He slammed down a worn copy of *Zen and the Art of Motorcycle Maintenance* on the counter. "It didn't help him no way to fix his chopper!"

Millicent gasped. Owen bit his tongue.

"Well, Mr. Pendejo, we may need to put in a request. What kind of bike does he have? Indian? Harley?"

"That last one. He got it off a biker user that needed to pay off his supplier down in Chimayo. He wanted too much, but my boy Rico got him down to a bus ticket to Vegas and a hundred instead. He even got my nephew Sheldon to take him to Albuquerque. The dealer, he come an' put sugar in the gas tank. He don't know..."

Owen was having a coughing fit.

"We have no 'Pendayhoe' on record" sniffed Millicent, her face showing her disgust.

"Sure, I got this one down in Taos," snarled Emilio. "What you take me for, some estúpido who don't know how to drive? I jest wanna save gas on this here no-good book!"

Owen was still coughing. Tears were beginning to roll down his pink cheeks.

"Sign here, please. I'll fill in the correct information and try to get you a better, er, more practical book."

"Gracias, Señor Wills."

"Oh," said Owen, "if you see Mr. Maestas, would you please tell him my wife and I are looking forward to having him for dinner next Friday."

Miss Brown would leave on Thursday.

"If I see him, I'll tell him. What time you want him there?"

"Seven would be just fine."

"Okay. Come, chica, hold onto your books."

Owen lifted down a giggling Sunny into the arms of a grinning deacon and braced himself for the three women. He heard Sunny laughingly squeal to her big friend, "You weally bamboozled him good. You talked tho funny! He doethn't know you don't have a boy at all!"

Behind him inside the bookmobile, Millicent was screaming something about vile smelly creatures. The day was getting better.

He gave the all-clear signal and waited for the women. Virgie handed him his cup as the three went ahead of him. He could smell her new permanent over the strong coffee as she hopped aboard. He'd have to come up with something clever to say about her God-awful frizz. Jovita slowly hauled her bulk up the steps and waddled down the aisle. Lita slipped in behind her large friend.

The wind came up as he stepped back up into the van. He inhaled the aroma of coffee mingled with the smell of approaching snow. He looked at the sky and checked his watch. He'd give them twenty minutes.

He couldn't wait to tell his wife, Miriam, about that quintessential rascal, Emilio.

"Ooh, *The Chalice and the Dagger*. That's the one where..."

"You've already read that one, Virgie. Go on. How about these new ones?"

While the other two women mulled over their decisions as carefully as if they were actually paying for them, Lita quietly asked, "Did my holds come in?"

"Of course, Mrs. Cordova, two new Johansens, Philip Yancey's *The Jesus I Never Knew*, and..."

"Thank you," interrupted Lita as she slipped the mysteries over the last book, *Liberalism is a Mental Disorder.*

"You gonna make Father Mondragon look bad," teased Jovita. "What you need that for?" She was eyeing the Yancey book.

"Oh, I'd just heard something..."

It was bad enough that her friends knew she did Bible study and honestly read the Book. After all, she was Catholic, but Lita had picked up the habit when her father had sent her away to be educated all the way to Albuquerque. She had boarded at Menaul School, a Presbyterian mission school. She had left home after her mother was gone, really gone. Mama, who'd really been gone ever since Lita's older brother died in a lumber accident, hadn't died for a few more years herself.

Some people said it was because they had had a bruja for a maid, but Tizto hadn't been a witch, just an Indian whose husband beat her regularly.

Yes, they'd probably shun her if they knew she actually prayed to God, bypassing the Virgin Mary altogether. At school, she had learned to be comfortable doing so. Perhaps it was because her mother had been absent and her own papa cold that she had found comfort in just, she liked to think, knocking on God's door and visiting with Someone who would love her.

Stuffing her books into her bag, she thought that praying in both directions as she did was nothing compared to voting Republican! That was something that would really get her judged ready for the loony bin! Sure, she had John F. Kennedy's picture along with one of Our Lady hanging in her sala, just like everybody else. No one but her grandchildren knew she kept a picture of Ronald Reagan in a cowboy hat behind her bedroom door. She would look at it at night as she read in bed or listened to Michael Savage on the radio. She thought President Reagan was right, that people shouldn't wait for a handout from the government, but should get busy. She thought they should help each other.

She had switched political parties, in her heart, when her husband, Ben, had had his first heart attack. She'd blamed the politicos in Santa Fe for making his job as a lawyer so difficult. That, and they were always putting pressure on questionable judges to let their corrupt compadres go free. Ben had laughed at her. He'd laughed all the way to his grave.

Virgie put her new romance novels on the counter and handed

over the old ones. "Oh, Mr. Wills, do you have a copy of Robert Penn Warren's *All the King's Men*, by chance?" she cooed.

Owen blinked. Millicent's head swiveled around.

"Mrs. Torres, I'll have it here for you next month."

"Oh, you're just wonderful!" she purred.

Jovita placed her Anne Rices in the return bin and put a book on Chekhov and a Dostoevsky on the counter. She turned to Miss Brown and whispered, "Don't you just love the way Russian authors use words? I find them so much more poetic than American writers."

She turned to Owen. "Mr. Wills, there's a new book out on English country gardens. I don't remember the title, but it was mentioned in a lovely article not long ago. Do you think you could find it for me?" She smiled and played with her thick braid, which hung over her shoulder and lay heavily on her ample bosom.

English country gardens up here? You've got to be kidding, he thought. Only Jovita would think of a topic like that.

"Of course, Mrs. Esquivel. Is there anything else?"

"No, except you should have a book for me, *The Armchair Gardener*, I think. It's supposed to have lots of shortcuts, especially about watering. Lo siento, I almost forgot. Here's some tea for Miriam." She dug down into her heavy tote and pulled out a large bottle and passed it to him as if she were serving high tea.

Not to be outdone, Virgie set her bag on the floor and pawed through till she straightened up with a cloth-wrapped bundle in her birdlike hands. "Here's a cheese for Thanksgiving. You tell your wife to keep it cool."

"Mrs. Torres, you know just the right thing to keep us going!" Owen remembered. "Your new hairstyle is most becoming. I'll have to tell Miriam."

Millicent had that glazed look in her eye, like she needed a Heimlich maneuver, as she handed the stamped books back over the counter.

"Thanks. I'm glad you like it," simpered Virgie as she patted her wiry curls.

Exactly sixty-two minutes after arriving, Owen was pulling up the steps and waving a warm goodbye to the women. As he turned on the motor, Millicent reverted to type. "You're not going to eat that awful cheese, are you?"

"Oh, I'm sure Miriam can find something to do with it," replied Owen, thinking of the glorious cheese with wine and crackers, maybe in front of the fire. He didn't tell the albatross that it was probably the same kind of cheese she had raved about that first night, when the staff had taken her to dinner at the Taos Inn. She had been agreeable that night. "Well, I wouldn't let a nibble of it pass my lips!"

After a few moments of silence, she was back. "That tea smells dreadful. Miriam's surely going to pour that out!"

"She will at that, right on her houseplants. Everyone around here pays a fortune for that tea. It's Jovita's own concoction and does it ever work! She makes it special for different problems. Say you have water problems, she might add oxidized lignite. Serious gardeners around here swear by it. She even ships some of it out of state."

"But she called it 'tea'!" choked Millicent.

"Oh, that's because she steeps it and because of the color. It usually looks like green tea. It must be the alfalfa in the goats' diet."

Millicent looked sick.

"Speaking of goats, that old goat was dreadful! I wish Mr. Maestas had been there today. I wanted to ask him about his Santos I saw in the Smithsonian."

"Uh-huh," replied Owen. The bookmobile was making a winding downhill turn, but in his mind he was already at home sharing the day and the cheese with his wife.

"Mrs. Cordova is interesting, a bit of a mouse. She must read the things she does to get away from an awful life. Look there, it's starting to snow. Will it keep up?"

Small, inconsequential flakes were hitting the windshield. Owen thought back a few years to the time when a blizzard had caught him in Los Santos, and Lita had taken him in for two days. Two glorious days in her lovely home, with Indian rugs on the wooden floors, heavy handmade furniture, and real Maria Martinez pots sitting around—four hundred years of history under one roof. Lita said the big black polychrome vessels had been traded at her father-in-law's trading post, which was now Chuy's General Store, for two horse blankets by a man from San Ildefonso. He could close his eyes and taste the strong Mexican chocolate and smell the piñon fire. Two days of laughter and histories of the village. He had helped her cart food to her stranded neighbors. "Probably," he mumbled.

***

That night, Jovita called Lita. Tomorrow was Wednesday. They always cleaned the church on Wednesday mornings, and then took turns sprucing up on Saturdays. "You got lemon oil? I'm out."

"Sure, and I'll bring plenty of rags. Benito and I picked up more ammonia in town last week."

Kitty Gato rubbed against Lita's legs, just his reminder that he wanted out. She tucked the receiver under her chin and opened the door for him, shivering as a cold gust blew into her warm kitchen.

"Good. We should have it looking beautiful by noon. Say, wasn't that a hoot at the bookmobile today? I thought Owen was going to split a gut, but he played right along."

"What was that all about? Emilio didn't say anything to me."

"He probably forgot. Emilio just said the other day that that mujer with Owen today was making everyone upset at the main branch and thought we were all stupid jerks. Anyway, Virgie and I decided to add some class. Do you think we overdid it?"

"No, I'm sure not. I wonder what Emilio did?"

"Oh, he played right into her stereotype, dumb Mexican all the way. He told me all about it when I called to tell him what we did. I'll tell you mañana. I promise, you'll laugh till you cry!"

"Great. Benito picked up a letter from Christina today. I'll have something to share as well, Miss Showoff! Good night."

Lita gathered up her supplies and put them by the door. She put the letter and picture in her coat pocket so she wouldn't forget them. Kitty Gato was crying at the backdoor. He thought it was too cold to be out at his age. She wrapped her sweater closer about her before opening the door to let him in. It was still snowing lightly and getting colder. She turned out the lights in the front of the house and made her way to her grandson's room.

She stood in the doorway for a moment, watching Benito study. The radio was on and he didn't hear her. How much he looked like his father. How messy his room was!

He looked up and grinned. "I know, Mamalita. 'Clean your room before you leave the house!'"

She laughed. "No, Smarty, I just wanted to say sweet dreams and that the temperature's dropping and it's snowing. Probably won't last all night. Now that you've mentioned it, a little picking up wouldn't hurt."

"Okay, Beautiful, thanks. Oh, you wouldn't happen to know anything about the Punic Wars, would you? These names are killing me."

"No, muchacho, but I bet they can wait till tomorrow. I'm going to bed now. Don't stay up too late with your housecleaning. Oh, if it's really cold tomorrow, would you drop me by the church on your way to school?"

When he nodded, she left him to Rome and headed for her room and Michael Savage. She smiled, wondering if Dr. Savage would like to help take on the Bureau of Land Management. She liked it best when she had the morning to work by herself. She'd hurry through, hitting the high spots, especially the chancel, and then she'd light votive candles and pray for her loved ones. She always prayed for her husband, Ben, her son, Phillip, and his beautiful wife. Oh, she prayed, too, for the living, for her grandchildren, Christina and Benito.

Albuquerque, the South Valley

The same Tuesday that Owen Wills and Miss Brown were enjoying Los Santos, Officer Nate Courtney sat hunkered over surveillance paraphernalia. He was in a tool shed across from Manuel Baca's place, down in Albuquerque's South Valley. The morning mist over the Rio Grande had burned off early and the clear blue sky hadn't seen a cloud all day. Some Sandhill cranes had flown over about lunch. Nate marked time by the birds. He was here by the time the neighborhood roosters crowed. Peacocks and peahens had screamed like injured cats till someone fed them. Down the road, the guineas, those great watch birds, screeched from their perches in the trees at cars, at dogs, at anything that moved. Dogs in this area barked at strangers, but rarely moved from their spots in the sun. Too bad guineas weren't dogs. Crows had come in the late morning, to work over the windfalls. Next week, he bet he'd be smelling piñon smoke. This weather couldn't last. It was a long, late Indian summer. When the wind was right, he would get dizzy from the smell of rotting fruit in the next orchard. He wished the sheep would hurry up and finish them off. Still, the aroma of bad apples reminded him that it was almost supper time. Darn, he'd forgotten, he'd have to hit the grocery store on the way home if he was going to eat more than fast food.

He was jolted from his reverie when the phone vibrated in his pocket. He quickly set his empty cup down on the orange crate table and snapped open his unit, simply saying, "Courtney."

"When are you going to call in, Nate?" It was the voice of his boss and friend, Luis Fernandez. "We've been out there way too long. The feds need something on this drug investigation, pronto."

"I'm just about out of juice," he answered, referring to his Palm Pilot, "but have you checked the email? I sent one at ten when Mona picked up Sadie and again at eleven nineteen when they came back," he explained. "Didn't think you'd want to know about the neighbors driving home or the after-school birthday party three places down at the Sosas'. I emailed again when Mona left at twelve forty-six and Mano and Sadie came out and changed the flowers in front of their Virgin Mary of the Bathtub."

"That's an Our Lady of Guadalupe, Nate."

"Whatever." Nate yawned as he scratched his rusty stubble. "Today, it's red and pink roses. Seems they change them every saint's day or something."

"Nate they're supposed to be red roses. Always red. Maybe this is it? Why don't you and Jerry trade off following them to Mass. Mano might be meeting someone.

"Nate, this could be a can of worms There are over three thousand family units in that parish. Checking them all out could get out of hand. Last week, for example, a fellow from St. Ann's came by and took pictures, remember? Seems the church's going to do a story about the Bacas' shrine in the church newsletter. Anyway, old Mano made poor Sadie move those flowers around three or four times. I liked the way she'd done them in the first place. He just stood there with his oxygen tank, poking at her with his cane."

"Poor Sadie, I'd hate to live with him," said Luis.

"Me too. He did help her get back up, but I think it was just so he could lean on her to help him up the step." Nate's jaw-popping yawn cracked over the line.

"Hang in there. Jerry should be there by the time your shift is over," cut in Luis. "Sure wish you had gotten something new for us, Nate. We need a break in this case yesterday."

"Yeah, yeah, hold on yourself. Here comes something. Never mind, only three lowriders and that long-distance biker. He's making his daily rounds. Usually he rides by in the mornings. He must'a had a big night, or maybe he overdosed on vitamins. I wonder how many miles that kook puts in every week? Well, they've gone on by. Okay, see you in the morning. Hey, I'll send another email."

Nate cut the connection and stretched the best he could in the cramped space. The little shed was in the corner of a one-acre field.

Come spring, it would probably be planted in alfalfa. He sure wanted to be out of there by then. Hopefully, the case would be closed. If not, maybe they could find another spy master. His allergies would be killing him by then.

He hated this kind of surveillance. His partner, Jerry Lucero, was home sick, or else one of them would have followed Sadie and her daughter-in-law. He knew where they'd gone, though. The three paper sacks had plainly been from Smith's Grocery and there were two blue plastic bags. Those would be from Dolly's, a little shop on Isleta, just down and across the boulevard from the pharmacy.

He poured more coffee, propped up his feet, and watched the old adobe and the cottonwoods. Since it was November, most of the leaves were gone. He'd been here for almost two months and had watched them turn from green to gold to brown and fall. Now the huge gnarled trunks loomed protectively over the south side of the low house across the road. Bet it sure had made a difference in the summer, before air conditioning. Nate appreciated passive solar. The old house, being adobe or maybe terrones, would be cool inside in the summer and toasty in the winter. He wished his own place was adobe. His utility bills would go down. Best of all, he wouldn't be able to hear the couple in the next apartment fighting, or worse, making up on the other side of the wall.

At five fifteen, the lights went on across the way. Without binoculars, Nate could tell it was the kitchen. He could make out the woman moving about. Wonder what's for supper? Guess I'm not the only one. She's letting the dogs out. They'll get Alpo and leftovers, I bet. Mano's turned on the television. Nate could just discern the faint blue glow around the edge of the blinds. Did that need to go in the record? Why not? It would give him something to do until Jerry showed up.

Nate turned on his CD player. Dave Brubeck's jazz seemed out of place in the dusty shed. The tall, lanky policeman identified with the musician. He scrunched his six five frame into the camp chair, picked up his laptop, and began recounting the last few hours.

Wednesday morning was not going well for Nate Courtney's boss, Luis Fernandez. After an unorganized rush getting to work, he had just started organizing papers for the day's meetings when his wife called. Her car wouldn't start and she had an appointment with two couples from California who were looking for homes. He arranged for his car to be taken home. When he called her back to say the car was on its way, she let him know that a toilet had overflowed and the regular plumber wasn't answering. Who should she call?

"Just turn it off at the wall and I'll take care of it tonight." Was his life a Morton Salt commercial or what?

Now he was on his way to a meeting with the feds and narcotics regarding Manuel (aka Mano) Baca.

Nate had emailed his report last evening, and Josh had brought his in early this morning. Nothing had occurred during the night. The Bacas had watched the late news and then nothing. Why bother bugging that house at all?

He took time to make three copies of yesterday's reports and hit the head before the meeting.

He noticed how seedy he looked in the bathroom mirror. He needed a haircut. Maybe there would be something new today and no one would notice his unironed shirt.

For months, all the agencies had been on to Manuel Baca and had tagged the old codger as one of the two masterminds of the drug traffic in the state. So far, the evidence against Mano was nada, zip, and zero. His supposed partner was in the state prison in Santa Fe, but nothing was on the books concerning Mano. Al Luna might be tucked away for trafficking, but drug business in the state continued and was growing. The agencies couldn't get a fix on Manuel Baca and his relation to Luna.

He was smart. Luis had to give the old guy credit. Manuel didn't do business on the phone. He put nothing in writing. He didn't own a computer. He was too old and dumb, or maybe too smart, to use one.

Luis sighed as he stepped off the elevator on the fourth floor. He knew in his gut Manuel was the key to the growing drug business, but he needed proof. Maybe this morning there would be something. Please let there be something!

The other men were already there when he reached room 405. Frank Quintana, the mayor's familial appointee to the narcotics task force, was busy trying to get powdered sugar from a Krispy Kreme off his pants.

Too bad he didn't know it was on his chin, thought Luis.

He sat down across from Frank and wiped his own chin, trying to send a message to the good-looking young man. Frank, Adonis that he was, paid no attention. If he didn't watch it, he'd turn to fat by the time he was forty.

"Hey, Franko, Louis is trying to tell you you've got doughnut on your face," growled Mitch Sweeney. "Wake up and come to the party." Mitch was head of the FBI office here. In the two years they had been working together, Luis had come to understand Mitch was still in culture shock, and had never learned to trust the locals.

Luis had thought Mitch had been sitting there dozing or watching the steam rise from his Starbucks. Couldn't the feds drink department sludge like other people, grumbled Luis to himself, or was it yet another silent message of superiority? Luis reached for the coffee pot, or, rather, one of those white plastic things with a glass liner, ubiquitous to every office.

Maybe the feds were taught the knack of watching with hidden eyes and took classes to learn to say things to put everyone else down? Mitch gave himself away, though. He chewed his nails down to bloody stubs. Not so much in control after all, Luis thought with a barely concealed smile.

Luis looked around the room, trying to focus his thoughts. Jesus, he hated this room. The walls were that sick hospital green and the chairs around the scarred table were fiberglass, out of style when he came on the force. These were so old and beat up that they would catch and fray your pants if you weren't careful. He'd had that happen more than once. It was as if the room was sending the silent message, "If you would clear up these cases, we wouldn't have to pull you back." Most of all, he hated the notices and pictures on the walls, crimes and problems still unsolved, victims and felons everywhere you looked. It seemed there were more of them today.

After what passed for a few pleasantries, the men got down to business. They each passed around their reports. They'd give oral ones, but maybe somewhere in all this fodder would be the kernel of an idea, a clue that would open up the case for someone else, hopefully someone here today.

Business was the same as it had been since they sent Albert Luna up a year and a half ago. Manuel Baca (aka Mano) was the only thing on the agenda.

Mitch took over. "Okay, I'll go first. We know that drugs are running through this state like chickenpox through a kindergarten class. Most are still coming from California. The drugs on Alfred Luna when he was picked up were a match to those in the tissue sample from the OD in Queens, according to the chemical analysis done by both crime labs. We know the drugs were grown in Mexico and processed around Bakersfield. The pipeline has to go through New Mexico. Since our last meeting, drug use is up not only here, but in Colorado, Texas, Oklahoma, Nebraska, Utah, and Arizona. California supplies most of Nevada and Arizona and points north. Sure, Arizona has lots coming over the border from Mexico, and there are drops from Mexico all the time down the southern part of this state, but all our evidence points to this frigging area as a main conduit for drugs. Guys, we know the Baca clan is involved up to its eyebrows. You gotta give us something we can go on!" Mitch's florid complexion had taken on a decidedly claret shade as he spoke, and his voice had become louder as he warmed to his subject. Suddenly, he spluttered to a stop.

Luis didn't need to open his file. He had it memorized. Nevertheless, he opened it, hoping it made a professional impression. He didn't bother to look down, as this month's expenditures were about the same as last month's.

"The Bacas don't get out much anymore. They have a neighbor kid who does most of their grocery shopping. He tosses the list and we pick it up. It matches the store's records and the bank's. There are no notes on it. We've checked for ciphers and have found none. All we know is that Mano goes through lots of oatmeal and Metamucil, and Sadie has given up canning. She gets enough canned fruit to feed a school. They eat at least a dozen eggs a week. They have their meat delivered, either from Sammy's Meat Market or it comes from that pig farm that Mano still holds title to, at least till it's paid off, in a couple of years. Alex Silva, who almost owns the farm, has been doubling up on his payments a couple of times a year."

Mitch's head popped up at that, but Luis continued. "Alex is not married, and besides his food and an occasional bottle of wine, he only spends money on art supplies and his investments in Mexico."

"What investments in Mexico?" asked Frank, quick as a road-runner on a lizard.

"A house in Guanajuato and whatever goes into it. Mexican authorities say it's nice. He goes down a few times a year. Oh, yeah, he's bought into an art gallery down there, too."

Mitch piped in, "Where does he get his money? Could he be doing deals for Mano in this Guanajuato?"

"His records don't indicate that," answered Luis. "His paintings are getting more expensive. Seems he paints in two different styles. He does big, bright, bold ones for the Mexican market and more subdued, smaller ones for a gallery in Santa Fe. We know he's making twice as much on his paintings as he is on pork. If Mano is using him as a runner or silent partner, we don't know about it. There's just no evidence."

"Real expensive, his paintings?" asked Mitch.

"My wife says she's dying for one," he answered. "I told her she could have one when I died. My insurance should cover it."

Mitch turned to Frank. "Can you get with the Mexicans and get a wiretap in his place down there?"

"Sure, Mitch. My department will do it as soon as possible," responded Frank.

"Back to the Bacas," said Luis. "Sadie still dresses her own chickens. She told Mona she's afraid of bird flu and will only eat her own. The only fish they eat comes from Long John Silver's. Mona and Junior Baca bring it in on Fridays."

"Old habits are hard to break," smirked Mitch.

The other men ignored the remark.

"Mano had four oxygen tanks delivered this month. Check number 9784 was written for the exact amount. Mano had six doctor's appointments. Other checks were written to the usual. St. Anne's for one thousand, Knights of Columbus for seventy-five, and Casa Angelica got two hundred fifty."

"Why so much this month, Lou?" asked Mitch.

Luis cringed at the familiarity. Mitch had asked as if the answer would solve all their problems. "October is the month Sadie was adopted. Remember, they gave the same amount this time last year. Next month it will go back down to twenty. Then there was five hundred to the Z.F.C. alone."

"What's the Z.F.C., anyway?" Mitch was getting his dander up again.

Luis turned to Frank. "You grew up in the Valley. You explain."

Frank wiped his mouth again. "The Zapato Farm Club. They're a bunch of old geezers who grew up in the Valley when money was tight. There wasn't money for shoes or much of anything else when they went to school, back in the thirties. Anyway, that really got to them, especially the no-shoes part, so, in the late forties or early fifties they banded together and started the club. They've bought shoes for kids for years. Basically, they buy a couple of kegs and charge the members and their amigos five, ten bucks to come get drunk. They buy shoes with the proceeds. Trouble is, most of them are dead by now, or can't drink on doctor's orders, or are like Mano and aren't healthy enough to make the meetings. In short, I guess you could call it a poor man's Elks Club."

"Crap, gentlemen, what we have here is a South Valley good old boy!"

Luis bristled. Why did he let Mitch get to him? "We've had the house bugged and have learned that Mona thinks her husband, Junior, is having an affair, and Sadie is worried about grandson Tres' girlfriends. Oh, and Mano has hemorrhoids. We know Sadie has names for all her hens and calls her husband a few choice names when she feeds them."

He looked at his nails and was glad they didn't look like Mitch's. He continued, "We also know Sadie likes the soaps, both English and Spanish ones, and that Mano is still blaming Junior for the tomato worms he had last summer. We know he ordered hay and he's out of sorts because it hasn't come yet."

"What's he want hay for?"

"He spreads it all over his place to keep down the weeds and save on water."

"Yeah, but it's getting to be winter," said Mitch.

"Sure," added Frank, "but you know how crazy he is. Crazy and lucky. Remember how you got in and bugged his whole orchard, and then how Mano's doctor wouldn't let him spray anymore! Then the old cuss had everything pruned?"

Even Mitch had to laugh. "We lost all but two cameras and three mikes. All lopped off and taken to the dump. He's such a foxy old coot; do you think his real name is O'Baca? He just stays at home and things happen!"

Luis added, "Sadie gets out more, but she mostly goes for plastic flowers or yarn. She sometimes goes all the way to the Heights when there's a sale at Hobby Lobby and Junior's wife, Mona, can drive her. I bet her family is sick of afghans and sweaters and scarves."

"Frank, you've been covering Junior and Tres. What's happening with them?"

It was good to be off the hot seat and pass it on around the table.

"Man, what a life Junior leads! A cushy job with the highway department, and all he seems to do is drive up and down the highways listening to salsa on the radio. He really is something with his Rolex watch and all those gold chains. You'd think even he wouldn't want to look like a has-been disco dancer."

"Frank," Mitch growled, "get on with it. We all have other work to do!"

Frank gave Mitch a winning grin and went on, "Other than that, he sees his chippie on Tuesdays and he and Mona, and sometimes Tres, have dinner with the Bacas twice a week. He always has to give the receipts to his dad."

He held up his hand to stop Mitch from interrupting. "Yes, we've checked the trash, and the receipts check out, no notes or messages, just a controlling old man."

"What about Tres?" asked Luis.

"He's having problems with some of his courses and a few of his girlfriends. He's a whiz on the computer, though, so if he can't cut it at the graduate level in business, he can always get on with some startup company. Speaking of startups, he's thinking of starting up his own sideline. Since the State isn't banning pit bulls, Tres is looking into breeding them. He does love those dog fights. He likes cock fighting, too, but I imagine dogs are more macho to Tres than birds. He's into some heavy research right now, looking into bloodlines and doing a feasibility study. One of his sweeties was telling her friends all about it last week at a bar. Funny, one of my men happened to be sitting at the next table. If he continues at the rate he's going, he should have a website up in about three weeks."

"One of the secretaries in our office will have a bitch she wants to breed about then and she'll be looking for a stud," said Luis.

"Really?"

"No, Mitch, but we can access his computer that way."

"That might be promising, Franko. Keep on it."

Frank flashed a frozen smile.

Goodness, thought Luis, Franko doesn't like nicknames either.

Luis had something bothering him. "Fellows, we know what Mano writes checks for, but we're also aware that he mostly deals in cash. That's how he prefers to do business. He has his lawyer acting as his bank. Mr. Skettering, the attorney, takes the Bacas a cash allowance every month, and Mano banks some of it so he can write checks. Guys, we need to find a way to follow the cash."

"Now, Manuel Baca spends big bucks. Recently we've learned from the BLM that Mano has a real estate deal closing this week. It will be in the next report, detailed, of course. The Bacas have just paid cash for six hundred acres just north of Socorro on the bosque."

"Shit!" exploded Mitch, as he gathered up his papers. "That bastard's going to own more of New Mexico than Ted Turner!" He slammed out of the room, and they listened to him swearing his way toward the elevator.

Frank gave Luis a wink. "Thanks, my friend, for not bringing that up earlier in the meeting. By the way, had you thought what a perfect place that bosque will be to grow pot?"

"Ah, Franko, what do you take me for?" asked Luis.

Frank just laughed as he picked up the remaining doughnuts and started for the stairs. Exercise or avoidance, wondered Luis. He sat for a few moments looking over the other reports, jotting down notes while things were fresh.

How much land do the Bacas really own?

How is information passed?

What does Junior do?

Hay. Where does that come in, or does it?

What about the pig farm?

Plastic flowers?

Real estate in Mexico? New Mexico?

He carefully extracted himself from his chair and was relieved to note that he had not snagged his pants or jacket. Maybe the day was looking up.

***

Perhaps it was looking up for Luis, but Nate was spending his day off following Mano and his wife to Mass.

Nate had had to call his date and postpone their trip to Madrid, an artsy little town on the far side of the Sandias. Kristy had wanted to shop in their quaint shops.

Once again he'd watched Sadie and their neighbor walk up the ramp to the church with Mano following with his walker. Nate would have sworn Mano was looking longingly at every cigarette butt in the planter alongside the ramp.

Inside Nate sat in his usual place, behind and to the left of Sadie, so he could keep an eye on Mano during the service and reach over the pew when they'd left to check for messages in the missals. Mano had slept through the Mass, except when Sadie elbowed him. It was another nada morning. Nate thought this was the dumbest of his boss' ideas as he made his way down the aisle.

When he exited the church, he used his cell phone to call Kristy and say he was on his way.

"Oh, Nate, it's you. Listen, I'm going to do something else this afternoon." Her voice quivered, "Nate, I've decided to do something else with the rest of my life. You're a great guy and all, but I don't want to spend my life always coming in second to any man's job."

"But, Kristy, wait."

"I've waited too many times already. Good-bye, Nick."

He listened to the buzz tone and stumbled toward his car. He sat behind the wheel for the longest time looking at the bird droppings on his windshield. Finally, he started the engine, deciding the birds had summed up his life rather graphically.

Mass had been held earlier that Wednesday morning in Los Santos.

At about the same time as the meeting in room 405 was taking place in Albuquerque, Father Mondragon was propping open the front door of the church for the second time that day. It was hard to do. He thought that if the door were a chair, you'd call it rump-sprung. He didn't know how to explain it exactly. It was as if the door had grown in places and no longer fit comfortably. One hinge didn't seem to work. It was rather like a sinner reluctant to come to church. Maybe an outward manifestation of an inward evil. My, he was getting good this morning, except it wasn't the door's insides that were the problem! It was the whole old worn-out building. When it was gone, the land grant church would not be replaced by the Archdiocese, which had its own properties to repair.

Maybe he should pray for some historical society to take an interest. Lita Cordova couldn't afford to rebuild her family's church for the community. That was for sure...

He turned and smiled as he watched his magpies coming back to clean. How they talked! Well, at least Jovita and Virgie did.

Estrellita was quiet. In comparison, she could have been a nun. She hardly said more than "Father, I have sinned," at confession. Sometimes he thought she'd have to make things up to have anything to say that would keep him awake. The other two wouldn't last a minute under a vow of silence.

Sometimes he worried about Lita. She listened intently to his homilies, but seldom mentioned them. He'd known her for years now, but he wouldn't say they were close. She kept pretty much to herself. Maybe it was only that she carried herself in such a patrician manner.

I guess her aristocratic genes must come out, he thought, her being a Robles. A Robles had come to the New World with Oñate. They were one of the few families in the state who still owned most of their land grant, even if it was small and much of it leased, to boot.

After last night's light snow, it was cold and clear, but warm enough on the roof so that the snow had melted and water had dripped from the ceiling all during Mass. The three women genuflected and crossed themselves before starting to clean. They were still stepping over and around puddles, chatting about where to begin their work when he went in to get the buckets. Every time it snowed or rained, he had to put them out to catch the water. "Hail Mary, hear my prayer. We need a new roof."

While lifting a bucket, a sharp pain raced across his chest. Surely he wasn't in such bad condition that a gallon or so of water would feel like lead?

"Now, Father, don't go wasting that good water. We don't know if we'll get any more. I mulched last week, so you be sure to put it on the beds out front."

No wonder Jovita's esposo left her, he growled to himself. He was dizzy. He knew he would do as this child of God ordered, but for a moment he would rather pour it over her head. He could imagine the looks on their faces as the icy water dripped from Jovita's round face and divine vines sprouted up, growing and twining around her body. She and Virgie Torres would be speechless at last! Virgie's mouth would turn into a big red O, the same shape as her thick glasses. Lita would probably just sigh and continue into the church to work.

Shame on me for having such ideas, he thought, as he gave the women a warm smile.

"Good morning again, ladies!"

The giddiness had passed, leaving him drained of energy. He was tired, but then he and his deacon, Emilio, had spent most of the night at the Taos hospital. Jaime Sisneros had broken his arm. The two men had driven him and four of the family down to the hospital, and had sat in the emergency room too many hours.

What a misnomer, "emergency room." You should be seen quickly if it was an emergency! Fat chance! They sat there for four long hours, Jaime trying not to show how much pain he was in, and his mama having hysterics.

So much for Jaime's athletic career, thought Father. No great loss to anyone besides Jaime. What could a five-four, one forty-three pounder expect to be able to do anyway?

He decided he needed a nap. That would fix things.

After hauling his water, Father Mondragon disappeared, leaving the women to their work.

Lita shook out a bandana and tied it over her head. At least the front of her head was covered. Her bun would have to stay away from cobwebs. "I think we sometimes bother him," she whispered, "He looks so tired. Maybe he's just in a bad mood. My Ben used to be that way."

"Oh, he's just a man," snorted Jovita. "Don't let him bother you. He just gets mad and stomps around like he did last month when he went off on that rant about the church in Mexico taking money from the drug dealers. Whoee! I thought he'd blow his top. Don't let him get to you."

Virgie asked, "How could we bother him? We're just like everybody else, same problems, same bills, same aches and pains."

"All right, already," laughed Jovita.

"Maybe we just talk about them a little louder," whispered Lita.

"Or perhaps he's got a crush on one of us," coughed Virgie, and gave a raspy smoker's chuckle.

"He's been here so long, he knows us too well for any of that," responded Jovita. "He came here, what, back in the seventies."

"'Bout that," called down Virgie, who was already up on a short ladder swiping at cobwebs. "He's christened my two youngest and all my grandkids."

"Mine, too, I mean grandchildren," nodded Lita. "Phillip, bless his soul, was baptized long before that."

Jovita changed the subject. "You were gonna tell us about Christina, Lita. You said you got a letter yesterday. She still liking New York?"

"Yes, and she likes the ad company. She's doing some modeling, too. She loves that."

"Who wouldn't, with all those gorgeous clothes?" called Jovita from behind the confessional where she was cleaning.

"No, Jovita, it's that she's making much more money doing that. You know how she is," said Lita.

Virgie pushed her glasses back in place. "She's too pretty to stay single long," she said. "She still got that same boyfriend, the lawyer?" Jovita stopped sweeping and leaned on the broom. "You must be so proud, Lita, having a real Cinderella. Her with a good job, a novio, and a real future."

Lita smiled, and Jovita continued, "Yeah, that girl's too much for us: college, that time she spent in Italy, and now New York. She always said she was gonna do big things."

"She's always done what she said," added Virgie.

"Hey, do you think she'd have time to do an ad campaign for **Queso de Cocina**?"

"We'll ask at Christmas," said Lita, taking a last swipe at the kneeler with an oil-soaked rag.

"Eeee, why didn't you tell us she's coming home already?" Virgie's voice was now coming from behind the altar where she was sorting odd vases. "I can't wait to hear about New York. I always wanted to go there. I had dreams of dancing at Radio City Music Hall. You think she'll tell all about her sweetheart? You sure about her and that lawyer? I don't like lawyers, now that your Ben's gone."

"Yes," answered Lita, wiping her hands on her pants legs. "She sent a picture."

"Ooooh, why didn't you tell us first thing?" demanded Virgie.

Jovita dropped her broom. "You keep too many secrets, Lita!" she put in as she briskly made her way up to the chancel area.

Lita quickly got her coat. Wiping her hands again to remove the lemon oil, she lovingly removed the photo. "It came yesterday. Benito went to the post office while we were at the bookmobile."

"Let's see, Clam Face!" said Virgie as she snatched the picture. She and Jovita moved under a window for better light. Lita watched their faces. She hoped they saw what she did. They were beaming like fairy godmothers.

"Oh, she's beautiful! Lita, you were a looker, but Jesus, Maria, y Jose, not this knock-down gorgeous!" pronounced Jovita.

Lita nodded. "She gets that from her mother. Remember, Bianca's mother was from India and her father was a tall Italian."

"She looks in love," whispered Virgie.

Both of her friends looked closer at her jewel. Christina was in a high-necked dark blue wool dress, smiling into the camera, while the rawboned young man beside her looked at her. No, he drank her in.

"I know he loves her! No man looks that hungry if he isn't in love," declared Virgie flatly.

What else could they say? With a sigh, she reluctantly gave the photo back to its owner. Lita lovingly returned it to her coat pocket.

Jovita picked up the broom. "When exactly will Tina be home?" she asked.

"She thinks on the twenty-second. It depends on work. She'll rent a car at the airport. She should be home by late afternoon," replied Lita, as she made her way to the pews to continue cleaning.

"That's too close to Christmas for a turkey. I'll fix some tamales to send over. That way, you can just visit," offered Jovita.

"I'll make flan and some cookies," added Virgie. "That way, we'll be there to get the news about him firsthand."

"She'll have more to talk about than her novio. Anyway, I thought you were gonna ask about an ad for us," huffed Jovita, as she wiped dust off Saint Joseph. "This old guy needs to be replaced. He's got so many cracks, and when he got wet last year, the wood expanded and the paint's peeling off. You think Emilio would carve us another Santo?"

"He's too busy. Anyway, he's just doing little ones for that gallery down in Santa Fe," put in Virgie. "His great abuelo did this one. Maybe he could fix it, though, after Christmas."

"He wouldn't have time before," agreed Lita.

"Did either of you bring steel wool? We need to give these votives a good scrubbing." She held one of the chipped red glass candle holders up to the light. How many times, she wondered, have you been lit? How many of my prayers to Our Lady have you heard?

"It's my turn Saturday. I'll bring some then," announced Jovita. "Just stash the ammonia behind the altar so I don't forget. Oh, I was going to tell you about Emilio!"

Soon, the three of them were giggling like a gaggle of teenagers.

"You were right, Jovita, when you said I'd laugh till I cried!" gasped Lita, wiping her eyes. "Emilio used to play tricks when he was young. It's good to know he still has a sense of humor. He's always been so formal with me. I guess I thought he acted that way with everyone."

"I think that's because you're so standoffish. We're done," stated Jovita in her "It's-all-settled" voice.

The women were glad to gather up their supplies.

With their coats on, they hurriedly put the buckets back in place, in case there were more leaks, and genuflected again before heading toward the door.

When Virgie turned off the lights, one of the chandeliers spit sparks. "Look at that fixture. My God, it looks like it's going to fall! Father Mondragon needs to get one of Pepe Garcia's boys to come fix it," whispered Jovita. The once-handsome tin chandelier, which was one of six, hung crookedly from the ceiling. On closer inspection, it looked as if the latillas around it were rotting. Where was the money to fix it? They looked at each other. The church was falling apart.

Ever matter-of-fact, Jovita summed it up. "Amigas, we need to pray for the building, not just the people."

Virgie held their purses and a bag of supplies while the other two struggled with the door. It took both of them to lift it shut. "Where's a man when you need one?" panted Jovita.

"We had just enough snow to make mud," coughed Virgie.

"Let's take ourselves over to Tessie's and have some coffee and a sweet roll. We can clean off our shoes on her grate."

"Virgie, you can always make an excuse for something good to eat," laughed Lita.

Jovita agreed to go, too. "Good idea. I gotta schmooze Tessie up. I read in that gardening book last night that Coke helps flowers bloom bigger and brighter. They like the sugar, just like Virgie here. I'm gonna talk her out of some syrup."

"Jovita, you can start with my yard. It didn't do so well last summer. I spent too much time helping you with your piñon suppers," volunteered Lita, as they made their way through the little plaza and around the mud holes in the road.

They entered the café, and sat at a booth that had Carmen Miranda's picture above Jovita when she sat down. Lita smiled. Tessie had pictures of Hispanic actors all over the walls, and they had chosen this booth. How fitting, she thought, as she compared the energetic Carmen to Jovita.

Last year, New Mexico had been hit hard by an infestation of bark beetles, and the beloved state tree was in serious trouble. All over the state, huge stands of the tree were dead. Los Santos was one of the few areas that had been spared. All the thanks for this phenomenon had to do with Jovita's efforts.

She and Virgie had chili suppers in the church hall at night for the workers she had coerced into carrying her tea and extra water to as many trees as they could. Even children were enlisted to scratch oxidized lignite in around the drip lines of the trees. She ordered it from over in Cuba where it was mined. It helped the trees draw nutrients from the soil and to get by on less water.

Everywhere else the Forest Service was having to not only cut down the dead trees, but pull the stumps, as well, to eradicate the eggs and curtail further infestation. The county had been impressed with the efforts of Los Santos. There had even been an article in the Santa Fe New Mexican about their heroic effort.

Since the nuts were so scarce this year, pickers were now trying to rent plots of land. The hard little nuts were going to sell for unheard-of amounts. Some said one candy maker in Albuquerque, who had a sheller, might go as high as thirty dollars a pound! Chinese pine nuts would be foisted off on unwary and undiscriminating palates.

⁂

The women were still talking nuts when Tessie brought their coffee and Virgie's roll. "Will the price of wood go up or down?" asked Lita.

Jovita tried to explain. "There's so much dead wood, it should be cheap. On the other hand, if there's a chance the infestation might survive in wood piles and next summer is dry, the State might put a ban on the wood. Someone with a big warehouse might buy up a lot of it to sell in small amounts. That way nothing else gets infected. That person would make big bucks. Everybody loves the smell of piñon!"

There was a moment of silence as the women each reminisced about the way the aroma of the burning piñon had enriched their lives.

Lita broke the spell. "Anyway," she said with a smile, "come next year, piñon money should be rolling into Los Santos, thanks to you. This is supposed to be a bumper crop year, and maybe some of those people who cash in will be thankful enough to spread it around enough to put a new roof on the church!"

"It would be a fair payback for all Virgie's chili suppers, even if we did use cabrito," agreed Jovita.

"Not that we all don't love goat meat, Virgie," laughed Lita.

Albuquerque, Late November

Luis Fernandez had spent much of the week after Thanksgiving at the Bernalillo County Clerk's office and the office of the County Treasurer poring over real estate transactions and tax records. So far, he had found sixteen parcels of vacant land and various pieces of commercial property belonging to the Baca family besides their residences.

These had been listed under various titles of ownership.

Manuel C Baca had title to most properties, but Sadie's maiden name was used, as well as Mano's mother's maiden name. Title was held by Mano's long-dead brother, Roberto Eloy Baca, Manuel C. Baca II, better known as Junior, and Manuel C. Baca III, aka Tres, on about a third of the properties. Other parcels were under the name of Mano's lawyer, Dwight Skettering, as executor.

Luis had sweet-talked the secretary at the treasurer's office after the second day and she had run off a program of all taxes paid by the Bacas on real property. He'd gone back to his office with forty-three sites. The next week, he sent Nate to Sandoval and Valencia Counties to check against the names on his list.

Plucky Nate added Mona's name and maiden name and came up with several more. In only three counties, they had found over sixty properties between them.

Luis had sent emails to the other counties in the state asking for acres and/or properties owned by the names on his list. Every day now, some overworked civil servant was sending him paperwork on two, three, even fifteen new land parcels. How stupid he had been to think the pig farm was all the Bacas owned besides their home! There weren't enough law enforcement personnel in the state to stake out or raid these properties!

By next week's meeting with Frank and Mitch, he'd have a clearer picture of the problem. One thing for sure, Mitch was right when he said Mano was going to own more land in New Mexico than Ted Turner. He just hadn't known how right!

And there were adjoining states no one had looked at. Luis closed the file. He hadn't made a dent in the flowers yet or figured out the question regarding the hay.

He pushed back his chair. It was time for lunch. He'd get a quiet booth at Los Cuates up on Lomas and think over a big lunch. Better make that a big bowl of posole, some sopaipillas, and lots of black coffee. He left a sticky note on his door and headed off. This problem made as much sense as one of those Sudoku puzzles his wife liked to work. No, those were easier. At least they were logical, if your brain worked that way.

***

While Luis Fernandez was driving up Lomas on his way to lunch with his favorite legal pad, Ricky Travis was thinking of his busy afternoon ahead. "Keep your mind on the business at hand," he told himself. He had to do about five more miles before he could turn around and head for his car. When he got back to Albuquerque, he'd have just enough time for a shower before his four-thirty appointment at Dean Witter. His brother had done some fancy footwork, getting this meeting for him. It was time to invest some more, especially now that he had money in his pocket.

Get rid of it quick before you know you have it and you're tempted to spend it. Before Karla knows you have it. She'd been hinting for a ring. Yeah, he wanted to marry her, but not before he was through with school. He had two more semesters to go for his MBA. That would be a good time for a wedding. He'd be seeing her later tonight. He grinned and the saliva dried on his lips and teeth. He wondered what she wouldn't be wearing. He leaned a little farther over the handlebars of his carbon fiber Trek. The sun overhead was catching the little rocks in the pavement and bits of shattered glass along the shoulder of the road. What could feel freer than having the wind in your face as you flew over and past these sparkling galaxies?

Too bad Karla didn't ride.

The smell of the high desert after this morning's rain was awesome! If he stopped, he'd only hear the wind. If it was summer, he'd hear the bugs and birds. If he listened hard, he could sometimes hear a train. He could feel the slight tightening in his calf muscles as he started up the long incline. It wouldn't be long now. As he crested the rise, he spotted the descanso, there, just beneath the horizon line of the next hill.

He grinned, thinking the crisp, arid bite in the air smelled like money. You had to admit, Tres Baca's granddaddy paid well. One thousand a trip and a Christmas bonus! "Christmas bonus" was a nice name for hush money.

He'd sure had a busy year between school and working for Manuel Baca, if that's what you called it. Travis preferred to think of it as training for a big race. Oh, and don't forget Karla. She was taking up a lot of time.

He pulled to a stop next to the little shrine with its garish purple flowers. He removed his crash helmet and wiped his brow. Before he replaced it on his head, he removed the metal cross sprayed with luminescent paint. He took a long drink from his water bottle as he listened for traffic coming from the east. The way he'd just come was empty, not a car. Assured that it was all clear, he quickly wired the cross among the purple plastic glads and checked to see that it was in position to reflect any lights.

Turning his bike around, Travis snapped his chin strap and pushed off down the hill towards his car back in Santa Rosa. The pavement thrummed, sending vibrations up his arms until he built up speed. He checked his watch. He had plenty of time, but he didn't like being late. Not good for business or for relationships. Strange, how he always had to wait for Karla. It took her forever to get ready.

"She's here!" yelled Benito.

Lita heard the front door slam and came running from the kitchen to stand in the doorway. She stood for a moment watching her family hugging, careless of the slush around their feet.

It was wonderful watching the love between the two most important people in her life. Christina, in long black boots and a new red coat, finally saw her and rushed to the low porch.

"Mamalita!" she shrieked, enfolding Lita in her arms.

Lita wanted the moment to last forever.

Tina's perfume was new, delicate.

Then they were holding each other at arm's length laughing. Some things hadn't changed. The silver loops, the open smile. She hadn't changed completely, but her hair! The sleek shoulder-length hair was gone. In its place was a mass of curls held off her face by a headband.

Benito brought bags and boxes in as the women headed for the kitchen.

Her granddaughter called out, "No peeking, little brother!"

As he went back for more, Lita looked around. What had been organized a moment ago was slipping into chaos. The red coat was over a chair in the sala. A purse was perched atop the refrigerator. She turned and there was Tina, pushing up her sleeves to help. Lita wasn't interested in food anymore. She had only been starving for this lovely tornado. Life would be back to quiet soon enough when Tina left again.

Lids were lifted. Tina had to smell everything.

"I invited Amy and Sunny for Christmas dinner. Say it's all right, Mamalita. I found a scarf for Virgie with the Statue of Liberty on it, at a street sale. Ooh, this smells good! Kip and I went to a flower show on a date and I picked up some seeds for Jovita. I can't pronounce their name, but if anyone can grow them, it'll be Jovita."

She yelled at her brother in the other room, "Snoop, I said stay away from my boxes!" She was pouring coffee into her favorite mug and opening tins. "Just checking," she said.

Lita couldn't keep up, and she so wanted to remember this visit as more than a blur. She's been home five minutes and I can't think! "Pour Benito and me coffee, too. Come, sit. Be civilized," she ordered. "Let's catch our breath."

"Now you're here, tell us about this Kip," said Benito as he sauntered in and straddled a kitchen chair. "Be quick! Jovita and Virgie will probably be here any minute and they'll want to know all about him. Tell us the good parts first!" He winked at his grandmother.

Christina laughed.

"Sweetie wants to know."

"Oh, it's Sweetie now and not my nosey kid brother," she teased, making him blush. "Maybe we should be asking you all about 'Sweet-ieee' and how the two of you are getting along? Been to the Ranch lately?"

Lita was in heaven.

"We asked first," he pointed at Lita. "Mamalita might not be asking, but she can't wait to hear."

"She can't wait to hear about the jobs, either," put in Lita. She opened a tin of biscochitos and put them between her grandchildren.

"Mmm, I've missed these," said Tina, taking a bite.

Benito took a handful.

Christina took a deep breath. Her long fingers toyed with a cookie crumb on the colorful place mat. She looked up at both of them, exhaled, and blurted out, "I know he's the one! He's just so..."

The phone rang. It was a friend of Tina.

That was the end of the conversation Lita had been looking forward to for such a long time. But there will be another time, she told herself.

***

In the week her granddaughter was home, the times the family were alone could be counted on half a hand. Tina ran in and out, meeting friends or having them in. The house was in an uproar. At least Lita learned about Tina's life and novio by listening to her friends grilling the girl. What a grand life she was having. How romantic!

Lita had forgotten how different it was when Tina was there.

Virgie and Jovita kept dropping in. Virgie always brought another gift of food in case Tina wasn't getting enough to eat. Tina had invited the Jenkins for Christmas dinner.

She had a surprise for Amy.

Benito had one for Sunny, too. He had fixed up Tina's old bike and had repainted it fluorescent orange for the little girl. They had also invited Emilio.

On Friday, Lita had Benito and Tina put a leaf in the dining room table. She got out the silver and put the young ones to polishing it. She carefully washed her wedding china and set the table. Tomorrow, she would finish the cooking.

On Christmas Eve, they bundled up and walked to church.

Lita was nostalgic as they met friends along the way and called out to each other "Feliz Navidad!"

No one could tell the church was in such bad shape unless they knew what to look for. The light from hundreds of farolitos bathed the old adobe walls in a soft glow. Jovita had thought to hang pine boughs over the door so one couldn't see where the door didn't fit at the top, at least not from the outside.

You could tell it was Christmas, mused Lita; the whole village was there, except for the dogs.

The service was lovely and cold.

It was snowing and icy enough that the roof was not leaking, gracias a Dios.

Father Mondragon conducted the service while Emilio assisted. The children sang and presented a shortened version of Las Posadas, as there had been too much snow to go door to door this year. All the extra candles made it festive.

At the end of the service, after the mariachi band had played the final hymn, Emilio thanked those who had taken time to fold and fill the farolitos and those who came early to light them. He surprised them all by saying, "Before Father Mondragon delivers the benediction, one of our own wants to address the parish."

Lita started as Christina rose and made her way to the chancel. What in the world?

"Merry Christmas, everyone, it's so good to be home and to be with you this most holy night," began Tina. She told her audience about the churches she attended in New York and how big they were. She explained to them how parishioners there gave endowments to these grand churches, while others gave memorials or honorariums for organs and stained glass and other needed things.

The congregation was captivated by her outlandish tale. Who could have so much money?

They were unprepared when she said, "I promise when I get back to New York I am going to start a drive that will enable our church here in Los Santos to get a new roof. It's what I need to do for all that each of you has done for me. Dios is good to us. I love you all."

The parish stood and clapped and cheered. There were tears and smiles all around.

Oh, my, shuddered Lita. What are we getting into now? After the benediction, friends pressed forward and hugged and thanked Tina.

"She's such a blessing," said Emilio at Lita's shoulder. "How proud you must be, mi amiga."

"Dumbfounded, you mean," she murmured in the crush. "Be there at one tomorrow, Emilio. You get to carve the turkey."

He grinned and the wrinkles around his merry eyes extended to the silver hair at his temples. "I have been on a holy fast all week in anticipation."

"I might have been on one, too, if I had to eat what you cook," she teased. "Don't be late. We don't want you fainting from hunger."

He gave a hearty laugh as he pulled his sheepskin coat over his wide shoulders. "Lita, I didn't know you joked."

After a few more minutes with friends, they were able to make their way home. It was good to hear the laugher and the familiar "Buenas noches" in the crystal winter air.

When they got home, Lita made everyone a quick cup of chocolate with plenty of cinnamon. With all the seasonal rush, it was the first chance they really had to sit and enjoy their tree.

"Look, Benito, here's the ornament you made the year you were going to grow up to be an astronaut!" Benito groaned when Tina held up the little stick man wrapped in tin foil.

"You stop it, chica. There are cowgirls and Christmas mice on there somewhere."

Who could forget Tina's trouble making the mice out of bits of dough after Ben told her she couldn't use the dead mice she had been saving for so long, the mice that the family had trapped or that Kitty Gato had brought home.

Kitty Gato! Where was he? He needed to go out before they went to bed.

Lita excused herself to look for the cat while the other two laughed and reminisced over past trees and family stories.

Kitty Gato was finally found in the clothes hamper and was rather indignant about being tossed outside. By the time Lita had her nightgown on, he was ready to come back in. Life was hard for him, he was so old. Come to think of it, he was older that Benito.

"Sweet dreams, you two. I have to get up early. Pull the plug on the tree when you go to bed, will you?"

"Sure thing. Buenas noches."

"We love you."

Lita was still smiling when she crawled into bed.

When she awoke Christmas morning at six to put the turkey on, she couldn't remember having finished her prayers. Oh, well, she'd have just as much to be thankful about tonight.

After putting on the turkey and having a simple breakfast of sweet rolls, orange slices, and coffee, they settled around the tree to listen to music and open gifts.

Benito was thrilled with his gift from his sister. In his wildest dreams he had never thought of a laptop. "Kip helped me pick it out. We thought you'd need it next year at college."

Lita gave him a computer desk for his room. It was small enough that he could use it in a dorm room. It was good that he was handy with tools, as it had to be assembled. He also received two hundred dollars to go towards either college or a new truck.

Lita was betting on the truck.

Benito thought he could come up with scholarships from somewhere. He'd have to work to pay for the rest.

That was all right. Lita didn't believe in anyone not working.

Benito gave Tina a stack of CD's he had cut for her after football and on Sunday afternoons. He was real proud of the Andrés Segovia. He knew she loved classical guitar, and had gone all the way to Santa Fe and checked it out of the library there in order to copy it. His personal favorite was his special mix of Good Charlotte, Out Kast, Alicia Keyes, Green Day, Blink 182, and Willie Nelson.

Lita was glad she hadn't had to listen to most of them being made.

"Wow, hermano, what a collection! You've thought of all my favorites and then some! I'll have something different to listen to every day. It must have taken days to copy all this!"

"I didn't copy all of them. I found the Mariachi Cantares por Amor at Hastings in Taos. Maybe Kip will like that one, since it's all love songs."

"I hope he does!" she said and threw the wrapping paper at her grinning brother...

Lita was amazed, not so much at her answer as she was that Benito had been thinking along romantic lines. He's growing up too fast, or maybe he's just grown up and I haven't noticed.

"I have another one for you; it's really from Sweetie, but I made the frame." He hurried out and came back with a picture tied up in brown paper.

When Tina opened it, she had to study it a moment before she figured it out. It was an aerial photograph of the ranch.

"Sweetie wanted you to remember you have a real home."

"Tell Sweetie I'll treasure it."

"Hugh and Mamalita had to have it made so the environmental engineers could study it for an impact statement. Sweetie talked him into making some copies. I have one, too."

As Christina opened Lita's gift, her abuela held her breath. Was it too redundant after the Baughmans' gift?

"Ooh, Mamalita! My favorite time of year! Did you know that this is when I get the most homesick?" She held up the picture for Benito to admire, as if he hadn't watched most of the paint being applied. It was a picture of their high valley in the fall with the aspens in the background and huge soulful cottonwoods casting lavender shadows on low-slung brown adobe houses. You could even make out the top of the church. It was painted with palate knife and thick brush strokes, much in the old Taos style.

"A good friend of Emilio's painted it. He stayed here with us a week in the summer to choose this perspective, and then he came back in October for a few days so his palate would have just the right colors. Be careful! The paint hasn't completely dried! Emilio made the frame for me and a crate for you to take it back in."

She opened her gifts. Christina gave her a long blood-red cashmere scarf and the kind of makeup kit that models used, complete with a small bottle of expensive perfume.

When Lita gasped, Tina laughed and said "Ben and I decided that it's time you start pampering yourself. If we hurry with dinner preparations, we'll have time to experiment on your face before our guests arrive. And when I'm not here to hug you all the time, you'll just have to wear this stole to know you're getting a hug from me."

Benito gave her a little cell phone. "It's to keep in your purse or pocket," he said. "Ya know your old car isn't much better than my truck. You'll be safer with this, especially next year, when I'm not around to charge your battery."

"Goodness, hijo, you are pulling me into the present! Thank you. You can't call me old-fashioned anymore."

"I won't be able to call you at all, until you buy a phone card. I didn't have enough left over to get one."

They were still laughing as they cleaned up their festive mess.

Lita and Tina then headed for the kitchen to finish the dinner, and Benito went out to shovel the walk again. Christina had just finished with Lita's makeup, just a little blush, and a dab of eye shadow in the creases under her brow, some faint eyeliner and lip gloss, when their guests started arriving. Lita felt she looked like a clown, but didn't have time to wash her face. Maybe no one would notice.

Emilio was the first to arrive. "Merry Christmas, everybody! Lita, you look exquisite," he boomed. "All your culinary efforts have made you as lovely as these epicurean aromas! Here are some flowers for your table and some remembrances for Ben and Tina."

So much for washing her face.

Tina grinned and swept the gifts and flowers from his arms.

"Gracias, Señor Maestas," Lita replied. "I'm glad you are so prompt. With all you've been wading through just now, I'm surprised you made it."

"Benito, please take Emilio's coat. I'm still busy in the kitchen." She turned back to her friend. "You look rather charming yourself. The green in that Pendleton shirt suits you. Make yourself comfortable. Tina and I won't be long."

Emilio surveyed his surroundings. He always enjoyed being in this tasteful room. The wood floors gleamed. The art work on the walls reflected several generations of Taos painters. Lita's abuelo and papa had both been patrons, sometimes giving room and board to a painter down on his luck. There was the new painting done for Tina, on top of a book case, leaning against the whitewashed wall where JFK had always hung. It had turned out wonderfully! He would have to compliment the artist when he saw him next. He turned to the fire on the short wall of the room and was pleased to see one of his Santos on the mantle. The figure's colored robes picked up the colors in the rugs and throws. This room would not be out of place in a decorator's magazine.

The only thing that wasn't tasteful was the tree. Ben had probably cut it at the ranch, and it was full of the ugly ornaments lovingly made by two generations of children. In its own way it was beautiful to the heart. At least they had put the scraggly little tree in a polychrome pot. Charlie Brown should be so fortunate!

Benito came up behind him. "It's ghastly, isn't it? Still, it's what Mamalita's Christmas is all about."

"Then, Ben, I'd say it was the most beautiful tree around."

Benito grinned. "Thanks for the name change." He started to say more, but there was a knock at the door. As he went to welcome the other guests, the cooks came from the back of the house to join the party.

Amy and Sunny came in with a platter of cookies and two small, brightly wrapped packets.

Sunny was jabbering away. She had measured all the ingredients for the cookies all by herself.

Lita knew the word "ingredients" came straight from Emilio. She could tell by the way he beamed. She could tell who had decorated the cookies by herself, too. They were a wonder of bright blue and purple icing and colored sprinkles.

After dutifully oohing and aahing over Sunny's contribution to the dinner, they opened their gifts from Amy.

Lita was charmed by her simple silver pin. She claimed it was perfect for all her sweaters. Tina pinned it on the shawl collar of Lita's cream-colored wool sweater.

Then it was her granddaughter's turn to squeal with delight

over the silver and onyx bracelet Amy had made. "I can't wait to show this off! Amy, you have really outdone yourself. Thank you!"

Lita had made Tina's friend Amy, a new smock to wear while working on her jewelry. It was not fancy, but totally practical.

Benito grinned when he rolled out the bike for Sunny. He had decorated the handlebars with pine boughs and red ribbons.

Sunny was thrilled to learn the bike had once been Tina's. For once, only for a moment, Sunny was speechless. Then her ecstatic chatter was only matched by her prancing. They all laughed when she told Emilio that she'd never need to be lugubrious again! Her only disappointment was that she'd have to wait for the snow to melt and the roads to dry up before she could learn to ride.

Finally, their feast was on the table and everyone's favorite deacon asked the blessing. Emilio checked to see that Sunny's head was down and then he bent his full head of salt-and-pepper hair. "Bless us, oh, Lord, and these Thy gifts that we are about to receive from Thy bounty. Lord, use each of us this coming year so that we may be more faithful servants. In Christ's name we pray."

When everyone chorused the "Amen," Benito fetched the turkey. While Emilio began carving, Christina presented a large envelope to Amy. "Feliz Navidad, amiga. I hope you like it."

They all watched in anticipation as a puzzled Amy slowly opened the document and began reading. Tears filled her eyes. "Oh, Tina! I've never had such a magnificent present!"

"So why the tears? Illuminate this old soul," shouted Emilio as he waved the carving knife in the air.

Tina touched Amy's arm and laughed at him standing in such a dramatic pose.

"Everywhere I go in New York, people compliment the pin Amy made me for a parting gift, so I had an idea. I was feeling really up one day when I was at a fitting in an exclusive shop. It was late on a Friday afternoon. We were doing a show the next day. Anyway, when the owner commented on my unusual jewelry, I asked her if her shop would be interested in carrying a line of it. She jumped at the idea and called her lawyer on the spot!"

"I had Kip look this contract over and he said it was airtight and more than fair for Amy. It's for three years. The shop will advance the cost of materials and pay Amy more than she could earn here for each piece. The shop will put a huge markup on everything. Those crazy people in New York won't bat an eye at those kinds of prices!"

"Wow! You're on your way, Amy. Congratulations."

"You're right there, Ben. We fellows should just turn the world over to these talented women and we'd all be in high alfalfa!"

As Emilio began serving the turkey, Lita watched the two young women. Which one was she happier for? Amy, who would be more financially stable and could make a name for herself, or for her granddaughter, who had pulled off a minor miracle?

"Does this mean I can have a dog?" asked Sunny.

"We'll see, honey," replied her mother, rolling her eyes. "Why don't you give the rolls to Lita so she can start passing them."

Taking the warm rolls from Sunny, Lita said, "Thank you, niña. Here, I'll take one, and then you help yourself and pass them on to Benito." Soon, all the plates were piled with food and conversation slowed as they began eating.

Lita paused, looking around the table at her family and their friends. How lucky I am to have so many good, kind people in my life. Gracias, Dios.

While the women washed the china and cleared the table for dessert, the menfolk put Benito's desk together.

Sunny helped by counting out the screws and looking after the screwdriver with the precision of a surgical nurse.

Then Ben showed her how to find and play Mine Sweeper. "Go to programs. That's right. Now push the pointer up to games. That's good. Now move over to the right and now down to Mine Sweeper. Now click here. There, you've got it! Now you're ready to play."

The women could hear "Pow. Look out! Here comes another

one! Direct hit! Way to go, chica! What a shot! Drop it! Drop it now!" They shook their heads and smiled as they put away Tina's great-grandmother's silver and Lita's wedding china.

"Will they ever grow up?" asked Amy.

"I hope not," laughed her hostess. "Why don't you go tell them dessert will be served in ten minutes? Tina will help me with the coffee."

Alone in the kitchen, Tina turned and gave Lita a hug. "Mamalita, I love you so much. I hope I can be as great a hostess as you are. You make us all feel so special!"

"Mi hija, you are the one that makes us feel special, but as to being a hostess, you start by putting the coffee on, and not too weak! Heat some milk, while you're at it, for chocolate for Sunny. I'll put the sweets on the table."

The choices for dessert were flan, biscochitos, empanadas, caramels with piñon nuts and Sunny's cookies. That should be enough, Lita thought. "What have I forgotten? Cream and sugar. That should take care of it."

Later, in the sala, Emilio appropriated the large rocker so he could hold Sunny. Benito stuck more wood on the fire and Tina poured another round of coffee. The girls settled on the sofa, Lita took the smaller rocker, and her large cat jumped in her lap and settled down to sleep. Benito sprawled in an ungainly pose in front of the fire.

"Mmm, this pot of coffee's even better than the sweets. Tell us, chica, how do you propose to accomplish last night's announcement?" asked Emilio.

"I don't know yet. Maybe we can auction some of your work. By the way, thank you for the little Santo. Southwest stuff is real hot on the East coast."

"I could make some jewelry," offered Amy.

"See, Emilio, that's a couple of thousand between the two of you just for starters. I have a friend at The New York Times that might do a story, say, around Easter. Perhaps we could drum up some sympathy donations then. We could always get the Zamoras to come do some mariachi concerts. Don't worry, there will be a way."

"I hate to bust your bubble, chica, but a new roof's going to cost big bucks. And before it can go on, some latillas need replacing and the old walls need to be reinforced."

"Yeah," added Benito. "Father Mondragon says he's always surprised to drive up and find the walls still standing."

"And don't forget the electrical problems, Tina, dear," added Emilio. "The reason we used so many candles last night was because we've been having shorts in the light fixtures."

"Pray for me then, everybody. I didn't know it would be such a big job! I'd better work fast."

"Amen," replied Emilio.

There was a sudden lull in the conversation broken only by the squeak of the rockers and Sunny's soft snores. They looked at the sleeping child with her blue-stained mouth and red ribbons from her bike draped around her shoulders. Her head lolled against Emilio's chest. They were silent for a moment while thoughts of naps floated just out of reach.

"It's been a most charming day, Lita, but I surmise it is time for me to carry this one home; that is, if you are ready to go, Amy?"

"I hate to leave. This has been such a perfect day, but you are right. I'll get our coats."

Lita said, "Tina, we don't want to wake Sunny. Go get a blanket. We can wrap it around both of them and Amy can carry their coats. I'll get some leftovers to send home with Amy and Emilio. Benito, will you take the bike?"

The big man sat in the rocker and watched Lita as she deposited the cat on the floor and rose from her chair in a fluid motion and made her way to the kitchen. He enjoyed the way she glided. She still carried herself like a ballet dancer or a young doe. Her movements never seemed hurried or wasted. She had gone through life that way. It was as if she wanted to be invisible, or was afraid to make a misstep and cause a change in the balance of the world, like that butterfly in South America.

In a moment, after soft "Thank-yous" and "good-byes," Tina and Lita stood in the doorway waving and blowing kisses as the little parade made its way down the road.

Emilio led with Sunny over his shoulder, both of them covered with a thick quilt. Amy was next, loaded down with an extra coat and bags of food for the two little households. Benito brought up the rear. He really looked funny bending over so low. He wised up finally, and just picked up the little bike.

"May Christmas always be so blessed, Christina."

"Yes, Mamalita. God loves us, no?"

Benito had just come back when Hugh and Sweetie arrived. Hugh stood in the doorway with a huge basket of fruit for Lita, and Sweetie had gifts for Christina and Benito.

"Season's greetings, everybody!" said Hugh. "I hope we're not too late?"

"Come in. Come in! Merry Christmas to you two as well. Benito, take their coats. Have you eaten? At least have some coffee and some empanadas."

"Ooh, we'd love some," said Sweetie, slipping off her coat and walking over to Ben. "Lita, you make the best goodies!"

"Sweetie, I love the aerial photo. Thank you for remembering me," said Tina. "What a charming necklace! Is it one of Amy's pieces?"

"Yes, I'm glad you like it." Blushing, she whispered, "Ben gave it to me for Christmas."

It was Ben's turn to blush. "Let me take your coats," was all he managed to get out. He hurried out of the room as Tina roared.

Sweetie had bought Christina a date book, because she was having so many dates now, after all. Benito blushed again when he opened his gift of men's cologne.

Hugh winked at Lita, and she rolled her eyes.

Sweetie told them all about the guitar her dad had given her as they sat around the table.

After a quick coffee and a nibble, Tina took them to the living room to see her painting, and Benito fetched his new computer for all to admire.

"This is great, Ben! Now we can visit all the time!" said Sweetie. "We'll have to get you an email address before I go back to school next week."

"Not too often, I hope," said Hugh. "Pumpkin, get our coats. We have yet to play Santa." To Lita he said, "My hands at the ranch need their bonuses and Father Mondragon needs his new sweater. Thanks for the break."

Benito walked them out to their SUV. When the door closed, Tina turned and grinned at Lita. "How does it feel to have your grandson in love?"

"About the same, I'd say, as having my granddaughter in the same situation." They both laughed. "Now, don't go teasing him," she warned. "At his age, he doles it out better than he can take it."

It seemed everyone in Nate Courtney's life was away for the holidays.

His new girlfriend—at least she might become one—had gone back to Virginia to see her folks. That's why he was still at the shed across from the Bacas' place. He'd given over his vacation time to Jerry Lucero, who was as bored with this assignment as he was.

Jerry's mom was real sick and this time off was Nate's Christmas gift to his coworker. Jerry had taken his family up to Farmington to see her and spend the holiday there, maybe for the last time.

Things were real quiet across the street. Junior had taken Mona and Tres to see Mona's parents in El Paso. Sadie had taken the season off and hadn't even put up a tree. She had called Furr's Cafeteria and had Christmas dinner delivered.

The only thing of interest all week was that the guy with the pig farm, the artist, had brought a ham to the old couple on Tuesday. He hadn't even gone in the house. Oh, yeah, and on Wednesday afternoon, Toby Luna, the little guy from Isleta Pueblo, had brought more hay and helped the Bacas put it in their small barn.

Nothing was happening.

Perhaps the El Paso police, who were watching the Bacas down there, would come up with something. On the other hand, sometimes a family trip was just a family trip.

iii

Manuel Baca liked doing business with the Indians. He had Toby down in Isleta, a Navajo guy over on the reservation just south of Ramah, and a woman, a Mescalero, down around Whitetail, who all grew marijuana for him.

It wasn't so much that he liked Indians, but he loved doing business on the reservations. As far as he knew, the tribal police were all pretty lazy and not above taking a bribe now and then. What he liked best about them was the fact that they didn't like outside agencies on their land at all.

His oxygen tank wheezed.

He'd be happy to have his family home from Christmas trips. They were supposed to be here in Albuquerque. And he'd be glad to get the pot and its smell out of his barn and hen house and delivered to the buyers.

He had to watch Junior all the time. He should have moved the pot before he left. Junior must've gotten his brains from Sadie, 'cause he still had all his. The lazy spick couldn't think for himself. Nah, he only thought of himself, and that was with his dick. As often as his son had his pants down, Manuel was surprised he had only one grandson.

Mona must be the smart one, 'cause Tres was a real go-getter. He was too rash, though, didn't think things through. But he had to give Tres credit; he was the one to come up with that Travis kid. He'd bumped into him up on campus. They had run together when they were little kids, but they'd lost track of each other when Junior moved his family up to the Heights into one of those swanky gated communities.

Tres had come to his abuelo right off. It had been Tres' idea to use Travis to mark drops and pickups using a bike. Mano rubbed his whiskers.

He and Sadie were always amazed that Mona didn't kick Junior out. That was why he had set up Mona's hermano, Lorenzo Gurule, in the funeral business. Financial bonds were stronger than marital ones, he thought.

He wished the doctor would let him have a cerveza!

There was no time to rest when Christina was home! After their big dinner, Lita thought things would calm down, but Benito was at the ranch with Sweetie, and Tina was running around buying bits of New Mexico to take back to new friends. Or she was down at Amy's little house, talking about jewelry designs and what colors and fabrics would be in next year. They thought it important to have the pieces designed to accent the clothes. When Tina and Benito were home, they had their heads together over that new computer, talking about it in a language foreign to her. She tried hard to hold on to every moment. This was the last year that Benito would be home, except for holidays, and her girl was here so seldom. She wanted them all to herself, but people kept dropping in. Father Mondragon, even, and Jovita and Virgie so many times she thought she'd scream.

Today was a whirl again as Tina stuffed her bags and Benito hauled them to the car with Sweetie's help.

Sweetie was there to be with him, but really to glean some bits of stylish information from her idol. Everyone seemed to gather to see Christina off.

"Go away!" Lita wanted to shout, but smiled instead.

Virgie and Jovita came with cheeses for her to put in her carry-on. Amy Jenkins brought some pins she'd been slaving over since Tina had given her the contract. Tina was a friend and a lifesaver for the Jenkins family, and Lita couldn't begrudge them a last good-bye.

Lita had baked more biscochitos for her to take back for a New Year's party. They were carefully wrapped, but she was afraid the cheese would crush them.

Suddenly, the rental car was packed, and Tina had hugged and kissed them all good-bye. "Look, Ben, I'm putting in your super CD right now. I'll enjoy it all the way to Albuquerque!"

Benito grinned. He seemed to puff up before them, he was so proud.

"You be good, chica!" someone called.

"Thanks for coming, sweetheart!"

"Thanks for the laptop! I'll email you tonight."

"Drive safely."

"We love you. Take care."

They stood in front of the house in the snow waving until the little car was out of sight. Benito thought he heard the horn.

"Mamalita, I guess that means Christmas is over," said Benito.

"It was so good to see her again."

"I love the scarf she brought me."

"Wait till you see my flowers!"

"Did she say when she could come back?"

"You can all come in for coffee, if you want, but friends, I have to tell you, I'm pooped."

iii

Christina smiled as she drove down the hill. It was good being home. She was lucky to have real people in her life. People you could count on.

It would be better getting back to Kip. She couldn't wait to see him. She couldn't wait to show him her painting either. When he saw it, he would know why she loved it here.

She was turning up the sound on the CD player as she came to the dip in the shade of the hill, right before the turn toward Taos.

That was when the deer broke through the trees above her, just a bit ahead. There was a magic moment when the sun spangled its rack and she saw it frozen above her. For an instant, she marveled at its proud beauty, and then it leapt.

Time instantly slipped into slow motion.

Tina's foot jammed on the brakes and she cut the wheel, trying to miss the animal. The car's tires hit the black ice in the shadowed patch. The lightweight car spun, rolled over a little berm, and dropped into Epie Vallejo's frozen field thirty feet below.

Leonard Salazar came along in a few minutes. Someone had called in the accident. He hurriedly slid down the embankment.

Who was the poor driver?

There was a good-sized deer, injured, unable to move. It was a no-brainer to see what happened.

"Oh, shit!" he whispered to the empty field when he looked in the car.

Christina Cordova's delicate neck was bent at an odd angle.

He wrenched open the door to feel for a pulse. Nothing. He gently closed her eyes.

The stag let out a plaintive cry. Leonard went over and put a bullet through its head. He just stood there for a moment, and then he started crying.

He had taken the kids from church to Eagle's Nest the day Tina caught her first trout. He could hear her laugh. Over the years, he had watched her spike volleyballs and dance with lovesick boys in the same high school gym. He had been to church Christmas Eve and heard her speak. This was senseless, and for some stupid reason there was music. The CD in the car was still playing Willie Nelson's version of *"What'll I Do?"*

Kip had come as soon as he could. He had flown into Albuquerque and had taken a shuttle as far as Taos. Emilio had picked him up there. Lita wouldn't let her grandson drive that road yet.

At first, it was awkward having a strange man in the house, but Benito warmed up to Christina's intended right away. The two of them had spent yesterday afternoon and most of today with their heads close together over Benito's computer. Lita was glad her grandson had another man to grieve with. It allowed her to hold her memories all to herself.

Kip had helped Christina pick out the computer, and since it was almost like his, he'd been able to show the other young man the ins and outs and all the shortcuts. In his grief, Benito was drinking in every scrap of information, as if in some mysterious way the very act of making the laptop do as he wanted would keep his sister alive.

Kip, bless his heart, had kept Benito busy until they had to hurry to get to the church for the rosary. Lita was glad the young man was there. She couldn't have addressed her grandson's grief yesterday or today. Kip was doing a heroic job of filling the void. She'd have to let him know how much she appreciated his being here.

While the rest of the house was involved with the laptop, Lita had held herself together the best she could. She answered the door till Virgie showed up, smiling and thanking neighbors for food and carefully making a list for thank-you notes.

After Virgie came, she took a long hot shower so no one could hear her cry. She dressed slowly for the rosary, making a ritual of the process to put some order in her soul.

When she was ready and had a face ready to meet the village, she had to hurry the men folk along so that they wouldn't be late. They arrived only a few minutes before the service began.

It was snowing outside when they arrived for the rosary, but all the people, so many friends, and the candles warming up the little sanctuary surprised all of them.

Lita was pleased.

Everyone seemed to be here, although the icy trip had been difficult for many. The old pews creaked under the combined weight of the mourners.

Old Man Ortiz coughed. She could tell it was him by the way he hacked and spat.

There was a collective murmur from the townsfolk when Emilio Maestas began the service in English. What could be more fitting? Maria Christina had been a woman of tomorrow in a larger world.

"Hail, Mary, full of grace, the Lord is with thee."

So many flowers! Their fragrance filled the room. Pink carnations from Jovita and Virgie, two huge poinsettias, the dark red kind, from Hugh and Sweetie, red roses from the University in Albuquerque and a lovely spray of white lilies—imagine at this time of year and all the way from New York! Floyd Patrick had sent a huge plant to the house. He would be here tomorrow.

"Blessed art thou among women and blessed is the fruit of thy womb, Jesus."

Someone slipped in late and the draft caused some candles to splutter out. Benito quietly moved from Lita's right and relit them as the rosary continued. Tina's novio sat on her other side.

Kip Stokes' height and blondness, as well as the cut of his suit, made him appear out of place. She reached out and touched his hand. You look in his eyes and you could see that his grief is just the same. He is one of us. Silly of me to think of him as the stranger with the lopsided grin, who shouldn't have had his arm around my girl in the picture she sent.

Lita thought of the photo she had lovingly showed Jovita and Virgie, the one where Tina was wearing the dark blue wool with long sleeves, it was the same dress she was wearing now. No wonder she looked so happy. This Kip was a fine young man. "Our Father who art in heaven..."

Christina had shown good sense choosing this man. He was a

Catholic, too! She noticed he didn't continue with the Our Father, a sure sign, and he had knelt and crossed himself when she and Benito had.

Someone else coughed.

"...now and at the hour of our death. Amen."

When Tito Andrade, along with Leo Zamora and his nephew, Epie, were playing their guitars and guitarro, and Jorge Gomez added the clear notes of his coronet, Lita began to cry. It was the same song, *"Tu Has Venido a la Orilla,"* that they had played when she had lost her son and his wife, and again at the rosary for Ben. Now, too, He had called out Tina's name and she would "seek other seas."

"Hail, Mary, full of grace..." Behind them a child cried. She could hear the mother cooing gently.

She and Ben had been taking care of their grandchildren while the young couple fixed up their house in Santa Fe. Philip and his wife were trying to work on the gas water heater themselves.

Now the baby girl was gone, too. So much sadness! All of them gone except Benito.

No, she must remember to call him "Ben." He didn't even want to be called "Benny." How was she to keep going? She had to find the strength from somewhere, God willing. There was still her Benito. He was too green, too young. She hoped she'd be there when he grew up. Please, Lord, show me the way.

Before she knew it, dear Emilio was thanking everyone for coming and inviting them to the funeral Mass in the morning and across the road to a dinner in the church hall right now.

Benito and Kip stayed with her to say their last goodbyes and watch as the funeral director closed and locked the casket. The trio slowly made their way back down the aisle.

When they stepped outside, the freezing wind caught their breath and shocked them back into the present. They were at least physically ready to be in the warm hall when they arrived. There, the smell of food and the fog of strong coffee reached out to hug them as surely as their friends. It seemed to hover protectively over everyone, daring the cold to creep in.

Tessie and her daughters were dishing up tamales, posole, green chile and venison stew, beans, and rice.

Tessie, Jovita, and Virgie had been cooking and calling friends and relatives ever since the accident.

Lita's home was full of food and here were mountains more. The dessert table was filled with cakes, pies, empanadas, and cookies. Little ones were racing about. Older children, mostly boys, were pushing and shoving at the head of the line at the serving table. Everyone seemed to be talking!

Death and food, codependents always, thought Lita as she picked at the plate someone brought her.

Kip was having a hard time with his plate. Everything was hotter than he expected. He was being a good sport, though, she'd give him that. And he was trying hard to keep up with the banter, some in English, most in Spanish. It seemed his grief was being pulled from him with the retelling of memories he had never shared of Tina's life in Los Santos.

"Oh, such a chica! So full of promise, our Tina. She, so pretty and full of dreams and promises of her own. Get Pepe to tell about the time she promised to take care of his sick calf! Hey, Pepe, come here!"

"Yeah, man, she done everything she say!" piped in Pepe. "That calf you call him turned into one fine bull. I got me lotsa blue ribbons and one fine herd off him, and all because of Tina. He was so sick I was gonna put him down, but she cry and say she can make him better. She did it, too!" Pepe nodded his bald head and patted his big belly as if to verify his every word.

Benito looked at Lita. It was a family joke that he was too young to remember firsthand, that his sister had brought the sick calf home and asked her abuelo to fix it. Ben had passed the problem on to Lita, and Tina had gone off to music camp. Lita had called the vet and the story ended with the Cordovas eating brown beans and rice for a long time that summer while Pepe rejoiced over his healthy calf. She looked back and winked. Kip needed to hear the whole story.

Ruby Abeyta's boy almost knocked over the dessert table when he pushed Lenny Hernandez. Virgie gave them both a good what-for and sent the whole pack of boys back to their parents. One would have thought she held a willow switch.

Mr. Milfort had everyone laughing about the way Tina had gotten Old Man Seis, bless his soul, to fix Mrs. Estepa's outhouse, God rest her soul. When she had been about eight, she had asked Onofre Seis, the meanest old fart in town, how to make adobes. She wanted to fix Mrs. Estepa's shed-like structure, which had lost its west wall during several heavy rains. The old guy had put her off, over and over, but finally melted when Tina got stuck in the adobe pit. She lost her shoes in the process—they had been sucked off when he pulled her out—but her tenacity had won him over. Not only did he make the bricks; he put them up as well. Tina hung in with him, telling him stories and singing him songs. She stayed with him till he got the job done!

Mrs. Lente swore that Tina had saved their orchard the day she fell out of an apple tree and broke her arm. It seems the bores had gotten into that one tree and if the branch hadn't cracked under her weight, they probably wouldn't have sprayed that year and would have lost everything. "That Tina, she was a godsend."

"She sure was," offered the Lentes' oldest son as he rocked back and forth with his new baby in his arms. "That chica, she was our talisman! She made everything better. Just like Christmas Eve! Remember? I got so happy, I knew everything was gonna be all right, `cause she promised she would fix things."

Didn't they realize she was just a big-hearted tomboy?

The stories continued and the food kept coming. It seemed that Tina's love and promises could fix all of Los Santos. Tessie came around with another pot of coffee.

Amy was picking up empty paper plates. She sent Sunny to

climb in Emilio's lap. The young mother looked as lost as Lita felt.

About nine, Lita, Ben, and Kip slipped out and went home. It would be a long day tomorrow and they needed their rest.

Once home, however, they weren't ready to be alone with their thoughts. Lita fixed Mexican chocolate with plenty of cinnamon and Ben opened tins filled with apricot empanadas and biscochitos. They sat in the kitchen around the table which still had a Christmas patterned oilcloth on it. As they ate the fruit pies and anise cookies, they shared more about Tina and more about themselves.

Benito laughed till tears rolled down his nose when Kip told of meeting Tina and how she had blown him away as well as blown him off.

"I mean it," he said, "The first time she smiled at me, I had to check to see if I still had my socks on!" They laughed at his rendition of his courting her, too.

Lita told of how afraid she was to let her granddaughter go off to New York where it was so dangerous. Strange that she had come home to die in a safe place.

When the oak kitchen chairs became too hard, they moved into the sala. Benito added a piñon log to the fire.

Lita sat back and watched and listened as the men visited. Her grandson was eager to hear of the Dakota ranch where Kip had grown up. Kip, in turn, was interested in hearing of Ben's plans for the ranch the family owned.

The lease with Hugh Baughman would be up the year after Ben graduated from college. Since a family who held a land grant wasn't allowed to sell, Ben had decided to come home and return the property into a working ranch once more. Hugh didn't want to extend his lease. All his friends who had enjoyed the hunting were now going to Africa or Alaska.

That led to talk of schools and the merits of the ones her grandson was considering. Kip told Ben how proud Tina had been of him and how excited she was when they had picked out Ben's computer.

She had thought he'd be able to use it when he went off to school.

Kip, Lita noted, was pushing all the right buttons. What a perfect brother-in-law he would have made. Yes, mi hija chose wisely.

Finally, it was time to say goodnight.

She had put Kip in Christina's room, hoping it would comfort him. At least the quilts and Hudson Bay blankets would keep him warm.

At the door, he had hugged her and started to say that if she needed...but had to stop. He could only hold her tighter for a moment. There really were no words.

Later, after her prayers to both Our Lady and The Father, she lay in bed. She could just make out the long, dry sobs coming from Christina's room upstairs.

***

Hugh Baughman's ranch hands had been working since sunup with tractors and a scoop to clear the way to the family plot up at the ranch.

He'd missed the funeral Mass, but Sweetie was there.

She had idolized Tina—hell, the whole family, for that matter. Jesus Christ Himself couldn't have kept her away. She'd tell him all about it.

Hugh had helped dig the grave, working at a fevered pace, it was his gift to Lita.

One minute he was grieving for his friend, Lita, and the next for himself, imagining if it had been Sweetie. What if he would never again see that tangle of burnished curls or hear her laugh? He couldn't work hard enough to chase his fears away.

Hugh had just made it back from cleaning up when the procession arrived. He hadn't expected so many! There should have been more folding chairs. The sun was out, but the wind coming off the higher slopes was damned cold.

Mercifully, Father Mondragon was keeping the committal service short.

He went to stand next to his daughter, the red head with matching eyes today, to be comforted by her vibrancy. He felt saved by her presence, yet guilty as he watched proud Estrellita Cordova gather up the tattered remains of what was left of her life.

Lita patted Benito's arm and came toward him. She thanked him for being so thoughtful and kind. Hollow eyes, on automatic, yet still the lady, thought Hugh. Benito and Tina's boyfriend helped her to the car. He and Sweetie would have to do something for their gracious friend, but Sweetie was due back in Dallas for school.

She should have gone back three days ago. Hell hadn't frozen over, though, and she had stayed for the funeral.

Dolores Maldonado's feet hurt. She had been standing all day. Nobody had told her about that when she'd gone to beauty school. They had also forgotten to mention chapped and swollen hands from perms and ugly nails from the dyes and rinses; oh, and the varicose veins. Don't forget the varicose veins.

She was tired all over, but had an hour and a half before she had to be at night school. She only had four more classes to go before she could become a medical transcriptionist and cut her losses at the salon.

She shifted the grocery bag to her left hip as she pushed the key in her lock. The tiny apartment was quiet and clean.

It had been ever since Petey had gone to prison. Dumb kid.

Dolores had taken care of Petey as best she could. It was hard keeping food on the table and a roof over their heads, not to mention keeping tabs on her brother.

Petey lived in his own world and didn't know nada about good and bad, right from wrong. How could he, when he had the IQ of a five-year-old?

Too bad he was twenty.

You promise a candy bar and he'd do anything you wanted. That was the problem, she thought, as she put the groceries away. That's exactly what had happened. Some cholos had given Petey a Pepsi for bringing a little girl to them from the park. Petey didn't know what they would do. Sheez, he didn't know what rape was! Somebody had seen Petey with the child.

She poured a cup of cold coffee and put it in the microwave. Dolores had just curled up on the lumpy sofa with the leftover coffee when there was a knock on the door.

"Ooh, whoo, Dolores..." It was her neighbor.

Millie Saavedra let herself in. "Your secret admirer sent you more flowers!" She stood beaming at Dolores over a bouquet of pink carnations in a blue glass vase with a large pink bow. "You sure you don't know him?"

Dolores closed her tired eyes. If only there were a real somebody! Not again, she thought, I'm too tired.

"Thanks for taking them, Millie. Wouldn't you like them? Since I don't know who sends them, I don't need them."

"Oh, I couldn't!"

"Sure, you could! I'm not home all day and you have pink curtains. They'd look great on your table. Please, take them."

"Well, if you're sure..."

"Absolutely." Dolores pulled herself off the couch so she could move Millie toward the door. "Anyway, you know I'm allergic to carnations. My nose is already beginning to itch."

Finally, Millie and the flowers left and Dolores closed the door.

She stood there a moment leaning her head against the door frame. Tears began to roll down her face. "God, will this never end?"

Pushing herself away from the door, she wished she could forget the flowers, forget Petey, and especially erase from her memory the two men who had come here that night. Maybe they had come earlier. All she knew was that they were here in the dark when she'd come in from school. They had roughed her up a bit, really scared her, and then they explained that Petey would be safe inside only so long as she followed directions.

The directions were simple enough.

On occasion, she would be sent flowers.

Wasn't that what all girls wanted, flowers?

When they came, she would have twenty-four hours to bake her little brother something, or take him something the same color as the flowers, but it had to be there in the allotted time frame. As long as she did this, the kid would be taken care of. If she failed, something would happen to him. She could be sure of that!

Petey liked Oreos best. Too bad. He'd only have them if something awful happened and she received black flowers. Tomorrow, he'd have to settle for something pink.

She usually went on Sundays. Her brother thought any day she came was Sunday, so what was there to worry about?

It was a good thing her old boyfriend's cousin worked at the pen. Sid could always find her brother if he was in the yard, and would deliver whatever goodies she brought.

At least she'd know Petey would get them in time.

What she didn't know was that her brother's cell was across from Alfredo Luna's, the drug lord. He sat like a spider and watched her brother, but Bad Al took care of the kid, too. Word was out that nobody messed with "Pete, the half-wit."

Sometimes, when the weather was nice and the road crews were out cleaning up litter along the highway, one of the prisoners would bring back a bandana and give it to Petey. The kid loved those things, no matter what color it was.

Since he was harmless, the guards would let him tie them around his arm or leg, or let it hang from his pocket for a few days. Once, he'd tied one on the bars of his cell. They had to take that one down.

Whoever found a colorful bandana knew Bad Al Luna was good for a pack of cigarettes.

No one ever knew who threw the kerchief-wrapped rocks for the road crew to find. Who cared, as long as the smokes were there.

When the weather was bad and the crews didn't go out, Dolores received flowers.

Alfredo Luna always knew when a drug deal went down in his territory. He had a pretty fair idea what his cut was. Everything was under control. He wouldn't have to do anything unless the kid got black licorice or a black bandana or some other damned black thing. It didn't matter.

Al was the enforcer, while Mano Baca was the brain.

Mano had figured all this out.

But just because he was off the streets didn't mean Al wasn't staying on top of his end of the business.

At seven thirty the next morning, a sleep-deprived Dolores Mendoza left a sack full of one dozen pink cupcakes with Sid Salazar at the gate and hurried on to work.

Sid helped himself to one, thinking it would go well with his coffee at his break. The other eleven found their way to a lucky Petey later that morning. It was too early to go to the exercise yard, and Petey was still in his cell, coloring in a book.

Petey giggled and clapped his hands when he opened the sack. Across from him, Alfredo Luna watched with interest as the kid licked the bright pink icing off the tops of the store-bought cupcakes.

Al hummed as he pulled a box from under his cot, withdrew a small notebook, and licked a pencil nub. Another seventy-five thousand had just been deposited in his account. He really liked the look of those zeros as he penciled them in.

Emilio had taken the time to build a lovely little cross with Tina's name carved on it, and Jovita and Virgie had decorated it with sunflowers and bright yellow roses they had bought at a crafts store in Taos. Virgie said the yellow flowers would brighten up everyone's lives, just as Tina had done.

"Tina was such a sunny personality," Jovita had said.

Lita and Benito had taken the descanso, the little cross, out one clear cold January afternoon and had driven it into the frozen ground where she had lost her life.

Lita thought the bright colors looked garish against the dirty snow.

Benito tried to grin and said at least it would remind everyone to slow down since there wasn't a guard rail. He had written a lovely letter (his grandmother thought) to the highway department, requesting a rail be erected to save other lives.

After a quiet moment of empty silent prayer, they went back to Virgie's, where she and Jovita had a meal ready. "It's good hot chili and tortillas to warm you up," Jovita announced.

Virgie's husband, Mel, had even joined in the conversation, trying to spark some life back into Lita. He told amusing stories about selling the flies he tied for the sporting goods store in Albuquerque. There was one about a customer who wanted to order Rio Grande Princes for her sons. He then had everyone else laughing about mix-ups at Fed Ex where he worked.

Lita had a headache and said she had to go home before dessert.

Ben had homework.

Virgie cut large slabs of chocolate cake for them to take with them. The icing was still warm, and it filled the car on their way home with the aroma of chocolate.

"I'm gonna email Kip and Sweetie and tell them about today, before I start on calculus," he said as they walked in the door.

"Give them my love. Tell Sweetie I want to hear her play her guitar when she gets back."

"Sure thing, Mamalita. Can I get you anything?"

"No, sweetheart." She struggled out of her coat. "You could eat my share of cake for me later."

"Your wish is my command!" He headed to the kitchen and came back with a fork and a carton of milk. "This is to help Virgie's cake go down," he said as he waved the carton at her on his way to his room.

When he and the cake had disappeared into his room, Lita went and got her shawl, her Tina hug. She wrapped it around her shoulders and sat in the darkening sala.

"Come on, Estrellita Cordova, snap out of it. You can think of something to do besides being overwhelmed. Ben would say, 'Get a grip,' but what is there to hold onto?"

She closed her eyes. For a moment, she could hear her grandson's CD. He was playing it softly.

All at once, she was rocking Tina, who was wrapped in a big towel after a bath. They were counting toes and checking the scrape on her knee, the time she fell off the fence. She had been playing Peter Pan and was more hurt that she could not fly.

When Lita woke, the room was dark and there was a blanket across her lap. Benito's lights were out. She had missed the Savage show. It was good to know that someone still cared about the world out there beyond Los Santos.

Tonight, she didn't even care about her little village.

"Holy Mother, help me..."

She hoped Benito had let the cat in.

Emilio shaved another curl of wood from an emerging St. Francis. This Santo was looking as gaunt and haggard as Lita Cordova.

She had been at the bookmobile today. Even Sunny had noticed, and asked Emilio why she looked so emaciated.

He was proud she had remembered the word "emaciated." She had learned it last summer. That chica never forgot a word!

He agreed with Sunny and said it was because she was still grieving for Tina.

Sunny had run over and given Lita a hug. On their way home, he'd asked her what she'd said to their friend.

"I just said I missed her smile."

"Me too, little one. Maybe soon we will see her laugh again. Sweetie will be coming back in a few weeks and she has always been able to charm Ben's abuela. What did you check out today?"

"It's a book about dogs. Mr. Wills says it will teach me how to train my dog and how to take good care of it."

"So, you still want a smelly dog? You haven't changed your mind since this morning?"

"Don't be silly!"

"Sweetheart, would I tease you? What does your mama say?"

"'We'll see. We'll see.'"

She made a face. "Emilio, why do grownups always say that when they don't want to talk about something?"

"Excellent inquiry. Perhaps it's because they want to say yes and make you happy, but don't have the energy or money to do anything about it."

"Mr. Zamora's dog had puppies. He said I could have one! That wouldn't cost anything."

"That dog is huge. Can you imagine a dog that size in your little house, sweeping all your mama's work on the floor with its long, wagging tail? You need a little dog to cuddle with. Read your book and then you'll know how much work it takes to make a good life for the right dog."

"I'll have Mom read it to me tonight, and then she'll know I can do it, and then she'll have to say yes!"

"We'll see."

"Emilio! You're no help." She left, letting the door slam.

He sighed as he ran his fingers over the smooth wood, checking for rough spots. If it were only as simple to make other people do as they should. The wood responded to the touch of his blade, but you just couldn't cut away people's problems. How he would love to shave their sorrows, sweep them up at the end of the day, and burn them in his fireplace. There were enough problems around here to keep him warm all winter.

He turned the little statue around and looked at the face. He worked with his smallest chisel, slowly, carefully, around the contours of the nose.

"Give me help in fulfilling your prayer, Señor. I try, but I'm not made for such things. It's one thing to identify the problems and quite another to do anything at all about them."

He removed a few more infinitesimal grains of wood. "Brother, you are going to have to assist me in my humble efforts."

***

That night at supper, Benito and Lita were going over their lists of all the things he would need for school.

Christina's little life insurance policy had left Lita a bit of money, after the funeral expenses. She hoped there would be enough for a sizable down payment on a new truck for Benito, but she couldn't say anything yet. She didn't want him counting on it.

Tina, after all, had promised a new roof.

"This letter from State says I should plan on six hundred a semester for books. I'm glad I got that scholarship. It will take care of the dorm and books and a third of my tuition."

"Don't forget to select a meal plan. You have to have one of those." She spooned more Spanish rice onto his plate.

"Yeah, which folder was that in?"

"Don't talk with your mouth full. If you keep that up, you'll never get a date! I think it's that one with the green border on the top."

He swallowed and spread butter on another piece of cornbread as he scanned the list. "I can't afford this, Mamalita"

"You have to eat! I don't want you living on fast food and vending machine junk. Someone's got to outlive me."

He let that slide. "How about I sign up for one meal a day? I can get a little microwave and do oatmeal and eggs for breakfast and have bologna for lunch, and peanut butter. I'll save lots that way."

"And how are you going to keep eggs and bologna?"

"Didn't you see this brochure? It's about renting mini refrigerators. They aren't much." He held up his empty glass.

"You have your computer and desk," she added as she refilled his glass. "They'll take up floor space."

"Yeah, and my CDs and player."

"Won't those do you a lot of good, though?"

"Aw, Mamalita, give me a break. What I really need is a truck."

"Yours should get you through the year, and if it doesn't, you can use my car. Now, don't make a face. It may not be as fancy as Alberto's or as new as you would like, but it's a mode of transportation. Your abuelo was so proud of that car and took such good care of it!"

"I like that, 'Mode of transportation'! Makes it sound like a foreign hybrid, instead of an eighty-six T-bird."

"You better," she tried to tease. "It means it will get you there."

They cleared the dirty plates and she cut him a large slice of peach pie.

"I'm supposed to bring extra-long sheets."

"We have Tina's already. They're white. They'll go with everything. You'll need some blankets. Hers were stolen, and all I have here are for double beds. Oh, put down towels, laundry soap, and quarters."

"How do you know all this stuff?"

"Remember how your sister used to say she couldn't do her wash because no one had change?"

"I'll need a bookcase. I bet I can pick one of those up cheap at a secondhand store or Kmart in Cruces."

Dorms, Cruces, microwaves—they all sounded so foreign and far away, she thought as she handed him his pie.

He looked at the growing list. "At this rate, I won't have any money left."

"That's why you're working for Hugh this summer. You'll make more than you would in Taos and you won't have to buy so much gas or any food. You can eat up there with the other hands. Tell you what, I'll bank the money that I would've had to spend on your food and you can have that to tide you over."

"Don't you go forgetting how much I eat! This pie's good. With what you save, I should be able to pay for everything!"

"Except that you eat beans and rice and cornbread. Those don't cost so much, and I get our cheese free for keeping the books for Jovita and Virgie. Maybe we could get you to sell cheese down there. That would give you some spending money."

"I could try. You ship me some samples after classes start. I bet other cheese salesmen don't know the names of the goats or whose grass they eat!"

Lita loved that, at seventeen, all things were possible for her boy. He would try anything and wasn't afraid of work. She didn't have to worry about him, thank you, God.

"You haven't gone to college yet, and your grades slipped at the beginning of this semester. Tina's death threw us all for a loop. Why don't you go study? I'll clean up here and straighten up the sala. The girls are coming tomorrow night to watch a rerun of CSI."

"Too bad I won't be around much this summer. They won't come every week for reruns and they'll be busy with milking and cheese. We could have some good times."

"We'll just have to make the most of the time God gives us. Now scoot!" She dashed her empty water glass at him and grinned when he ducked.

How would she get along when he was gone?

She should buy a computer so she could email him. Maybe she would do just that and he could show her what to do before he left.

Where would the money come from?

Did she have anything she could sell?

Emilio rolled back his right shoulder, bent his elbow at a little more than a forty-five-degree angle, flicked his strong wrist, and followed through as his line sailed across the dappled light. He watched with satisfaction as the line unrolled in a tight loop and the leader settled gently on the surface.

His casting had improved after studying a book he'd checked out from Owen's bookmobile. If you really want to learn anything, you had to find a great teacher. The book had been written by a lady, Joan Wulff. She was older than he was!

Even though this boulder-infested stream didn't demand a great level of casting skill, he derived a substantial amount of pride in the soft ease with which the line sailed through the air. At times, it seemed that the casting was almost more important than the fishing.

Interesting? He wondered if there were any parallels between this art and that of Santo carving.

He picked the line off the water, made one false cast, and laid the Rio Grande King back on the water inches from the boulder at the head of the pool. It was not his most productive fly, but he loved to fish with it because it was a classic local pattern. With a practiced flick of his wrist, he mended the fly-line once to keep the current from dragging it from the sweet spot behind the boulder.

One last cast and he would call it a day.

Four sweet Cutthroat later, two for himself and two to share with Amy, were sufficient. He had to fish for two families. Amy and Sunny could always use more protein.

Not bad, considering the cold water temperatures. Fishing would improve as the water warmed later in the summer.

He was thankful that the State had chosen not to stock hatchery rainbows in this creek. The rainbows put up a much better fight and were more fun to catch, but the Cutthroat were far prettier, and their pinkish flesh was superior in taste.

Emilio carefully removed the fly, dried it on his shirtsleeve, and placed it in an Altoids box with a mix of nymphs, small Wooly Buggers, and a couple of Royal Coachmen. The flies had been a Christmas present from Mr. Torres. The box of flies went into his shirt pocket along with a single spool of leader material. Emilio fished light. His best fights today were too small to keep and had to be released. They'd be there later in the season or next year. They'd be wilier and harder to catch, so the thrill would be greater.

What more was needed, except maybe an apple or burrito, for an exquisite afternoon? He hadn't lost a fly nor tangled his line in the underbrush and had four fine fish. Emilio reckoned he had experienced a perfect day.

For some reason, the fish lying in the leaves reminded him of Lita. She had lost her luster just as surely as these fish would if he left them there much longer. He took an old towel from his backpack, wet it in the stream, and rolled up the fish. After packing them away, he started downhill, across Lita's rented-out property towards home.

He realized that most of his life had been tied to Estrellita Roybal Cordova.

Even his love affair with words began because of her. He had been picking berries with his grandmothers. One had been the daughter of a medicine man and the other a war bride from Ireland. His grandfather had gone as a doughboy to Europe in the Great War. He'd lost a leg but gained a nurse wife. She had been an orphan with black, curly hair, blue eyes, and what she called a well of fey.

As the two women rested on a rock, Lita had ridden past. She was a bit younger than he, with thin legs reaching only halfway down her pony's side. When he had started to tease her, both his abuelas reprimanded him.

"Shame, Emo!"

He'd come back into their circle of chastisement, and after a few moments of self-pity, had been caught up in their conversation.

"That one will surely be a votress," stated the lilting voice of one grandmother.

His other grandmother nodded wisely and said, "Our people call her kind a Spider Woman."

Emilio sat pretending to be bored, but couldn't wait to find out what a votress was. When he opened the big dictionary and read the meaning of the word, he imagined Lita dressed in filmy, white Roman robes, a vestal virgin tending sacred flames.

Years later, he was surprised to hear that she'd married, and then laughed at the joke on himself when she had a baby, thinking it was rather out of character for a vestal virgin.

The word "votress" had caught him as surely that day as a barb hidden in one of his flies. Since that day, words for him had become magical. The way they felt rolling around in his mouth was glorious. Their sounds and meanings flavored his life and made it palatable. He built his inner life with exotic syllables and colored the world around him with a vibrancy that others seemed to lack.

Now, in the spring, the aspens were differing shades of celery. When summer arrived, they would turn a darker, more intense green with celadon backs. Autumn was his favorite time, for in the fall when he looked at the aspens, he didn't think a mundane gold, but rather gamboge or turmeric or butterscotch.

He loved the breezy afternoons when there was always a tumultuous symphony of color, as the leaves were tossed every which way. Evening light was amethyst, never purple. The sound of strange words rolled over him constantly. Bouillabaisse, salmagundi, syllabub.

He once had seen an ad in the back of a magazine and had ordered scuppernong jam. He had been disappointed in the flavor. The appellation was much more exotic.

After stowing the towel-wrapped fish, he turned toward home.

He should have brought Sunny with him. She was old enough to be quiet. She should learn to fish. Her young mind was like a sponge. Perhaps this summer. It would be amusing to show her the habits of the trout and the food they eat, the differences between the mayflies, the stoneflies, and the caddis. "Etymology." She would love that word!

When he reached the village, he made his way down a back alley towards Amy's place. He passed Jovita's and waved to her through the apricot blossoms. She had spent the afternoon tenting her young vegetables with chicken wire. Gallon milk jugs covered baby tomatoes and whatever else she needed to protect them from the cool nights. She was now in the process of sifting self-rising flour on her plants to take care of the early bugs. Her chickens would see to the insects when the plants became stronger and the wire was removed.

"Hola," he called as he leaned his rod against the low adobe wall.

A grin spread across her wide brown face. "Any luck today? I want the guts for my compost." She never stopped. It was either gardening or goats with Jovita.

"Guts I gave back to the stream, but I'll give you the heads. Sunny won't eat them with the heads on. She says they're watching her."

"You take good care of Amy and her girl, Emilio. Wish you'd been around when I was growing up."

"I was, but I was too busy growing up myself to think about anybody else."

She laughed. "We could have all used you back then."

"Since we're on the subject of helping, have you and Virgie spent much time with Lita lately?"

"We clean together. We watch TV. She's worried Ben is having an affair with his computer. His grades are going to pot and they both still grieve over their girl."

"But what about her?"

"Emilio, you know her." She flipped her long, thick braid over her shoulder. "Lita should've been a poker player, like my ex. She holds her cards real close."

"You're right about that. Something tells me you and Virgie ought to cheat."

She laughed her deep laugh. "And you, a deacon! Go on. You

got fish to fry. Virgie and I will do what we can. Wait right there. I got some early yellow squash in the green house. You can leave the heads as payment."

Jovita never quit. You had to give her that. After she shed that no-good husband, her life had taken on new meaning. Now she was about the most productive person in the valley.

He grinned to himself as he sliced the heads from the fish. He thought his payment was shy of what he really owed.

"Here are six small ones. I needed to get them off the plants so they won't die when I transplant them in the morning." She handed him the summer squash and flicked the fish heads to her chickens. "After they clean those, I'll put the rest in my compost. Deacon, you sure you want us to lean on Lita? Somehow it don't seem right."

He picked up his rod and winked, "Sometimes, Jovita, I don't think God expects us to play fair."

"In that case, we'll try." She dusted flour at him.

***

Emilio knocked on Amy's door with the fish, but took one look at Amy's table and invited the Jenkins to his house to eat. There were metal fillings and bits of unfinished jewelry all over the surface of the table, and the kitchen counter looked worse.

Amy stretched her thin back, looked at the mess in front of her, and quickly accepted the invitation. Sunny followed him home to help set the table.

Both her top front teeth were now missing. It was a good thing fish was easy to chew. He thought she said, "And when I have a dog I'll have somebody to talk to all the time and he can sleep with me and..."

"And what will I do when you neglect in communicating with me every moment?"

She smoothed the calico placemats. "Silly you, Emilio, I can't tell you all my secrets."

"So, chica, what is the name of this dog? Curious Clifford?"

She hooted. She had finally returned those two books to Owen after Christmas.

"Maybe you could name it Waldo and when it was lost, you could say, 'Where's Waldo?'"

She giggled so hard he thought she'd lose her balance. When she came up for air, she said, "What a stupid name for a dog! My dog will go with me when I ride my bike."

Next to her nonexistent pet, the bike that Ben Cordova had fixed up for her down at Tito's Garage was her favorite possession.

Amy and Emilio had spent their spring taking turns huffing and puffing along beside and then behind the wobbly bike. Also swabbing scrapes with hydrogen peroxide. Now, Sunny rode everywhere she could.

He chopped onions, garlic, and frozen chiles, browning them in olive oil while Sunny carefully wielded the biscuit cutter. Then he diced the squash. Fresh ground pepper was added, along with the squash, to the vegetables. After it finished cooking, all he'd need to do was add some salt.

Sunny watched as Emilio carefully heated lard in his big cast-iron skillet, rinsed the fish and breaded them in cornmeal.

Amy was chipper over supper, her worried frown almost erased. Her mouse-brown hair was pulled back in a simple ponytail and the oil lamp on the old table did fascinating things for her bone structure. Emilio had no use for the man who had beaten her, yet, without him, she and Sunny wouldn't be in Los Santos.

"How's the business coming along?" he asked over coffee and store-bought cookies.

"I had the name changed on the new contract," she replied. "It's now 'Tina's.'"

"Ah, another one of us keeping her alive."

"Emilio, it just made sense. She was the one who thought the whole business up and brought me that first contract. If it hadn't been for her, I wouldn't have money in my account or a roof over our heads.

You know as well as anyone she talked Lita into renting me our little place for next to nothing."

"Amy, I know Tina's grandfather got that house in payment for legal work and that there wasn't anybody to rent it to around here. I know Lita plows your rent back into the church, so you're tithing even if you're not Catholic." He just had to get that last part in. "She's pleased the varmints haven't moved in and destroyed the place"

"She had to help me get the roof fixed..."

"That's what landlords are for, chica. Now, in return, for Lita, you make beautiful jewelry and sell it to those snobs in New York. That will make Lita happy, not the money."

On and on they talked, pricing, branching out, name recognition. Emilio was the only other artist in the community besides Emily Higgenbotham, and she only lived there in the summers. She and her husband spent their winters in Arizona. Amy and Emilio had adopted one another. He was family.

He nodded to Sunny, asleep on the sofa. "She needs that dog."

"I know, but not a big one and not a puppy. I don't have the room or the time."

"I'll see what I can do."

Amy took the flashlight, and the big man picked up the sleeping child. It wasn't far, but Amy was tired, and why wake this baby whose face looked like an old woman needing dentures? He grinned at Amy and gestured with his chin at the little girl.

"Those teeth better come in soon or she might swallow that upper lip."

"And pray they come in straight!"

That night, Emilio dreamed of a beautiful young woman at an elegant dinner. There were candles on the table and flowers in crystal vases. She slowly unfolded a cutwork napkin and spread it in her lap. He woke with a start and grabbed a pencil and paper. He reminded himself of his grandmothers and could almost hear them chuckle as he wrote, "Emily Post, table manners, Sunny."

"I think I got prostrate problems!" claimed Virgie as she swept down the aisle.

"You can't have that!" called Jovita from behind the altar where she was going through the junk that always accumulated there. She held up a bow from some forgotten flowers to the light to see if it might be reused. "Anyhow, it's 'prostate' and only men get that."

"Then why do I have to get up so many times at night?"

"If you'd stop drinking coffee and Cokes all evening, you wouldn't have to. Isn't that right, Lita? Me, I sleep like a baby. How about you, Lita? Lita!"

"What?"

"You sleep okay?"

"Some nights."

The cousins looked at each other. Virgie shrugged. Jovita tried again. "Lita, you think little Sunny ought to get that dog she's always going on about?"

"Why not? It would make her happy."

"But a dirty dog in your rent house. It might damage the place!" put in Virgie as she adjusted her glasses.

"Who cares?" sighed their friend.

What could they do to jump start her? Jovita had had it. She raised her voice. "Lita, you gonna cook beans for the Fiesta again this year, or are you gonna serve'em hard and dry like you are?"

Virgie gasped. Jovita was rarely so hard on anyone.

"I guess, I mean yes. May I borrow your roasters again?"

"Sure, three Crock-Pots and three electric roasters. That ought to be enough."

"I've saved ham hocks," said Virgie. "They've been in my freezer. I'll send those over to give some flavor. Onions, garlic, and chile aren't enough. I like how ham adds a little something. Mel always wants ham in his beans."

"I swear, you spoil that man," snorted Jovita.

"All right," said Lita. "But it's still two weeks away."

"Has Tessie told you the road crew's almost finished with the new guard rail?" asked Jovita. "She's gonna miss the extra business when they're gone. Isn't often she gets extra regulars around here."

"How much longer do you think?" asked Lita.

Jovita winked at Virgie. Their friend was taking an interest. They'd have to tell Emilio.

"Maybe a week. You know how men like to make a job last as long as they can!"

Virgie piped in, "Tessie says there's a big fellow, wears lots of gold jewelry, that's the boss. At least he acts that way. Tessie says he's a real big tipper!"

Emilio knocked on Lita's door.

"I'm coming," she called. "Come in while I let Kitty Gato out and pull the plug on the coffee. Do you want to take a cup along?"

"No, thanks, I've already had two cups. Thanks for going with me on this great adventure. I've never done anything like this."

"I'm the one who should be thanking you," she said as she grabbed her purse. "It seems like years since I've been out of the house. I'm in need of an adventure myself." She didn't speak again until they were going past the church. "I can't believe Amy finally broke down and said Sunny could have a dog. Why isn't she going with you?"

"She wants it to be a surprise for Sunny."

"What if it isn't the right dog?"

"Oh, we have plenty of rules we have to go by. I have the list right here." He patted his shirt pocket.

She gave him a quizzical look.

"It has to be small."

"That makes sense. It will eat less and that house is so small there's not room for a big dog."

He nodded and held up a second finger. "It has to be female."

"Why? The pound spays and neuters all the animals."

"Sunny thinks females are easier to train. She's been doing her homework, and I won't argue with her."

"Anything else?"

"It can't be a puppy, and it has to be trained."

"Goodness, we are looking for a paragon, aren't we?"

It was a fine morning to be out. Emilio had his window down and the smells of spring and freshly turned earth filled the cab of his truck. She broke the short silence.

"Why did you ask me to come along, really?"

"I suspected you needed a break and some new surroundings."

"And?"

"And I need someone with good sense to take control," he laughed. "I'm afraid I'll get in there and end up coming home with a whole kennel full of dogs. I don't know if I can leave a single one there, and you are to curb my sensibilities. Anyway, you can remind me I'm going on my trip next week and you would have to come feed them all for two weeks."

"Don't you worry. I'll keep a short rein on your appetites." She smiled, "I think I'm too much a cat person."

They chatted about the church, the village (what was the difference?), and his upcoming trip to Germany. He was being honored at an art museum in Frankfurt. They had purchased a collection of his Santos for their new Native American display and invited him to come for the grand opening. Emilio said he wouldn't have gone, but the round-trip ticket was too good to pass up.

They pulled up to the low slump rock building and sat for a moment listening to the ruckus they had caused. They couldn't see the animals behind the fence, but there was no doubt the dogs knew they were there.

"Shall we?" Emilio got out and came around and opened her door. "Remember, I'm depending on you."

She patted his arm. "Trust me."

The woman behind the counter looked like she could handle twenty-mule teams. These animals appeared to be in good hands. "Are you looking for a lost dog?"

"No, but we're here to find one," answered Emilio.

They explained about the lonely little girl up in Los Santos and how badly she needed a dog.

The woman listened and then picked up her keys. "Follow me. Don't let the noise or the smell get to you. Sam will be here to clean up any minute." She opened the door, and the noise and the offensive odor hit them.

"Don't put your hands near the cages," the woman said as she shouldered her way forward.

Lita had never seen so many dogs. Seemingly dogs of every size and color one could imagine were here. Some had deep, fearsome barks and some yipped sharply. Some lunged against their cages, while others wagged their tails expectantly. A few crouched in fear at the back of their cages, shaking, with their tails between their legs.

"The small ones are back this way," said the woman turning to her left. "Here we are. Now, here's a healthy Chihuahua cross."

Emilio looked at Lita.

She shook her head. "It's a male and he'd freeze in winter."

There was a Pekinese with a blind eye, a feisty toy poodle with an earsplitting yip, and a pug that snarled at them. Lita kept shaking her head. She literally pushed Emilio past a cage where a nondescript dog looked at them with running eyes. They were almost through when they came to a cage with two dogs keeping each other company.

"These two have just come in," said the woman.

When they peered into the cage, the little dogs pranced to greet them. They didn't bark, but sat with their button noses pressed against the bars. The blonde one licked at Lita's finger when she reached towards the cage.

"These are sisters. Real beauties, aren't they?" Emilio and Lita looked at the two dogs and both their hearts melted.

"Their owner was going to Paris and didn't want to be bothered with them anymore. Silly bitch, excuse me, but some idiots don't deserve animals. These are small for Havanese. They're almost full-grown. They might get to seven pounds. One of them ought to do. They've been house-trained and have been through obedience school."

Lita looked at Emilio and nodded.

"We'll take the one with black ears," he said.

"You'll need to get her groomed," the woman said. "Sometimes they pick up fleas and ticks from the other cages." She reached in, picked up the little dog, and firmly shut the cage. They turned to go, when the remaining dog let out a whimper.

Lita didn't know how it happened, but she heard a voice that sounded quite like her own saying, "I'll take her sister. We'll take both of them!"

Emilio grinned.

"We can't leave her here," Lita was almost pleading.

"Good choice," said the woman, looking kinder than she had initially. Before Lita could change her mind, her arms were full of wiggles.

Soon, the dogs had received their shots, and Lita and Emilio had filled out the paperwork. Their new tags were heart-shaped. Emilio pulled out his wallet and counted out his money. Lita had to use her credit card.

Fifteen minutes later, they had dropped the dogs off at a groomer suggested by the pound.

"What have I done?" moaned Lita. "Why didn't you stop me?"

"You just beat me to the solution, Lita. I'm proud of you."

"But I've never done such a foolish thing in my life! Benito will think I'm crazy. What will he say? What will Kitty Gato do?"

"We'll find out, won't we? Come on. Let's go to Taos Books and see if we can find out about these prizes. She said Havanese, didn't she?"

"Yes, she gave me their papers. Here they are." She fished them from her purse. They went to the bookstore, and were soon in the right section.

"Here's what we're looking for," said Emilio, paging though a book on small breeds. "Havanese...toy breed, related to the Bichon Frise. Listen, Lita, they were brought to Cuba by seamen as gifts to the ladies there."

"How romantic."

"It's thought they were used in Europe as circus performers but became lap dogs."

Lita was reading over his shoulder. "Looks like the only things they need is grooming and affection. It says at the top of the next page they don't shed. That's a relief! Oh, see here," she pointed down the page. "The poor things almost didn't make it out of Cuba because of the revolution. Now most are found in the U.S."

"I wonder how much they cost?" whispered Emilio. They went to the information desk and the nice salesgirl helped them find what they were looking for. Lita gasped when she saw sixteen hundred dollars and up, depending on the breeder.

"Oh, my, Emilio, I didn't know we had such extravagant taste! I better buy this book. Everyone here has been so helpful, we can't just walk out."

"I hope they don't have such expensive taste. We need to go buy dog food."

They thanked the clerk, who was nice enough to give them directions to PetSmart.

Soon, they were looking lost inside the pet store. Thankfully, there was a helpful clerk who led them around.

"I bet he's on commission," whispered Emilio, as the items in their basket kept growing. Dog food, two cases of canned and two ten-pound sacks of dry, collars, leashes, vitamins, toothpaste, little rubber toothbrushes that fit over the finger. There were combs and brushes, shampoo and flea powder, wicker baskets, and plaid pillows to fit them. They selected small bowls with paw prints for food and water, complete with matching place mats. They drew the line at travel cases, but did get several toys. They reasoned the dogs would be lonely without each other. At the checkout stand, Emilio noticed some doggie treats. They had to have those. The clerk came running up with scented wood shavings that he said were foolproof when it came to training. They didn't want any accidents...

Emilio borrowed a phone and called the groomer. Lita wished she'd brought her phone. The dogs wouldn't be ready for two more hours. As they were loading most of the supplies in the back of the truck, Lita hooted when he said, "I'm such a fool! If I ever hear that you told anyone I bought wood shavings, I'll swear you are a prevaricator of the highest order! I wade in wood chips!"

"But not scented ones, Emilio..."

"Hush, woman, and let me take you to lunch. It's been a long time since you surprised me so thoroughly."

"I must have spent two months' allowance today! You'll have to treat me to a very big lunch. I may be going hungry."

"I don't know. Did you read the ingredients on those cans of food? They sounded fairly enticing."

He told about his plans over lunch. While in Germany, he was going to study for a week with carvers in the Black Forest area and attempt to pick up some new skills or at least some new tools to use in his work. He admitted that sometimes he felt he was stagnating in his craft, forever using the same themes, the same techniques. He dreamed of trying something new.

"Well, I'm ahead of you. I'm trying something new. I've never owned a dog of my own. We had lots of dogs at the ranch when I was little, but they were working dogs, not pets. Ben was allergic to them, so this will be my first."

"God works in mysterious ways."

"I think you planned this, you old fox."

"Lita, who said, and I quote," (and he mimicked her very well) 'I'll take her sister. We'll take both of them!'?"

"Touché."

They finished their meal and went to a few new galleries before it was time to pick up the dogs.

"Do you think I should sell some of the paintings at the house or ranch?" she asked. "They seem so old to me. I have no idea if any of them have any value, but Tina did promise a new roof."

"Why don't you have them appraised first and then think about it? Ben might need the money in a few years more than the church does now."

"I thought you'd be all for it, Deacon Maestas."

"To me, the church is the families who worship together. Some of us are as bedraggled as the building. Sometimes I think we'd be better off having a nursing home rather than a sanctuary."

"We are rather dying on the vine, aren't we, with the young ones moving away."

"Some of us, Lita, but today you jumped into a new wineskin."

They were surprised when they picked up the dogs. Forty dollars each! They were assured by the owner that their nails had been filed, they had been dipped to rid them of fleas and ticks, and their ears had been treated and cleaned, all before an absolutely marvelous shampoo.

"You're just going to love how they smell now." The man made them feel as if he had done a mountain of work and they were shysters to inquire what they had spent their money on. "And shame on you," the man lisped. "The darlings were all matted. You haven't been taking care of these babies as they deserve!"

"That's right, we haven't," smiled Emilio. "In fact, we just got them from the pound."

"My, aren't they the lucky ones, and you, too, of course. You know they are rather rare? I'll just get the precious darlings now."

They hardly recognized their dogs. Each had a pink bow holding back her bangs exposing inquisitive black eyes. They knew they looked nice and they pranced about the lobby as Emilio and Lita paid their bills. The new collars and tags had been left in the truck, so Emilio scooped up her pet and presented Lita with a soft ball of fluff. Never in a million years would she admit that the little thing smelled "divine." Emilio then picked up Sunny's dog, and looking for all the world like a first-time father, led the way awkwardly to the truck.

"Will such high-falootin critters mind riding in a pickup?"

Both dogs were well-behaved and settled down right away, but after a while, Lita's dog crawled onto her lap and then looked up as if asking permission. Lita found herself nodding and talking to a lap dog, of all things. Emilio was faring no better, for he was telling the little dog with black ears all about Sunny.

As Lita listened to him talk to the dog, she became aware that he constructed a world with his words that was tangible. He used them in such a substantial manner. His words are real to him, she thought. She wished she felt that way about her own vocabulary. Hers was adequate, but she felt she used words as other people used slipcovers or paint. They kept the basic shape, but the idea was more real to her than the word itself. Sometimes it was like looking at trees through fog or snow. You knew the tree was there and sometimes glimpsed a limb or trunk, but mostly the reality was hidden by the word. Oh, how dreadful she was at expressing herself. She must try to do better.

"I think you should have been a writer, Emilio."

"I never had the training."

"Still, you have the right talents, the love of words, their sounds and meanings, everything about them. You also love to tell stories."

"It sounds grand, but being a loquacious raconteur does not give me the gift or the ability, although it does make me appreciative of those who spend their days with a pen or a computer." He reached into the bag at her feet and handed her a sack of doggie treats.

"You do the honors. Let's see if they'll sit up or something." Two little heads cocked to one side and both plumed tails began to wave as she opened the bag.

"Sit. Sit up," she commanded, and the dogs tried to obey in the bouncing truck. "Oh, my!" she gasped when a warm little tongue touched her palm as her dog took its reward.

"So what are you going to name her?"

"Maybe Dora, short for adorable."

"Or that old saw, 'Dumb Dora,'" he said.

"Scratch that name, then. She's soft and warm and about the same shape as a sopaipilla. I could call her Sophie."

"Ah, the goddess Sophia..."

"I don't like that. It reminds me of the Da Vinci Code."

"What's wrong with that, Lita?"

"I can't keep from thinking that the author had some political agenda. Making people question their faith. Poor Virgie got so upset she cried for weeks and refused to clean the church last year. No! Never Sophia!"

"She's about the color of pampas grass and she will be pampered. How does Pamplona sound? Oh, I forgot. Sunny says short names are best," he reminded her.

"Pam sounds oily, so that's out."

"She's almost the color of taffy," he suggested.

"That's a sticky man's name, you remember? 'Taffy came to my house and stole a marrow bone.' She's also the color of the inside of a ripe banana. I could call her 'Chiquita.'"

"She's also the color of candlelight," he said.

"Candy is sweet and short for candle, in a way, but that is like taffy, sticky. Short names you say...I'll call her Glow! That's soft and bright and warm, all rolled into one, like candlelight."

"I wonder what Sunny will name this one," he said, fondling two black ears. "Are you going to the party tonight?"

"Of course."

"Would you permit me to give you and Ben a ride?"

"We'd be happy for the lift. Thank you."

They were already pulling up to her house. Emilio helped carry Glow's paraphernalia inside. He borrowed Lita's pliers and attached the little license to the leather collar. "There you go, sweet thing," he crooned when he buckled it on. "I believe it's time you spread your wood chips, Lita. This dog is dancing way too fast. I'll let myself out."

When Lita opened the back door to take Glow out, Kitty Gato started in, but stopped dead. The cat was almost twice the size of the dog. When the cat hissed and raised his ruff, the dog was smart enough to know who was in charge. Glow crept forward and rolled over, exposing her underbelly. Kitty Gato sniffed once and marched in with his tail twitching.

"That's better than I'd hoped for, little girl. Come on, let's hurry."

The dog started following and then took off exploring the yard, needs forgotten. Lita spread the wood shavings in a corner by her trash bin where she'd never gotten cosmos to grow.

"Come here, Glow. That's a good girl. Here's where you do your business. Now, go!" The dog squatted, but saw a cricket. She was off. She would pounce and the cricket would jump. Pounce, leap, jump, jump, right, right, left, right.

"Inside," Lita commanded. Glow looked up, but instead of following, ran to the wood chips. Lita was as proud as a mother realizing her first born was potty-trained. They went in and the dog began to explore while Lita started supper.

Ben hooted when he met Glow. "Mamalita, this isn't a dog, she's a wind-up toy!" He was soon down on his back in the middle of the kitchen floor, laughing as Glow licked his face.

"At least you got something friendly to replace your grandson," he teased.

"You should be so well-trained!" she bantered back. "Now go wash up. We need to be at the party in an hour."

Glow had her supper while Benito and Lita tried to eat. They kept watching the dog as she ate.

"She cleans up after herself and doesn't leave crumbs," beamed Lita. "I hope Sunny's dog is as clean."

She told Benito how foolish she had been at the pound and all that had happened that day.

"I'm going to call you Softie from now on!" He smiled and said, "Mamalita, I'm so glad you finally did something for yourself."

"Oh, but it wasn't for me! It was for Glow. I couldn't leave her there all alone!"

"Are you sure?" He winked. "I think you both hit the jackpot."

Dark clouds were moving in when they left home. Big, heavy drops begin to hit the tissue paper on the gift. "Hurry!" she called. "We don't want the present ruined."

"It won't matter. Sunny won't remember this one."

The party was just cake and ice cream. It was too bad Mrs. Vargas' kids had pink eye. There were only adults to help Sunny celebrate turning six. After the food, Sunny started opening gifts.

Virgie had brought a puzzle and Jovita a book. Lita had knitted a red sweater and Benito had a bottle of nail polish for her (Sweetie had suggested it in an email). Emilio gave her a big box. She squealed as she began unpacking cans of dog food and toys and doggie treats.

"Oh, Emilio! You think I'm going to get my dog!"

"Why don't you go to the bathroom now and wash your face," suggested Amy.

"Thanks, everybody!" called Sunny as she dashed off. The adults all listened expectantly and laughed when they heard the excited scream.

"A dog!" Sunny was back in no time with a wriggling mass of black-and-white fur. She was giggling as it licked her face. "She's perfect! Thank you, Mama!"

"You're very welcome, Sunny. Now, put her down so we can all get a good look at her."

Lita thought it was comical to see the adults bobbing and weaving their heads this way and that as the little girl and her tiny dog bounced around the room.

"So, what you gonna name her, chica?" asked Jovita.

Sunny picked up the dog and looked into her eyes.

"Her papers said Doña Merced," suggested Emilio, "but her ears make me think she'll be a good listener...for secrets."

"I like Doña," announced Benito. "Sunny, you can always say Doña, do this and Doña, do that. Then you'll have one mixed-up pet."

"Don't be silly. Her Name is Tima."

"What kind of a name is Tima?" Virgie asked.

"It's short for 'última.' I said you were perfect, didn't I, Tima?"

"That didn't take long, and here I was betting on Waldo," said Emilio, rubbing his hands together.

"Girls shouldn't have boys' names," pronounced Sunny. No one pointed out that 'Sunny' sounded quite like 'Sonny'.

Lightning flashed and the rain started in earnest. Emilio said, "Ben, Lita, let's race to the truck. Does anyone else need a ride? I could come back."

"Virgie and I are fine. We came in Mel's car!" shouted Jovita over the noise of the rain on the tin roof.

"Sunny, feliz cumpleaños!" grinned Emilio. "I'm thrilled you have received your fondest wish. Amy, thank you for sharing this event. It was truly an última moment!"

The three dashed for the truck. They were wet and laughing as Emilio moved the pickup out into the road. "I hope your dog isn't afraid of thunder," sang out Emilio over the sound of rain and squeaking wiper blades. He drove past their house and turned around so he could let them out as close to the porch's overhang as possible.

"Goodnight...and thanks," said Benito as he jumped down from the truck.

"Yes, thank you for a wonderful day," murmured Lita.

'Welcome back," he replied.

They were astonished to find Kitty Gato and Glow tangled together in the wicker basket. Benito called to the animals. He picked up an old umbrella and the dog and headed out. He stood by the wood chips to keep Glow dry. Lita waited at the door.

"All's well for the night," he said, "but don't think I'm going to make a habit of this. It's just she smells so good right now, and if she gets wet she'll smell like dog."

Kitty Gato rushed past them. Benito shook out the tattered umbrella on the back porch and left it there. Lita put Glow back in her basket and went to get ready for bed. Benito went to email Sweetie the events of the day.

When Lita came out of her bathroom, she was surprised to see both the dog and the cat on her bed. Kitty Gato rarely slept with her, joining her only when it was very cold. He must be jealous and protecting his territory.

Lita closed the door and patted Ronald Reagan's picture. The sports were still on when she turned on the radio. She looked at the clock. Seven more minutes till she would learn what to think about the rest of the world.

She crawled into bed and Glow snuggled up to her, licking the lotion on her hand.

"I think I'm going to love you, little one. You too, Kitty Gato." She stroked the dog's head. Emilio was right. It was good to be back.

When the music for the Savage Nation started, she winced. It was so loud and abrasive. That was probably why he'd picked it, but she wished he'd selected something more melodic to play. Then she smiled. She bet Dr. Savage would like Glow as much as he did his dog, Teddy.

On a Thursday, after he had fed his pigs, Alex Silva was in his studio sanding the gesso he had put on the boards earlier in the week. He'd used rabbit gesso. He liked the way it made a finished painting look. When covered with the oil glazes, it would take on the appearance of marble beneath the transparent colors.

Tchaikovsky was echoing off the walls at such a volume that he almost didn't hear the phone.

"Who the heck?" He ran to answer, hitting his elbow on the door jamb and bumping his shin on the coffee table in the tacky living room.

"Hello...Hello?" Too late. The phone was dead. He shoved the cell phone in his back pocket. He'd go make lunch and maybe they'd call back. He rubbed his elbow and limped to the kitchen.

He let the phone ring a second time while he spread mustard on the bread and looked for some halfway-crisp lettuce as he answered, "Silva here."

"Mr. Silva, this is Tito at Los Hermanos Farms calling. Your order will be leaving here tomorrow evening, that's Friday, the seventeenth, and be at your place on Saturday, by seven a.m. This order is even better than your last. If you have any questions, please call by four your time. The number here is (559) 311-2947."

He opened a beer, ate his lunch, and called Mano. The jerk could have given him a heads-up so he might save some on a plane ticket, but no, the old coyote kept his secrets. Sadie picked up on the third ring.

He had to be careful. Mano had let him know his phone was tapped.

"Yo, Sadie, you beautiful babe, is Mano around?"

"My life? Just one canvas after another."

"No, I haven't found a girl yet. I haven't had time, Sadie."

"Well, that's good to hear."

"Uh-huh, ya don't say..."

"Uh-huh, uh-huh, listen, Sadie, I do want to know all about Mona's new car, but I need to have a word with Mano."

"Yes, I'll wait..."

He sure didn't want to be here when that shipment came, and he knew Mano didn't want him here, either.

"Mano!"

"Yes, I'm fine. Listen, the reason I called is, I gotta go to Mexico on some business this weekend and my workers are on lock-down till finals are over. You think Tres could come down?"

"Yeah, Mano, I'm glad you liked the Christmas ham."

"You bet, it's been a long time since I've seen you. Mano, the pigs are friggin' fine! I'm told they're even the best ones yet."

"Yeah, yeah."

"You ask him, hear?"

"And call me if he can't come. I'll have to find another pig-sitter."

Alex slammed down the receiver before he said what he really wanted to say to the old cuss. Being a pig farmer was the last thing Alex ever thought he'd be, but here he was.

After he'd gotten his M.F.A., he'd borrowed some money from Manuel Baca to tide him over until he'd made a dent in the art market.

He often wondered if it had been Mano's guys who torched his gallery before his insurance went into effect. He had to get a job to pay back Mano and all those friends of his who'd entrusted him with their work.

Mano had been real big about the whole thing and was selling him this sty bit by bit. The old man took most of his profits from the livestock, so it was a good thing his paintings were hot.

By next year, he figured he'd have the Bacas paid off and he'd get away from here as fast as Seabiscuit. He'd sell to the first idiot who came along and move to Guanajuato! Mano could shit in the wind.

He had to admit, every time one of these shipments came in, Mano sent him an envelope full of cash. That had gone a long way towards his gallery in Mexico.

He wasn't sure why Mano always ordered from Los Hermanos, because Alex felt their livestock was inferior to the suppliers he did business with. He must be related to them or something.

He went to his bedroom and booted up his computer.

It's a darned good thing I love my place in Mexico, he thought as he keyed in www.americanairlines.com and made his reservations. He'd leave in the morning. He'd fly to San Antonio, change planes, and land at the Leon/San Miguel de Allende. He'd take a cab from there and should be in his own home by three.

Then he phoned Yvonne to say he was coming and set up a dinner date.

Next, he called Jimmy.

Jimmy was his top worker; he'd come and check up on things Sunday afternoon, be sure there was food and water for the animals, and get Tío and Chuck to muck out.

Tío was an old fellow from Socorro who was good at what he did for Alex when he wasn't nursing a hangover. Jimmy and Chuck were students at NMIMT. Jimmy would graduate when summer school was over. Alex hoped Chuck could carry the load by himself. He didn't want to take the time to train another worker.

Luckily, he had several paintings ready to go. They were small and they'd fit in his carry-on. Too bad they were the wrong style. These would sell for more in Santa Fe. That's all he needed to take besides his passport.

He liked traveling light.

***

Up in Albuquerque, the tape came to a stop and Lt. Gordon transcribed the last of it.

She quickly applied some lip gloss and adjusted her skirt. She knew hunky Frank Quintana would be pleased with the information she was delivering. It was about the pig guy they had under surveillance. Much to her disappointment, he was on the phone and didn't look up. So much for lip gloss and orthodontia! He'd just held out his hand and taken her report. As she turned to leave, she heard him say, "Gotta go." She paused at the door and heard him dial and ask for Luis Fernandez.

What was she going to have to do to get his attention?

The semi driver had picked up his load by four-thirty on Friday afternoon. He did this for two reasons. First, he would be going east, away from the setting sun, and secondly, it was already warm in southern California and he'd have to drive across Arizona with this load. One hundred sixty-eight piglets smelled bad enough at any time, but in the daytime, the stink was more than he could take. At least at night it was cooler so it didn't stink so bad.

He guessed it was kinder to the animals, too, not having to swelter in a metal trailer, so that might be reason three.

By the time he was outside Flagstaff, Coast-to-Coast was on the radio. He stopped at a truck stop about midnight and went in to fill his thermos and hit the head.

He rolled his beefy shoulders before he went through the heavy glass door.

"Hi, there, stranger. Long time no see," said the waitress.

He couldn't remember her name. Molly? Polly? Holly? He couldn't read her name tag. There was a spot of catsup on it. She was wiping the counter with a gray rag.

He was glad his wife had sent a hoagie with him. He wouldn't want to eat here.

"Where ya heading?"

"Only to Socorro, then back to Albuquerque, and home to Needles." He put his thermos on the counter. "Fill this up, will you? Just black. I gotta be home by tomorrow night, early."

"Gotta big date, huh? What's the missus gonna say?"

The driver grinned. "We're chaperoning the prom at our daughter's school. I hope I make it back in time. It's gonna be close."

"She'll love that!" she said, rolling her eyes as she set the filled thermos in front of him. "At least she'll be safe as long as the dance is going on. These stupid kids these days."

He shook his head. "Our Trish, she's a good girl. She's not into the drug scene, but you never can tell about the rest of them!"

He put down his money and, nodding his thanks, made his way out the door.

He and his wife were lucky to have a kid as smart as Trish. Cute as a button, too. He was glad she wasn't the kind that wore all black, one of those weird ones that wore bolts and safety pins stuck all over. Or tattoos. Those really got to him.

Trish had wanted one of those, a little lady bug, but her mom said "Sure, just as soon as you move out." He had agreed with his wife, and that was the end of it.

By the time he got back in his cab, call-in time was over and the radio show had moved on to its scheduled guests. The first guest tonight was talking about all this gold the Confederacy had hidden all over the South during the Civil War. Callers in the next hour would probably be pumping the guest for clues. He could just see them packing their picks and shovels as they talked.

He guessed that wasn't any more stupid than him buying a lottery ticket once a week. He figured they probably had a better chance of getting rich than he did, but he didn't have to take time away from work and get dirty. He'd just keep filling his ashtray with tickets.

He'd won five dollars a few months back. That was after he'd started carrying a playing card with the number eight on it in his wallet. He'd heard about that, the lucky number eight, from a lady on this same show. He couldn't remember if it only worked once or not, so he kept carrying it.

When he got to the weigh station just inside the New Mexico border, he was first in line. The lights were all on inside, which meant someone was there and he'd better stop.

They had new chairs, blue, since the last time he'd been through here, and the men on duty were leaning up against the Coke machine.

The younger one finally came out.

"Phew! You always haul such shitty smells? Let's hurry up. Maybe we'll get a good wind and blow it back to Houck, or maybe even Sanders. Poor little piggies, you're off to grow into good ham sandwiches."

The driver filled out the necessary paperwork and was soon back on I-40. He was feeling sleepy an hour later and stopped at the huge Giant truck stop outside Gallup.

After a fill-up, he went in and took a shower and had a Denver omelet and a side of hash browns. When he went outside, the cool high desert air felt good.

He felt sorry for the pigs and hosed them down, spraying between the slats on his rig. He hoped he got some water into the trough that was up against the back of his cab.

He checked his watch. He didn't have to hurry. They didn't expect him till seven.

He switched stations (he didn't believe in UFOs).

He moved the dial, "...Remember, Pepe, the current resident of the White House is so Spanish-illiterate that he referred to Cinco de Cuarto in front of the Mexican Ambassador earlier this month. No way is he going to make it perfect for you. You are a legal resident, aren't you?"

He moved the dial again. This time he hit a classical FM station. The announcer's voice was ageless and precise, enunciating the composer's name stiffly, like she was giving the word at a national spelling bee. 'Rahk-mah-nee-nauf!' He didn't like that voice. He bet he wouldn't like the radio host either. Then the music started. He hated it.

He liked the music they'd be playing at the prom later tonight, and that was saying something!

He listened for a little while and switched to a CD of David Halberstam's The Best and Brightest. His wife had given it to him so he could learn enough history to help Trish with her homework. He was a third of the way through and found it was better than he'd expected.

By the time he crested the drop into Albuquerque on Nine Mile Hill, the sun was making it over the top of the Sandias, but the city was still dark and lights were twinkling. The green of the valley looked almost black as it filled the groove it had formed over the eons. From this distance, it reminded him of a kind of moss back East that grows between the bricks and rocks and in small crannies in the old graveyards, only this was darker. It was always a treat to see this place. He knew the city was here, but still it was always a surprise. Even heading in from the east, you wound through the mountains, came around a curve, and there it was, spread out below you like one of Coronado's lost cities. After traveling so many miles, you didn't expect it to be there.

Coming in from the west, as he was now, Albuquerque was no less of a marvel. The only hints of civilization were the glow on the horizon and the billboards.

He liked driving along highways where those ads were banned. They got in the way of his imagination. He liked to think of himself as an explorer or settler, and billboards spoiled the pictures in his mind.

Every time, by gummit, it made him catch his breath, seeing this place. He'd like to show it to Trish someday, just like this. She'd love it. She'd like the thin air, too, that made the lights sparkle.

Right outside of Albuquerque, you could still see the stars, millions of them. California didn't have stars anymore, not like these here. Going north from here, on the way to Denver, the light pollution gave way to the whole Milky Way. That ol' Van Gogh feller wouldn't have done himself in if he'd seen those stars. No, sir! He'd still be painting.

In another twenty minutes, he'd made the turn south onto I-25 at what was called the Big I. It sure had changed. Now, there were walls to keep neighborhoods quiet, and lots of turquoise paint.

He was going south now, passing the hospitals. Their parking lots were already filling up.

He maneuvered into the center lane, as those fools speeding to get to the airport (so they could wait for hours) sped by on his right.

He could live in a place like this. Not so much crime, not so many druggies.

He shook his head at all the cars parked at the casino south of town. He felt sorry for all those families who had someone inside losing the rent or the grocery money. That was one bad thing about New Mexico, all the places to gamble! Other states, you saved up and took just so much money with you to places like Vegas for a vacation, but this was here twenty-four/seven, right in your own backyard.

Praise God, he didn't gamble, except for his lottery tickets.

By seven, he was pulling up to the pig lot. That same nice kid was coming out of the little house, waving at him and pointing him around back where they'd unload.

José Jimenez. That was his name.

José helped him open the back of the trailer. When the wobbly chute-like ramp was in place, the kid got in and herded the wiggly, squealing bodies toward the exit.

"Hey, Mister, there's a fresh pot of coffee inside. Help yourself. Throw me up the hose. I'll wash down the inside for you."

Such a nice kid. "Thanks, you just talked me into it."

He made his way to the house. "Home" wasn't the word to use to describe the place.

He poured coffee and stood watching José's shadowy form moving around inside the trailer. He watched for a while and then wandered around for a bit. It felt odd going into someone's home you'd never met.

The living room wasn't much, a couch, a coffee table, and a little television with a phone on top. He hadn't owned a set that small since he'd first gotten married. There was a little bedroom. The bed was neatly made, but the mattress looked lumpy. The cotton curtains were really serapes thrown over a rod. There was only one other room besides the bathroom, and it was a mess.

It looked like a crazy person spent his time in here. Pictures were leaning against the walls and furniture. The floor was covered with blobs of paint and footprints. The smell of paint and turpentine permeated everything.

It takes all kinds.

If he'd left a room like that, his wife wouldn't feed him till it was clean. He was heading back to the kitchen when he heard the door slam.

The driver waved his coffee cup around. "What kind of person is your boss, José?"

"Kinda weird. He paints a lot. Did you see his stuff?"

"Yeah, some of it is kinda wild."

"He's down in Mexico right now. He took some paintings to a gallery down there. He sells out of one in Santa Fe, too. Nice enough, I guess."

"Must be, if you're working here, but there ought to be something better for a smart guy like you, even if your parents named you after a comedian. You go to school here?"

"Yeah, two more semesters, then I'm outta here."

"Then I guess this is an okay job for a while," He handed the kid his clipboard with the paperwork. "Just sign in the usual spot, and I'll be off like a dirty shirt."

The young man signed the paperwork and the man said "Thanks. Nice doing business with your boss, and thanks for washing out my trailer."

"No problemo. It was good t' see ya again."

The driver took off for Rosa's Papel in southwest Albuquerque. It would be a light load going back, but it would pay for most of the gas. The man who owned the company was from Belize and was making a go of his business. José, back there, was a lot like the man he was on his way to see. Both of them were hard workers.

Tres Baca watched until the big rig turned back on the highway. Then he got to work.

First he sorted the young pigs by their ear tags. Odd pigs went to the back pen where he fed and watered them.

Next, he mixed up a mash for the even-numbered animals. He stirred in plenty of Epsom salts and glycerin. He wanted to get this part over with as quickly as possible, so he stirred more glycerin in the water.

He put on his headphones and turned on his iPod. He pulled on a pair of rubber gloves and waited.

He pulled from his pocket the four filled condoms he'd found in the rig and washed them off. Some of the pigs had gotten a head start. He always volunteered to wash out the rig so he could double-check. Grandpa always said it was the little things that got you caught.

In a matter of minutes, he was wading through shit.

In some ways, it was like looking for Easter eggs in a bog. His father and grandfather should have to do this once in a while. They didn't think he did squat. He'd like to see them all hunched over, pawing through this stuff and trying to keep an eye on which pig needed help.

He'd learned the hard way when he first started this, and now every time he saw an animal take a dump, he'd rush over with white shoe polish and put a daub on its back. Each pig was supposed to have eight condoms full of drugs. He couldn't account for the four in the trailer until later.

Eight times eighty-four. Jesus! This was going to take all night!

When a pig had eight white spots on its back, it was put into the pen with the odd-numbered ones.

Only when all six hundred seventy-two rubber-wrapped packages were in hand could he stop. He had to be out of here before Jimmy and the guys came at noon tomorrow.

When things slowed down, he mixed some soapy water and washed the little treasures. He couldn't wait to get in the shower himself.

He always brought extra clothes to wear afterwards and burned his old clothes in the rusty oil barrels Alex kept for trash that the animals couldn't eat.

There went another one. That made eight for her. He'd better watch more closely and not get ahead of himself. It was always the little things...

He'd much rather have stuffed their mouths at the California location. If he were in charge of the market costs, they'd go way up. Nobody knew what shit he had to go through, and no matter how many showers he took, his mom would always complain that he smelled like crap early Monday morning when she came to pick him up at the bus station.

She had dropped him off at the bus station yesterday. He'd ridden the bus as far as Socorro and had gotten off to take a leak. He'd gone into the men's room and changed clothes with one of his girlfriend's brothers. When he'd handed over his ticket and a C-note to the kid who'd been waiting for him, he told the teenager to be sure to keep the jacket on so his tattoo wouldn't show. He traded his wraparound sunglasses and baseball cap for a worn-out straw hat and a set of car keys. "The car will be back here Sunday night. Thanks, pal."

"No problemo," was the reply. "Thanks for lunch. I ordered you another green chile cheeseburger and fries. It'll be out in a minute. The check will come with it."

Nobody appreciated all the preplanning and hard work he did. No matter what he did to keep the family business going, his mom would still bitch about how he was smelling up her new car. She'd gripe all the way home. Too bad he couldn't have driven his own car rather than take the bus yesterday, then he wouldn't have to listen to her.

Six more packets to go and he could hose the oinkers off.

He didn't want anyone to see the shoe polish or they might get wise. He wouldn't be done with this project even when he got home. He had to deliver it all to Uncle Lorenzo at the mortuary today. Then in a couple of days he'd have to take it to the airport. He took all the risks!

Jerry Lucero was back from Guanajuato in time to give a report to the committee. Mitch and Luis were there when Jerry came in with cassettes and papers tucked under his chin. Frank came in right after, and they were ready to begin...

"Frank, before Jerry starts, what did you come up with on the Baca kid?"

"We know he said he couldn't go to Socorro—seems he was going to have a heavy date—but he'd been in a fender-bender last week and his car was in the shop. I pulled my men off when we knew he wasn't going anyplace. He'd have to borrow his mom's new car, and from what I know, she wouldn't let it out of her sight."

Mitch was already livid. "Way to go, whiz kid! Just what did he do all weekend? You don't have a clue, do you? He might have been down at that pig lot, or in Vera Cruz, for all you know! Give me a break!"

"Not so fast," said Frank. "One of my men followed Mona's car Friday afternoon. She took the kid to the bus station. My guy checked, and Tres bought a round-trip ticket to Cruces. We called Socorro and the police down there were looking for him. He got out in Socorro to take advantage of the rest stop and then boarded the bus four minutes later for the ride to Las Cruces. See, he has another girl down at State."

"There's nothing we can do about that now, Mitch," said Luis, earning a grateful look from Frank. "Let's see what Jerry brought us and we'll have a better idea where to go from there. Jerry, what do you have?"

"I'm not sure what you're looking for. I might have missed something important," said the young man, giving Mitch plenty of room.

"Just get on with it," growled Mitch with his FBI scowl on for good measure.

"Here are my written reports," said Jerry as he passed them out. Luis winced. He could hear it coming.

"That so? Who would have ever guessed?" Mitch was in a foul mood today.

Jerry blushed. "I flew on the same flight and picked up the rental car. Thanks for thinking of that. Mr. Silva took a taxi and went straight to his house.

"Sir, if you would, put this disk in; it's a copy. The federales in the department down there insisted on keeping the original."

When the computer came on, Frank hit the lights and all four men watched the screen.

The first thing they saw was a picture of Alex Silva coming through his front door. Different cameras focused on him from different angles as he made his way through the house. Mr. Silva was a handsome man. Luis could just hear his wife sighing.

"The policía dubbed in the phone calls from the bug on his line," whispered Jerry as they listened to Alex Silva's deep-voiced conversation with a husky, sexy voice.

"What are they saying?" asked Mitch, who wasn't as good with his Spanish as he should have been.

"Just the usual," answered Frank. "Minus the sweet talk, it's supper for two at eight."

"I picked him up when he left for dinner. That's why the picture's jerky. I was driving and trying to keep him on the camera at the same time. He was out of my sight for three and a half minutes while I parked, but the officer who was waiting at the restaurant said he just waited in the lobby and didn't speak to anyone. This next bit is from a camera in the maitre d's boutonniere."

Frank let out a low whistle. They watched as a gorgeous young woman entered and kissed Alex on the cheek. She was dressed to kill in a black dress cut low enough that the maitre d's camera left nothing to the imagination.

Mitch kept asking what they were saying, so Luis kept a running monologue going, leaving out the really personal comments. The only other sounds were Frank gulping and Mitch's hard breathing.

"Two guys from their department followed them home. That's why this part's clearer than mine. I went straight to headquarters, so I wouldn't miss this next part." Jerry looked around the table. These guys were just like their counterparts in Mexico. They looked like spaniels begging at the dinner table.

It was hard to make out what Alex and his companion were saying. Luis kept making shushing noises. It sure didn't look like they were making any deals, drug deals, anyway. He sure as heck didn't talk business to Lydia while he was licking dribbling wine off her throat. He couldn't ever remember licking wine off his wife.

Mitch and Frank sat closer to the screen as the couple moved to the bedroom. Frank bit his lip so he wouldn't say something stupid like, "Now for the good part." Mitch wiped his face as Alex slowly undressed the woman and she, in turn, teased him while she unbuckled his belt, slithering up to him in her lacy blue lingerie. Her lithe arms went around him, her hands kneading his hard muscles.

He pulled her against him as she pushed his pants down to his thighs, kissing him deeply all the while. She waltzed around him as he struggled with his pants and shoes.

"God, he's hung!" gasped Mitch.

The woman's hands could be seen stroking Alex's bum.

"Ven aquI, querida," whispered Alex, turning in her embrace. He lifted her in his arms and carried her to the bed. He skillfully removed her skimpy lingerie and flicked her nipples with his tongue.

Mitch loosened his tie.

Nate blushed again.

Luis heard one of them say, "Wow!"

"I'll leave you all to your voyeurism for a moment," said Luis. "Frank, will you translate? I just remembered something." He made his way to the elevators so no one could hear him call his wife. He then quickly called his secretary and asked her to make reservations at that new Italian place everyone was talking about. "Oh, and send her a dozen roses, too...Of course, red."

He slipped back in the room just in time to hear Mitch say, "Man, oh, man!" He glanced at the screen in time to wonder how Lydia's bottom would look, up in the air like that. The couple writhed and groaned, murmuring endearments.

"Mi corazón," Alex whispered.

"Mas, mas, maaas!"

"Mi amor."

Soon, their passions were spent and they cuddled for a few moments in each other's arms. The woman sat up, smiling, and leaned her tousled hair over the hair on Alex's chest murmuring, "Necesito más ahora mismo." Her hand caressed his thigh.

Later, Jerry said, "The men didn't get cameras in the john, but here's the tape of what they said. Do you want to hear this now?" he asked, turning to Luis.

"Why don't we send that home with Frank? That okay with you, Mitch?"

"What? Oh, yeah. Then what happens, Jerry?"

"That's on disk two. More heavy wet sex in the morning. Out for an early breakfast, and then he walked her to her bodega. The bodega, Casa de Sueños, is a real classy furniture store. I went in when he left, but I couldn't afford anything there to bring my wife."

"You didn't tail him?" Mitch was back to being sarcastic.

"The guys down there did. Do you want to see him go home and go to bed?" asked Jerry.

"Good to know our stud muffin has to sleep like normal men!" joked Frank.

"Jerry," asked Luis, "did he make contact with anyone else while he was down there?"

"He also had an appointment in the early afternoon. He went to his gallery, the one where he's part-owner. One of the policewomen went in undercover while he was there, but all he did was talk to the guy running the place—I guess that would be his partner—about the art scene and what prices they thought they could get for the paintings he took down there. Here's her tape. You can send it to the decoders after you listen to it, but it sounded pretty straightforward to me."

Jerry put the small tape in front of Luis.

"Thanks, Jerry. That was a good job you did down there. If any of us have any questions, we'll be in touch. Do you have anything to add, Mitch? Frank?"

Mitch shrugged his shoulders, but Frank grinned. "Just a couple of questions. Did you get her last name, Jerry? If you go down again, do you need some help?"

"Enough, Frank. I suppose that little show was sufficient to distract us from anything else today. Next week, same time, same place, but each of you better come up with something!" Mitch sat there holding his head as the other men filed out.

Luis headed for his office to wrap up a few more things before heading home. He needed to pick up a bottle of wine on the way.

Frank was still in a cloud when he pushed open the heavy door to his unit's offices.

Whomp!

He looked down and there was Lt. Gordon on the floor. Papers were everywhere. She had never looked so charming.

She was blushing and trying to get up. "Sorry, sir, I didn't know you were coming through."

"No! I'm so sorry! I was thinking of something else. Here, let me help you." Her hand was small and soft. She did look enticing with her hair disheveled and her shirt tail out. He knelt down and began picking up her spilled reports. When he lifted his eyes, they felt glued to her knees. He had never noticed she had dimples on her knees.

Things were looking up for Lt. Beverly Gordon.

Rio Rancho, New Mexico, May

At nine in the evening, after the rosary was over and the receptionist and other staff had gone home and the front door was locked, Lorenzo Gurule, president of Lasting Peace Mortuary of Rio Rancho, adjusted the light in the prep room, flexed his hands in his latex gloves, and bent to work, putting the finishing touches on the face.

A little more blue under the lower lashes before he sponged on the heavy Max Factor, the kind they used on stage. He carefully used the eyebrow pencils in gray and brown to delicately shade the temple, the sides of the nose— oops, that was a little too much! When he was through accentuating the lines on the brow, he stood back and appraised his work much the same way a window dresser would look at the drape of a scarf.

He had dressed the body earlier, before Mrs. Klein's service. Gray slacks, light-blue shirt and navy blazer. Lorenzo insisted on his departed looking their best. He chuckled to himself when he used more energy than necessary to lift the inert form from the gurney into the casket. He shook his head. It had been some time since he had done this.

Silly to forget the difference in weight.

He leaned into the casket model #pwo-639 (pressed wood, oak with white satin lining). It was designed for cremation.

The shoulders were just a little crooked. There, that was better.

Before he finished with the makeup, he crossed the gray tile floor and retrieved a bottle of formalin from the shelf above the assistant mortician's sink. He returned to the casket, unbuttoned the blazer, and poured the embalming fluid over the belt line, thoroughly soaking the fabric. Looking again at the body with an expert eye, he pushed on the left side and tucked the shirt tail further into the pants. When the torso looked right, he straightened the red-and-navy striped tie and buttoned the jacket again.

Always careful, Lorenzo placed a towel over the belly area and carefully, tenderly, arranged the hands in a restful pose. Lorenzo was proud of the way he worked with hands. They said so much about an individual.

He sighed as he sponged makeup over the knuckles, across the back of the hand up to the wrist. No one would notice his handiwork at a service.

Too bad these weren't real hands. They looked so natural against the navy blue when he removed the towel. He added a ring.

The face was fine, as well, considering that it was really a rubber mask.

Giving the body one last critical look, he realized this was some of his best work. In many ways it was art.

The head, neck, torso, arms, and legs were filled with high-grade cocaine. The formalin had been used just in case airport security opened the casket. He closed and locked the lid to keep the smell in, and placed a hazardous material label next to the lock. Let them think George here had died of some highly dangerous contaminant.

A few more of these going out would be it. He'd have enough then to leave his silent partner with a building that was paid for. He was going to open his own mortuary outside of Austin. He still had family near San Antonio, and it would be great to be closer, but not in their back pockets. The Austin area was just far enough away to give him a sense of privacy.

His sister, Mona, was the only other one not living in the hill country, other than their parents in El Paso. She probably wouldn't ever speak to him again if he left the business here in Rio Rancho, but, face it, he wasn't the criminal type.

It was a shame she had married into a family that leaned that way. He didn't know much about the operation, only that his nephew, who worked for him part-time, would drive the van every time a body was shipped out with drugs or shipped in with money. That rarely happened, the money part. It had been over a year since he'd received a casket with cash inside.

He didn't mind the ship-outs too much. It was kind of fun making dummies look real. Ship-ins were a different ball of wax.

New York and San Francisco would send real bodies and wouldn't bother to embalm them. Street bums or OD's mostly, he guessed. He wondered about those corpses. What sort of lives had they led to end up as mules for a dealer, without even the dignity of a potter's field? Some of those bodies were past ripe!

On second thought, maybe he'd go to San Saba or Llano or New Braunfels. A little town where everybody knew everybody; there wouldn't be any disposables there.

It was stupid that at a time of national security, when airport security was so tight, that guards never opened the caskets. Tres would go up with the paperwork and they'd ask what he had and pass it on through. These guys, who were hired to keep America safe from death and destruction, were too squeamish about the dead to open a casket or body bag and take a peek.

Jeez, it could be bombs in there, and they'd just check the paperwork and send it on!

Lorenzo had always sent a lot of decedents back East. Mostly Jews who'd come out when the town was just getting started, back in the sixties.

He used to send cremains, never Jews, but since 9/11 it was illegal to ship sealed containers. Families had to transport those themselves.

When he used to ship drugs in urns, he'd put the drugs in the bottom of the vessel and top it off with the ashes of the same dogs that had been used to carry the drugs to Albuquerque. They'd always been long-haired so the incisions wouldn't show, and had come in family cars. Narcs never thought to check a family pet.

Tres also brought Lorenzo the drugs to ship out, like this shipment. He had no idea where the kid got them. Best he didn't know. Tres also took care of the dogs used as mules. He'd euthanize them in the prep room and cremate them after the heroin had been removed from the body cavities. Lorenzo had only cleaned out the ashes. The extra ashes went into bags and then into the dumpster behind Gringo's Bar and Grill.

As Lorenzo was finishing up, he thought of Manuel Baca's other deals. Like how did he pull them off in Colorado, or in Central America, or the Southeast?

He bet Tres didn't know any more than he did. Such a little blowhard, his nephew was, always going off in wild directions, just like his mother. Sure, he was in grad school, going after an MBA, but Tres was crazy! One time he had big plans for fake antiques; another time he was talking up an Internet scam. Lately, he was excited about pit bulls and dog fights. He couldn't seem to settle on anything.

He was cleaning up the prep room when he heard a knock on the backdoor. The knocking grew louder as he made his way down the back hall.

He froze when he opened the door. A man was standing there with a gun pointed at him. It took a moment for Lorenzo to realize it was a police officer.

"Mr. Gurule? I'm sorry if I frightened you. My partner and I," he motioned to the other officer in a defensive position behind the patrol car, as he holstered his weapon, "were going by and saw the lights on and didn't see your car."

"Whew, you scared me!" sputtered Lorenzo.

"There's been a rash of break-ins in the area, kids coming in and spraying graffiti everywhere."

"Thank you, then, for stopping. Would you two like some coffee?" Now, why did he have to go say that? "We had a rosary earlier. I'd hate to pour it out. I was just cleaning up the prep room. We have a ship-out in the morning." Why was he going on so?

"Who died?" The officers were both following him down the corridor.

"A man from California. He used to live here with his daughter. The altitude was too much for him, he had a bad heart, so he went to live with his son out in the Bay area."

"Why come back here?"

"The daughter had gotten a pre-need policy for him with the former owners when he lived with her in Rio Rancho."

"Who is she?" asked the older officer.

Lorenzo was thinking fast. "Her husband was transferred to Denver three years ago. I'm only taking care of him till he can be sent home tomorrow. Say, will one of you fellows hold the door open so I can roll him out to the hall?"

"No problem. What's that sticker for?"

"It's a hazardous label."

"I thought you said he had a bad heart."

"He did. He had a quadruple bypass out there."

"Poor man. Died on the table, did he?"

"No, the surgery went fine, but they gave him some bad blood and he came down with AIDS. It was more than he could take. He took his own life. The sticker's there to warn people to be careful because of the AIDS. Oh, the coffee. This way, gentlemen."

He ushered them into the break room. "Help yourselves. I just have to finish up his paperwork and I'll be with you."

When he got to his office, he could hardly stand up, his knees were shaking so badly. The writing on the form didn't look like his, either, as he filled in the shipping label, DeMarco's Funeral Home, Newark, NJ.

He always created a name to go with the casket—what was this one? Oh, yes, George Satterfield. Lorenzo took a deep breath before returning to the break room.

"This coffee hits the spot. Where's your car, anyway?"

The president of the funeral home looked at the young officer. They wouldn't let up.

"I took a limo home yesterday. I knew I'd be working late tonight and my turn signals are on the blink, pardon the pun."

The officers smiled. "Good thinking," said the older cop. "People aren't used to looking for hand signals at night. Jeff, you ready?"

"I'll go out with you. That way, you'll know the place is locked up for the night," said Lorenzo. "I'll get the lights. See you outside." He pulled the plug on the pot and poured the liquid down the drain. The receptionist could wash it in the morning.

When he finally waved the officers off, he sat in the limo taking deep breaths. Mano Baca was going to shit green apples when he got his last mortgage payment check. Lorenzo knew the old man expected him to be under his thumb for a long time, but he couldn't take much more of this! He'd borrow the money to pay the bastard back, sell this place, and get the hell out!

He'd forgotten to check the flower room. Damn!

He let himself back in. He still had the casket key in his pocket, too. He put the key on top of the paperwork on the casket for Tres in the morning. Lorenzo wouldn't be back until after his nephew had gone tomorrow.

What was it his mama had said? "Keep your nose clean and your pants pressed." That was it. He checked the flower room to see if there were any deliveries that needed to be watered for tomorrow. It was his responsibility to keep them fresh.

He made sure the right CDs were ready for the Simpson service at ten in the morning. That family was in such a bad way that he wanted everything to go perfectly for them. To have a son commit suicide over a breakup with a girl was unthinkable to Lorenzo.

When he got back in his car, he was thinking about what the girl must be feeling. Lorenzo hoped she felt as guilty as Ted Bundy. He drove slowly to Gringo's to have a drink and call Kitty on his cell phone. Kitty Lubinsky, the love of his life, was his fiancée. She had already moved to Austin and was working as a secretary in the Anthropology Department at UT. It wasn't a great job, but it was a start. He and Kitty were going to have a fantastic life! He needed to hear her voice to know everything was going to be all right.

Mano had said his phone might be tapped at home and work. Lorenzo didn't want anyone knowing where he was going when he disappeared. He didn't want anyone to know about his future with Kitty.

On the Road to Los Santos, May

Owen Wills was making his way to Los Santos. It had been raining all day and the road was slick. He hoped someone besides Lita Cordova would be there today.

Emilio was in Germany, and he understood Sunny had her new dog. She'd have other things on her mind besides books.

He'd been pleased when Lita had called him about bringing her some books on dogs. He'd told Miriam that their friend was showing a bit of interest in the world again and had gotten herself a dog. He'd had quite a search. Sunny still had those two other books.

All at once, there was a bicyclist racing downhill towards him in the middle of the road. Owen slammed on the brakes.

The rear of the bookmobile slid to the left. It caught the back wheel of the bike as it whizzed past, sending the rider tumbling into the gravel on the far side of the road.

Owen jumped out and was running back to the man when the stranger picked himself up, threw Owen a Hawaiian good luck sign, and sped off.

Shaken, Owen crawled back into the driver's seat.

"Whew, that was close!" He pushed back the nonexistent hair that used to cover his forehead and sat there for a moment. Where had that guy been coming from, anyway?

He was sure he'd seen that fellow before. Where was it? That flashy bike and purple crash helmet were hard to miss. He'd have to ask Miriam if it was the same rider they'd seen last fall when they'd driven the back way to Silver City to see her sister. His wife would know. She was good at things like that.

Lita must be waiting by now.

He started up again, checking his rearview mirror and slowly getting back in the proper lane. She would have to wait a little longer. The road was too slick for speed.

Sunny and Lita were the only ones waiting today. Sunny had

brought her dog to meet him. It sure was a cute little thing! She had it sit up and roll over, but mostly she hugged it to herself like a rag doll.

Both customers seemed more interested in the dog than they did in the books he had to lend. Sunny was soon off, with her dog at her heels. He and Lita watched her pick up the dog when she came to a puddle. They laughed.

"Are you as careful with your dog, Lita?"

"More so," she answered. "I'd have brought Glow to meet you also, but I didn't want her to get wet. If the weather is nice, I'll bring her next time."

"I'll be looking forward to meeting her. She seems to have brightened your spirits!"

"Yes," she agreed. "I should have had her long ago."

"Here are the books on dogs you called about. If they aren't enough, you may want to borrow Sunny's."

"Thank you, Owen. You are so good to me."

"My pleasure. You better get on home to—Glow, is it? I need to head back myself. The roads are treacherous and Miriam's going to worry. Say, while you and Sunny were waiting in Tessie's, you didn't happen to notice a cyclist on a bike, did you?"

"No," she answered. "Sunny and I spent our time admiring Tima."

Lita tucked her books under her raincoat as she made her way around the rear of the bookmobile and headed for the church. It had felt good to return that Rabbi's book, When Bad Things Happen to Good People. Father Mondragon had suggested it to her to help her overcome her grief.

She smiled. It would have saved her reading that book over and over if she had gotten Glow two months ago. She had wanted to bring her dog along to introduce her to Owen, but she had to clean the church today, and the weather was so bad. She didn't want to get the little dog wet.

If the weather had been pleasant, she would have sat in the plaza and read the new books about caring for dogs and their training. With all this wind and rain, she couldn't stay. She ran and made it inside as the rain increased. When had they ever had such a wet spring?

Lita was cleaning on Tuesday instead of Wednesday. Virgie and Jovita were busy all this week with the new kids and all the extra goat's milk. Their business needed them more than Lita did.

The sanctuary was dark and musty, making her feel like she had walked into a dank cave. The buckets were almost full from the roof leaks. She lugged a couple out to the flower beds and, knowing Jovita wasn't around to see, dashed the rest out the door.

She kept her coat on against the chill and hurried with the sweeping and dusting, trying to outrace the plinks and drops in the empty pails.

Rolls of thunder reverberated in the empty room, and the sound of rain on the roof increased, making her feel like she was inside a popcorn popper, except that then she would be warm. The buckets were half-full already. She'd need to empty them again when she was finished if it was still raining.

She might as well use some lemon oil on the chancel. She could call Jovita tonight and tell her she wouldn't need to do it tomorrow. That woman was so busy! Oh, wait! Tonight was CSI. She'd see her then.

It was still pouring and the buckets needed emptying again.

"God, if you won't tell Jovita, I won't either." She tossed as much water as she could out the door.

If the rain didn't let up, Benito—"Ben," she corrected herself—would come looking for her when he got home. She figured that would be about six, which would give her time for some serious prayers. She found some matches behind the altar and lit a votive. Amazing how the light of one little candle could make a glow in an empty heart.

She thought of her dog. She'd light a candle for her, too.

She set the candles back on the votive stand and knelt.

"Holy Mary, help us." Plink.

"Dear Mother, what are we to do?" Plunk.

"Our Father." Splat, hiss.

Her candle had gone out. A new leak! She got up and lit another candle and knelt again. She had just bowed her head in prayer, when that was doused. Up she came. This time, Lita moved the heavy cast-iron stand before she lit another votive.

She went behind the altar to find something to catch the water. She came back and thumped down a tall glass vase where the stand had been. There was a satisfying plink in the vase. It was a little higher-sounding than those plunks in the buckets. She settled herself down again for some serious prayer with a cacophony of leaks playing not-so-soothing background music.

"Almighty God, do something! This church is falling apart and Los Santos isn't doing any better! Everyone is in as much grief as I am over Tina's death. They all expected her to pull off a miracle. You know and I know she couldn't have done it without You, but at least she would have tried! Help us!"

Lightning flashed and the lights went out, leaving Lita with only the light of one votive.

"Okay, God, Mother Mary, and you, too, St. Joseph, help us in the best way you can!"

Kersplat! A wide section of the north wall slid to the floor. Water had worked its way under the bond beam, soaking into the old adobes. Wet mud was all that was left of a wall that, moments ago, had been twice as thick. Four to six inches of mud had fallen away from each brick, and water was running down the wall.

Lita screamed. She jumped up and carried her candle to the wall.

Light reflected in the running water. The mud was everywhere. One window looked to be tipping inward ever so slowly. She rushed back to where she had been praying.

"Okay! That's enough! I know you don't like to be talked to like that, but I mean it! WE NEED HELP! And no more of that showing off!"

Lita pulled up the hood on her rain coat and started to leave, but ran back to say, "Amen."

She had to find Father Mondragon. She really needed Emilio, but he was in Germany. Father Mondragon would have to do. She could call Benito from the parish house, and he could come get her. Why didn't she carry that cell phone?

Somebody had to get busy tonight. Maybe the Pachecos and the Oteros. Oh, let Father worry about that! She ran out into the downpour, hoping she would find him.

***

Later that evening, Lita had just enough time to reheat last night's venison stew and take a hot shower before the girls arrived. They had brought their electric roasters and Crock-Pots for Lita to use the next week. Jovita had also stopped by the church hall and gotten a large coffee pot. Virgie had come with containers of frozen soup. The men working through the night needed something to eat.

"We can heat this up while the show is on and make the coffee," said Lita.

"Jovita and I can take it to the men down at the church on our way home."

"You two have no idea how awful it was when the wall came down! It's such a mess. It will take weeks to fix!"

When Lita told about cleaning the chancel, they decided it would be best if they redid everything when the men were through patching up today's disaster. Who knew what a mess they would leave? Jovita and Virgie would be through with the goats by nine, and so if they met after ten and the milk had been stored, they would have at least two hours to work tomorrow.

Virgie plunked down her old Crock-Pot unceremoniously on the counter. "You can keep this old thing a couple of weeks if we need it. Sounds like we'll be using it a lot." The Crock-Pot had seen better days. There were chips in the enamel and the handle was broken off the lid.

"You sure that thing works?" teased Jovita. "I remember you using that at the Last Supper."

"Go on, you got yours the same time. Yours just looks better 'cause you never cook."

"That's the truth," agreed Jovita, patting her ample hips. "I'm always thinking I should watch my diet."

"Before you start, have one of these. I saw them in a magazine. They looked so good I thought we needed them tonight." Virgie reached into her roaster and removed a plate mounded with what looked like little cookies. She had taken mini pretzels, melted a chocolate-covered caramel on each, and then pressed a pecan half down into the warm chocolate.

Lita put on the coffee, while Jovita fine-tuned the television. The three of them settled down with their hand work to watch CSI.

Lita had to put down her work when Glow jumped in her lap. It wasn't long before the cat joined them. She sat there stroking their fur as the credits rolled.

"Lita, you're never gonna be able to do anything again with those animals all over you!" said Jovita.

Glow growled, which surprised them all.

They were getting into the crime scene when Benito came from his bedroom. Virgie beamed at him when he helped himself to a handful of her treats. "Hey, these are great!"

Lita was embarrassed when he took another helping. Jovita laughed and said, "I better have mine now."

On the screen, one of the agents was cutting into a maggot-infested corpse. "On second thought, I'll wait awhile, at least till this part's over. Ooh, look at that!" gasped Jovita.

"Yuck," blurted out Virgie, "how can you watch that? I'm gonna hotten up my coffee, and check on that soup. Anybody want anything while I'm up?"

Lita stopped petting her animals and leaned forward when the scene shifted to the crime scene. She watched closely as the characters sifted through the victim's garbage with gloved hands, searching for clues.

They were always so careful not to contaminate any evidence. She watched as they sacked and labeled each item.

Virgie sat back down in the other rocker. "What have I missed?"

"Only all the clues they need to solve the case."

"Shush," said Virgie when Gus Grishom was asking a colleague to go with him to the morgue. "I think they're so cute together." She said. "Do you suppose he's getting interested in her?"

"Virgie! They're going to the morgue to see if they missed something. How romantic is that?"

"So? Last week he called her at home."

"Last week she cut herself on that metal and had to go get stitches," responded Jovita.

"But he called and asked how she was feeling!"

"And he asked if she'd found out whose fingerprints were on the compost bag!" said Lita. Virgie could be so exasperating!

When the bad guys were caught, it turned out Lita had been right. She had thought the husband and wife were in on it together. When the last commercial came on, she called Ben to come help load the hot soup and coffee urn into Jovita's truck.

"He's such a fine boy, Lita. I wish I had one like him at my house. I could use a gofer with a quick smile."

"I won't have him much longer, Jovita. I better get all the good I can out of him now. He's going to work at the ranch this summer and soon he'll be off to school."

The rain had stopped. They took the food out to the car; and then they visited a while longer on the porch.

Lita watched as they backed out onto the road, then she turned off the porch light. She hurried the dog and cat out the back door.

She was missing the first hour of her show. She wished Michael Savage came on in the daytime. Sometimes she'd like to call in. As it was, he got to do all the talking.

She picked up the plates and cups. She'd have time in the morning to wash them.

She paused in Ben's doorway to say goodnight. She used to stay up till her son Philip was finished with his homework. She even managed to keep awake till Tina was through with her studies. But time had caught up with her. Benito was almost grown, she told herself. Anyway, she didn't know anything about calculus.

She curled up in bed with a book, the dog, and the radio. She'd prayed enough for today, she told herself. Maybe she should lie low for a while and keep to herself.

Michael Savage was telling a sad story about an old man who had a pet monkey that turned on him. She wondered what he was really talking about. Was the monkey a person or the government? Lita yawned. She'd figure that one out later.

A little after midnight, her grandson came into her room. He tiptoed over and removed her glasses. He gently pulled the cover up and switched off the light.

Who would do this next year?

Early Saturday morning, Epie Vallejos was working on the acequia. The sun wasn't quite up yet, but there was just enough light for him to open the gate and begin watching the water gushing into his ditch. He leaned on his hoe for a moment, and then decided to whack some weeds over by the road. He'd probably find more trash there, too. Those thoughtless men working on the guard rail had been throwing their lunch bags and bottles and cups onto his property.

He turned west and was making his way in that direction when the sun topped the peak behind him and caught the windshield of a car up there where poor Tina Cordova rolled her car last winter.

Thinking someone must be having car trouble, he yelled and waved his battered hat. He started moving as fast as his arthritic knees would allow. The man up there waved back and closed his trunk. The hombre got in his car, a long dark-blue or black one. Epie couldn't tell with his cataracts. It sounded expensive as it roared away.

Epie stood there in the middle of his field scratching his head. He replaced his tattered straw cowboy hat and returned to his work and his own worries, never dreaming that he had just witnessed the beginning of a milagro.

If he hurried, he'd be home for breakfast. He turned and missed a gust of wind blowing dust up by the road. In the morning sun, it turned to gold. Then, all at once, there came a light morning rain out of the west.

Father Mondragon announced at Mass on Sunday that the congregation would have to move what they could from the church to the church hall. The archdiocese had decided that the structure was unsafe, and until something could be done, they would have to meet in the church hall across the street.

A few men had loaded up their pickups with statues, the altar, and years of religious paraphernalia, and hauled it across the street.

That same Saturday, Junior Baca climbed over the fence into his neighbor's yard and knocked. It was only six forty-five, but the lights were on all over her downstairs. She liked to watch the early morning news, or rather listen to it, as her macular degeneration was getting bad. He heard the sound level of the TV go down before the door opened.

"Morning, Mrs. Simpson."

"Is that you, Mr. Baca?" She squinted at him. "Why, good morning, neighbor. What brings you here so early? Come in for some tea?"

"Ah, sweetheart, I've already had mine."

He pointed to his work hat with the Highway Department logo on it. "I have to make a run up north to check on some work the department's been doing. I just remembered you saying that your car needed an out-of-town workout. I was already in my car when I thought I'd better come ask."

"Oh, you darling. I was just telling Liz Baxter, when she drove me on my errands yesterday, that my dear Harold would be so upset the car hadn't been on the road. He always believed the engine needed a chance to blow out the stop-and-go garbage. That's what he called it."

Harold Simpson had bought his wife a new Volvo the week before he died. A few months after that, Gertie was refused a driver's license renewal because of her eyesight. But she wasn't about to give up her beautiful car, Harold's last gift, and what did doctors know? Maybe her vision would clear up. She might need it. How lucky she was to have such thoughtful neighbors!

"Liz and I filled her up yesterday on the way home. Come in, come in. I'll get the keys."

In a matter of moments, Junior saw the unmarked car three houses down from his, as he passed his own street. "Suckers!"

By seven-twenty, he was honking the horn at his honey's. When he went in, Lovey was still in the shower.

He checked his watch later as they were leaving her place. If he hurried, they'd be there by ten. A good-looking woman, a beautiful day, and all that money. What else could a man want?

***

Lita wasn't cleaning this morning. It was her turn, but Virgie couldn't do it last week, so they had swapped mornings. They were all supposed to meet at the church, but Virgie called to remind her that she didn't have to show up. She was glad! After last night's rain, there would be so much mopping!

She did have things to do. Benito was taking her down to the general store. She had to buy the beans for the Fiesta. She only had a few pounds at home.

"Mamalita," Benito called over the noise of the engine. "I could pick the beans up for you on my way home from work."

"Don't be silly, chico. It's a beautiful day. I've been cooped up so long! I have my cart in the back and I need the exercise."

"Sure you want to walk? It's two miles uphill on the way back."

"I wore the walking shoes you gave me for Mother's Day." She wiggled her ankle at him. "You want them to grow cobwebs? I have my jacket if the weather changes," Lita paused. "Maybe you can look at some new trucks during your lunch hour. I've had an idea. We could sell some of the paintings—if they're worth anything, that is— and you could use the money you make on the weekends in Taos and at the ranch this summer working for Hugh to help with school."

She still couldn't say "college." That sounded too far away.

"You don't want to sell your paintings!"

"Phooey, I've looked at most of them all my life, and so have you. Maybe it's time someone else looked at them. Anyway, I've called a conservator in Santa Fe, and he's going to come give me an estimate of their value."

When he started to object, she changed the subject. "Listen to this rattletrap! Even my little Ford is better than this! I hope it gets you home tonight."

"But, Mamalita..."

"Hush. I want to stop on the way back from Chuy's and check Tina's flowers. Those road workers might have damaged them when they put up the rail."

They both fell silent, each thinking the guard rail had come too late to do them any good. Ben left his motor running to make sure the old battery wouldn't conk out on him. He lifted his grandmother's cart out of the truck bed and put it up on the store's porch.

"Don't buy too many beans. They'll get heavy on the way home."

"That's why I wore my sweat suit. Don't worry about me, hijo. You have enough to worry about with this old truck. Be safe. See you tonight," she said as she hopped down and reached for her cart.

Her grandson sputtered off in a cloud of blue smoke. She went in the store. She could hear Jimmy Chewiwi in the back. She took a moment to look around. She bet he hadn't painted the place since he bought it from her father-in-law.

It had been Benito's great-grandfather's before that. It had been a trading post then. The buffalo head still hung behind the cash register.

Instead of the things she remembered from childhood— pots, saddle blankets, tack and jewelry—there were now cans of vegetables, soups, and laundry soap.

The plastic bags of beans were stacked between the soft drinks and motor oil, just beneath the jars of salsa sauce. Imagine anybody buying salsa! She must have some lazy neighbors if they bought their salsa. She shook her head.

Jimmy came from the back in time to help her load her cart. They visited about the old days for a while, then about his business and the Fiesta. Yes, he was going to roast chile again, and his wife would make fry bread.

It was almost nine when she stopped by Tina's descanso. To her right, the alfalfa in Epie's field looked beautiful. She'd have to tell Virgie.

The cross and plastic flowers were canted a bit to the left. Look, someone had put a little cross among the flowers. Wasn't that sweet. They'd even painted it with reflective paint, so people driving by at night would remember her girl.

***

The morning was perfect. Junior felt like a million with the sunroof open and his sweetie snuggled up next to him. Her long red nails played up and down his thigh. He couldn't wait to get back to Albuquerque to celebrate. Hell, after the pickup, he'd surprise her and stop in Taos or Santa Fe. Maybe one of those rooms with a Jacuzzi. Or they could stop at Ten Thousand Waves. He pulled her closer and she giggled. He could just imagine her nude body at the spa. Heads would turn, and she was all his!

She pretended to be frightened by the boulders perched on the cliffs above them on their right as they sped toward Taos. She leaned playfully into him as they rounded the sharp curves.

"Ooh, hurry, Junior, I gotta pee!"

"First chance, sugar."

There was no hurry. Soon, he pulled into a filling station and enjoyed watching her mince her way inside to the restroom. He decided platform heels were about the sexiest shoes he knew of. They sure accentuated her long legs and round little ass. She must be completely redoing her hair, she was in there such a long time. Junior bought some candy bars and left a big tip for the woman behind the counter.

***

Lita stepped back to check her work. Was that any better? She'd always thought the bright yellow flowers were wrong.

Her left heel hit a soft spot and she lost her balance. Goodness! She had fallen backwards and had mud all over her sneakers and the bottom of her pink sweats.

She bent her right leg in order to push herself up, and the ground gave way under her foot. Looking at the ground for a better way to get up, Lita noticed an edge of plastic sheeting.

That's odd. She pulled it back and, "My God!" She was sitting on a pile of money wrapped in bubble wrap! Stacks of it! She looked at the little cross with its beautiful yellow flowers and began to cry.

"Thank you, Christina! I've found your promise!

"Oh, thank You, Blessed Mary!

"God, You did hear my prayer!

"Dear St. Jude, thank you for the impossible!"

Tears were running down her face. "Thank You, Jesus. You heard me! Thank You!"

"Hurry, you can't be seen!" a voice seemed to say. She began frantically pulling the stacks of bills out of the ground. There were canvas bank bags bulging with hard shapes at the bottom of the pile.

How was she going to get all this home?

She pulled off her jacket and started removing the cash. Where to put it? There was no room in her cart. She hurriedly dumped the bags of beans out and put the miraculous gift in their place in her cart, putting the bank bags on top.

She tossed the bags of beans in the hole and stuffed her jacket—sleeves, pockets, hood and lining—and placed it over the blessed miracle.

Was this really a miracle?

"Don't doubt," she thought, as a gentle breeze picked up and brushed against her cheek.

"Fingerprints!"

Lita knew about fingerprints. Just last night on CSI...! She yanked the beans back out of the hole and tore the bags open and poured the little speckled pintos back into the hole. She covered everything as best she could again with moist earth.

"Eeeh, I've left footprints everywhere!"

She ran across the road and pulled a clump of weeds.

She hurried back and began sweeping backward towards the pavement, erasing every sign of her presence she could see from the moist earth.

She pushed the empty plastic bags down the sides of the cart.

She put the weed broom on top of her jacket and started for home as fast as she could. Her mind was working overtime.

"Hail, Mary, this is a miracle, no?" It must be the answer to all their prayers! What else could it be?

Lita didn't like thinking what else it might be. What if she'd stumbled onto something illegal, like on television?

No, God wouldn't play with her like that! God did work in mysterious ways.

She had a stitch in her side. She hadn't moved so fast in years.

Unaware of her surroundings, Lita didn't smell the lilacs spilling over the wall as she passed Juanita Delgado's house. She didn't see them tossing in the breeze. She didn't know the pins had fallen from her hair and was oblivious as it whipped about her shoulders. She kept repeating, "Holy Mary, Mother of God, pray for us sinners..."

Jovita looked up from the flowerbeds at church and waved.

Lita was oblivious. Jovita stood and watched as a mud-spattered Lita trotted past her. After so many months of Estrellita going around like death itself, then she gets a dog and we think she's all better. Now mi amiga has gone completely mad! "I'm glad Tina isn't here to see it!"

Virgie had been up milking at the ranch and was hurrying to get the milk in the refrigerator before she joined Jovita at the church to clean. The milk cans rattled as she hit a bump where the dirt road met the pavement. She saw Lita hurry past and wondered why she didn't respond to her horn. She'd have to call. Virgie'd never known Lita to roll in the mud like that! Whatever was the matter? She lit another cigarette and ran the scene over in her mind again. Jovita would have an answer that made sense. Virgie inhaled deeply as she turned toward home. Jovita could always make sense of the strangest things.

***

Junior pulled up in front of Tessie's and ushered his mistress inside. The smells of strong coffee, chile, and garlic pulled them to a table as surely as if they had been strong-armed.

Tessie was glad to see the flashy man again. He'd been a good customer back when the road crew was working down where poor Tina, God rest her soul, was killed.

"How you been? I thought you fellas were all through." Tessie smiled at the big man. Even with all his gold chains and fancy watch, he was a big tipper. Usually, duded-up hombres were lousy tippers. Oh, well, they could only spend their money once.

"Two of your best lunches. You got some of that good stew? Add two apple pies with ice cream. I've been telling this sweet thing how good they are!" He planted a kiss on this sweet thing and said to her, "See! They're all here, and some of them are autographed!" He swept his arm around the café, indicating all the posters. "They're all hermanos! Tessie here can tell you about each one. Look, there's Antonio Banderas!"

The sweet thing giggled and Tessie raised an eyebrow.

"Why don't you start by giving this pretty lady a salad and the story about how you got that picture of Benicio del Toro. I have to check out the work and see if they did it right. I'll be right back."

The sweet thing looked over Tessie's shoulder and pointed at the first Hispanic to win an Academy Award and asked, "Is that Desi Arnaz?"

"No, that man with the nose is José Ferrer. He's dressed as Cyrano de Bergerac. Speaking of dressing, what kind do you want?"

Junior let out a false laugh. He pecked his honey goodbye and stepped out the door. The two women watched as he took a deep breath of fresh mountain air and strolled to his car.

Tessie looked at the woman, who shrugged and waited for her salad. Tessie sighed and went back to the kitchen.

Junior passed the corner that Lita had turned up a few minutes earlier and made his way around the south side of the crumbling church. He stopped at the stop sign and turned right, heading for the drop site. The DeMarcos in New Jersey were good people to do business with. They always paid. No problems, ever.

He pulled his official cap and vest from under the seat as he glided to a stop at the new guard rail. He looked around. No one was in sight. That old geezer must have been out earlier. Junior could see water still standing in the field. He backed up right behind that silly little cross. He pushed a button and popped the trunk.

Junior moved quickly for a big man. He scuffed the ground till he found what he was looking for. He leaned over and flipped back the plastic sheet.

"What the ..." Mierda!

Instead of money, there were beans! He dug his hands into the dry legumes and searched for something, maybe a marker.

Christ on a crutch! All hell was about to break loose. He jumped in the car and peeled rubber on his way back to the café.

⁂

Tessie was standing with bowls of stew and large mugs of coffee on a tray. She'd been making her way carefully to the table where her good customers would be eating when Junior rushed in.

What a change in a man! He threw bills on the table and grabbed his floozy.

"We gotta go!"

"But, Junior!"

"Now, I said!"

The painted lady began to cry.

"Shut up!" he roared as he pushed her out the door.

Tessie put down the tray and watched the silver car speed out of sight. She picked up the salad and the money. She shook her head. She guessed heads were gonna roll at the Highway Department. Somebody must'a screwed up big time.

⁂

Lita pulled her drapes and locked her door. Then she hid the money under her bed. That was stupid. That was the first place anyone would look! What was she going to do? She had to go to the bathroom. She was shaking. When she washed her hands, she looked in the mirror and began laughing hysterically. She looked like La Llorona!

She took a quick shower and put her muddy clothes and shoes in the washer. Her mind was on fast forward.

The phone rang. It was Virgie.

Lita heard herself talking. "I don't know how it happened...I fell...I think I fainted...I don't feel well."

The lies were coming thick and fast!

"No! Don't come. I don't want anyone catching whatever it is I have. No, I haven't taken my temperature yet. Yes, I will.

"Oh, Virgie, dinner? That is so sweet of you. Just make enough for Benito. I really don't think I'll be able to eat anything...

"About six?...That will be great. Thank you."

She then called Benito. Dios forgive me. I'm going to do it again.

When Ben came on the other end of the line, she began lying again.

"Benito, I didn't get home with the beans after all." (That much was true.) "Why don't you pick up a fifty-pound bag there in Taos? Chuy's beans looked old. I'll pay you back tonight, or better yet, put it on my credit card.

"I know Sweetie's coming in. Virgie's bringing in dinner. You'll have plenty of time to go up to the ranch. I don't feel well. No, don't worry. I'll be fine."

Maybe that money was evil. Dios mio, she'd never told so many lies!

Sweetie! That was it! Maybe that would work? Lita'd always liked the ranch house looking clean when Hugh's daughter came home. She'd drive up there right now.

When she started the car, she had an idea. Opening the trunk, she ran into the house and grabbed some sheets from the linen closet. She pulled the money from under the bed, carefully wrapped the parcels in the sheets and carried them out to the car. She locked them safely in the trunk.

She then took the trunk key off her key chain and put it down in the bottom of a sack of dry dog food. She picked up Glow and let the cat out.

"Come on, honey, I want to introduce you to someone."

Soon she was driving to the ranch.

❧❧❧

Junior glowered all the way back to Albuquerque. The goose in the car with him hugged her arm rest and sniveled as far as Santa Fe. After that, she fixed her face in the mirror on the visor and gave him the silent treatment.

After they passed Bernalillo, she started in on him. It was the worst tongue-lashing Junior had ever experienced. He had never heard her use words like that. Soon they were screaming at each other.

When they pulled up in front of her house, she jerked her door open and hissed, "Give me back my key, you bastard!"

Junior threw the key at her. It missed her and landed in the grass several yards behind her, someplace where she'd have to look for it a long time.

As he drove off, he thought, And I was thinking of leaving Mona for that bitch! Mona never talks that way to me! Sure, she spends money, but when you think about it, Mona isn't so bad.

Junior stopped and refilled Gertie's tank and returned her car. He went straight home and left a note for Mona saying he'd be at his parents'. He left in such a hurry he didn't lock the front door.

A car followed him out of the gated community.

Screw 'em. He had bigger worries!

What was his papa going to say? As far as Junior knew, they'd never been stiffed before!

❧❧❧

Lita and Glow pulled up in front of the ranch house where she had grown up. Some folks called it a hacienda, but that was too pretentious.

The door flew open and Sweetie came running out to greet her. "Mamalita! It's so good to see you!"

"I meant to come earlier and have everything ready for you, but the time slipped away."

"That's not all that's slipped away! How much weight have you lost? Come in and I'll make you a sandwich. How about a Coke?"

Sweetie led the way through the house. Lita followed more slowly.

As she passed through the sala, she noticed her father's rocker still sat by the big fireplace. She was flooded with feelings she had forgotten. There she was in a pale blue starched dress with a big bow in the back. She was flirting with her papa.

It was the summer after her brother died. "Papa, are you glad I'm a girl?" she'd asked. To this day, she could feel her world shatter when he'd replied, not even looking up from his book, "No, mi hija. If you were a boy I wouldn't have to worry about the rancho, but you're just a girl, aren't you?"

She had fled the house and tried to run away. Hours later, one of the hired hands had found her up in the mountains, cold and hungry. The blue dress was torn and stained.

"Are you coming? It's almost ready." How fortunate Sweetie was to have a father who thought she was special.

"I forgot Glow. She's still in the car. Let me get her."

"I'll go," the girl sang over her shoulder as she raced out the door.

Soon Lita was hearing squeals, then the babble of baby talk as Sweetie came back in with Glow in her arms.

"Mamalita, she's adorable! Ben never told me how small and soft she is! Come on, Glow, I'll get you something to eat, too."

Lita followed along in their wake, saying, "If you start spoiling her, I'll have one fat dog that won't live long. She can only have a little bit."

"Tell me about your last semester," said Lita, as she sat down at the old kitchen table. "How does it feel to be a graduate?"

"Like I should know more than I do. I'm just glad to have it over so I can be back here." Sweetie set a huge ham sandwich in front of her. As she poured the Coke, she continued, "It's really scary. Ben is so lucky! He has this wonderful ranch to build his life around, and it's all he's ever wanted. I don't know what I want to do."

"Benito's told me you've been writing songs."

"Oh, I'm not very good yet, but it would be fun to sell one. Would you like to hear my latest?" Her eyes twinkled.

"Of course. How can I tell if you're any good if I can't hear what you've done?"

"Let me get my guitar."

Lita let Glow out the kitchen door and watched her sniff about the old fountain and bite at the dandelions. She wished Hugh would spend a little more time and effort on the grounds around the house and less on the high meadows. Sweetie came back into the room with her new guitar and Lita called the dog back in.

"All right, now. You and Glow sit right there. I'll play the tune first, and then I'll sing what I have. It's not finished yet. You don't have to like it."

Sweetie bowed her head over the strings and began to play.

Lita was amazed at the melody. Sweetie was really talented if the rest of her music sounded this charming. She began nodding her head to the rhythm

Sweetie began to sing. Her voice was clear and sweet, but, oh my, the lyrics!

He says that I'm all frigid
When I lay in bed all rigid,
That it ain't the way a woman should behave.
Well, he might get his rocks off,
If he'd only take his socks off,
And it wouldn't hurt none any if he'd shave!
He just grinds his molars,
When I wear pink plastic rollers,
And slather purple night cream on my face.

"That's all I have so far. There's going to be a verse about food. She wants cordon bleu and he wants catsup on his stew, and one about her wanting to go out while he just wants to stay home and drink beer and watch sports on TV."

"Sweetie, that was an unforgettable tune, quite lovely, really, and you have an angel's voice."

"So you don't like the lyrics, huh?"

"I would say it was clever if I didn't know who wrote it, but Sweetie, you're my girl. I changed your diapers and watched you grow up. Those words aren't you." She looked at the fragile child with the halo of burnished curls. She tried again, taking care to treat her words like antique lace. "I feel your songs might be more meaningful if you wrote about what's real and important to you. These words don't sound like you at all." She was relieved to see Sweetie smile.

"Maybe not, but they sure sound like my mama. Boy, did she make a wrong turn when she left Daddy! How about my coming to serenade you with another one later? It will be a nicer one, I promise." She was fingering her necklace, the one Amy had made. "How's Ben?"

"Excited about seeing you," laughed Lita. "Glad to be graduated and anxious for school to start and still wanting a new truck."

"I know. In every email he has to say something about this or that model. Now tell me about you. You need to gain some weight. Have you been making Ben cook?"

"It's just me, chica. That, and the doctor tells me I should drink bottled water." Here she was lying again, but this is why she'd come.

"Are you?"

"I'll get around to it."

"I'll see that you do!"

"I don't want Ben to worry. Please don't say anything. My, this is a good sandwich!"

"Hello, Lita!" It was Hugh coming in the kitchen door. "Did I hear you say 'sandwich'? Sweetie, I wouldn't mind one of those myself."

Sweetie rose to make another sandwich and Hugh continued. "So how have you been, Lita? Sweets here keeps me up on Ben, but she doesn't say enough about you. Did hear about this dog, though; she was a real surprise!"

He reached over and scratched Glow behind the ears. He winked at his daughter and said to Lita, "I guess parents aren't romantic enough to talk about, you know. Especially when there's Ben to chatter about."

"Daddy!"

Lita enjoyed listening to their banter. Hugh got up and helped himself to a beer, teasing Sweetie all the while. His daughter gave as good as she got.

Lita looked at the clock. Time to get down to business. Virgie would be showing up at home, and she needed to be there.

"Hugh, I'm needing to get some appraisals on some of the paintings and stuff still stored here. Would it be all right to bring someone out in a few weeks?"

"Sure thing, Lita, anytime. Are you thinking of selling some of your antiques?"

"I'm not sure, Hugh. The money might be tempting, depending on what they're worth. It might be enough to make a difference, with college starting in a few months."

"Don't I know that!" He smiled at his daughter. "Do you have any idea how much girls cost these days?"

"Speaking of money, Hugh, could you start Benito this week instead of next? There must be something he could do around here to help get ready for summer. Maybe fix the fencing down by the goats or work on that fountain out there."

He reached over and patted her hand. "Is there anything else we can do for you?"

"No, just work him silly."

They were such good people. She hated using them like this. "I best be going. Ben will want to eat as soon as he gets home. He wants to come see Sweetie tonight."

"Good. I'll talk to him when he gets here, before he gets sidetracked."

Sweetie walked Lita to the car and held the dog while she got in. She stood and watched till Lita could no longer see her in the rearview mirror.

When Lita got home, she let the air out of one of the T-bird's front tires. Next, she climbed under the hood and loosened a few belts and removed a few screws from several hose clamps. She pulled a few wires and went in to call Tito's Garage.

She was sure the car wouldn't go anywhere without the missing parts, and she also knew that the only parts she would have to pay for were the missing screws. She could see her husband, Ben, ranting about the damage she'd done to his beloved car. Tito was as honest as they come and as slow as was possible for someone who was supposed to have good sense.

If she told him she'd lost her trunk key, he'd work around it. He'd think she'd find the key someday and so he wouldn't think of ordering a new one. She was too frugal for that kind of extravagance, and everyone knew it.

Tito arrived right behind Virgie.

Lita met them at the door in her winter robe and a hot water bottle under her arm. Her cough was worse than Virgie's smoker's cough. Under cover of a vigorous hacking spell, she saw Tito and Virgie exchange glances.

Virgie put supper in the oven and fed Glow. Lita was amused at how far her friend stayed away from her.

Tito never even came in the house. He simply hooked up the T-bird to his tow truck and shouted that he'd call with an estimate in a few days. Lita croaked to Virgie, who passed on the message, "No hurry."

When they were both gone, Lita let out a long breath. The money was now safe till she could think straight. She went and changed into pajamas and her scruffy house shoes. She hung the robe back in her closet and wrapped Tina's shawl around her shoulders. She let the cat and dog out and settled down with a cup of tea to make plans.

First, she'd have to miss Mass tomorrow. When was the last time she'd done that? Maybe she could talk to Father Mondragon. That would help.

She had made another cup of tea and was letting the animals in when Benito came through the front door.

"Mamalita, what's the matter? Are you really sick? Here are the beans." He slung the gunny sack onto the kitchen counter. "Where is your car?"

"Not so fast, hijo. Let's do things one at a time. Thanks for the beans. How much do I owe you?"

"You don't. I put them on your credit card."

"That's good. Tito came after the car. I went up to see Hugh and Sweetie today, and when I got home I noticed a low tire. I can't seem to find the trunk key, so I saved you some time changing a tire. You don't want to be late. They're expecting you this evening. Your supper's in the oven. You can eat as soon as you shower." She stopped abruptly. She was talking way too fast. She never did that. Fortunately, Benito didn't notice, or he would be on to her.

"Great, I'm starving! What are we having?"

"I have no idea, but it'll be good. Virgie brought it over."

"How come she cooked for us?"

Lita sighed. She hated lying to Benito. "I don't feel so good. Don't worry. It's just a little touch of something. Whatever it is, I don't want you to catch it. I think I'll go take a rest now while you get ready and eat, and then I'll fix myself a little something. We can't have you getting sick with graduation and the Fiesta both next week. If Tito doesn't hurry with my car, I'll need you to cart the beans down to the church. Enough about me. How was your day?"

"Mamalita, I saw the greatest little truck! I'll tell you all about it tonight when I get back." He headed for the shower. It would be lonely without him here every night, but she didn't want him around right now. She did want him around; she just didn't want him involved in her business.

Lita was in bed by the time her grandson came in later that night. She'd tried staying awake to see his excitement and hear his plans, but the adrenalin rush she'd had for most of the day had finally left her. It was all she could do to stay up till it was time to put Kitty Gato and Glow out one last time. She didn't even turn on the radio. She opened her Bible instead. She chose John's Gospel and read:

In the beginning was the Word and the Word was with God. He was in the beginning with God. All things came into being through Him, and without Him not one thing came into being.

Did that mean that the money was from God?

What has come into being in Him was life, and the life was the light of all the people.

The light shines in the darkness, and the darkness did not overcome it.

The money certainly would bring life back into the valley! It was clear as day she was meant to find it! That fit right in with the imagery about light. Lita yawned. She was almost nodding off when the words from verse 16 jumped out at her. From his fullness we have all received grace upon grace. "Yes," murmured Lita.

She switched off the light and snuggled down into the bed. Glow let out a sigh. Lita's last thoughts were of all the gifts and graces she had received.

"Thank you, God. Amen."

Something was happening at Mano's place.

Junior had pulled up in a cloud of dust at four. The only call that had gone out was to Mrs. Benavidez, who owned the half-acre behind the Bacas. Sadie had called to say that her grandson would be happy to rototill the empty lot and put down hay to keep the weeds down. No charge. Couldn't neighbors do for each other? Anyway, keeping down the weeds would be good for Mano's health. Mrs. Benavidez was pleased to help Mano and Sadie. They had always been such good neighbors, blah, blah, blah.

Nate Courtney, who was listening in, wished they'd get to what was happening!

Mona arrived at five-thirty with Tres.

Junior had come out of the house and had hugged his wife, something Nate Courtney had never seen before.

What was going on? The three of them stood in a tight little huddle, then Tres went stomping into the house. Mona put her arms around her husband and comforted him as he sobbed in his parents' yard. Nate watched until they went inside hand in hand, then he put a call through to Luis Fernandez.

While Nate was talking to Luis, Tres was tossing bales of hay over his abuelo's back fence.

He'd just gotten through with one dirty job and now he was going to have to spend his Sunday doing another one.

Luis Fernandez arrived shortly at the stakeout shed to keep an eye on things himself. It wasn't that he didn't have complete faith in Nate and Jerry, but he felt in his gut that things were starting to happen. He had to be there. He had just settled into a lawn chair when the call from the Bacas went out to 911. Mano was down!

The two men looked at each other. Nate shrugged. It took eleven minutes for the fire truck and ambulance to arrive with lights flashing and sirens ripping apart the quiet afternoon. The two men waited till the ambulance left, followed by Sadie and Mona in her new car and Junior and Tres right behind.

"I'll call the hospital and have them relay info on Mano to me," said Luis. "Looks like there's nothing for you to do around here. Why don't you go home and have a hot supper and a good night's rest? Tomorrow might be a real kick."

"Thanks, Boss. I'm glad you were here when that 911 went out."

"Me, too. See you tomorrow. I might call if Mano doesn't make it."

Nate locked the door to the shed as they left. "That'll be fine. I'll be home tonight."

Millie Saavedra wasn't sure what to expect when Dolores Maldonado opened her door Monday night, but surely it wasn't the scream that issued when the young woman saw the bouquet.

"Oh, sweetheart, I didn't think you really loved him. I guess it's over, huh?" Millie stepped in and put the florist's arrangement of dried flowers spray-painted black with a large black bow on the tiny kitchen table. Millie felt the arrangement was in bad taste, maybe worth a few tears, but this agonized scream was something else.

"Let me make you something cold to drink. You just sit down. This must be a shock, after getting all those pretty flowers for such a long time. What's it been, two years now?"

"Oh, Millie, I wish I could tell you."

"Dolores, I thought you were too smart to get mixed up with a married man. Is he one of those big políticos?"

"No. Nothing like that! Millie, when do I have time to have an affair? What clothes in my closet would suggest that I even date?"

"You got a point there. Maybe after this semester when you get your new job, you'll have some money to take better care of yourself." Jerking her thumb at the gruesome bouquet, she added, "All I got to say is that whoever sent you these has a nasty sense of humor."

Dolores started to cry. Millie busied herself with the ice and glasses. The soft drink fizzed as it hit the ice. When she finally handed her neighbor a glass, she served herself and sat across the table.

"So, what you gonna do now?" Millie cocked her head to one side like a parrot and clicked her dentures.

Dolores took a long sip of her drink. "Go to class tonight. Then I'll have to keep on going. I guess I ought to start really praying. Maybe I'll go back to church."

Millie arched her eyebrow. This wasn't what she expected to hear. Then again, Dolores wasn't like most young women she knew.

They drank in silence. "You'll need to be getting ready for class,"

Millie finally said as she rinsed out her glass. "Now don't go asking if I want your flowers. The answer's no. But I'll take them to the dumpster for you if you want."

Dolores laughed. "I can do that on my way to my car. Thanks for being here with me. It was better, having you here."

Millie patted Dolores on the shoulder as she passed on her way to the door. "Call if I can help," the older woman said.

Dolores sat for a while wondering how many different flowers, pods, and weeds made up the arrangement. It was really well done. Too bad it had to be black. That made her shopping tonight easy. Licorice, and chocolate-filled Oreos, two of Petey's favorites.

***

Earlier that morning, Lita had gone to Mass. After confession, she told Father Mondragon that she had found something and had no idea who it might belong to. She wanted to know if it would be all right to donate it, give it away. He suggested that she wait a while and see if there was anything in the lost-and-found section in the classifieds. She said that was a good idea.

She was fixing herself some lunch when the doorbell rang. It was a young man from the bottled water company in Taos.

"Mrs. Estrellita Cordova? I'm Jim from Crystal Springs Bottled Water. I have a delivery for you. Where do you want me to put it?"

"How much water are you talking about, Jim?"

"Fifty five-gallon jugs and one cooler unit I can set up for you in your kitchen. That's where most folks want it."

Sweetie, you overdid, as always, bless your heart.

"I guess we ought to store the water on the back porch. Come on in, and I'll show you where you can put the cooler in the kitchen."

"They're pretty heavy. You think you'll be able to change them by yourself?"

"Yes, you'd be surprised how strong I am."

It only took Jim fifteen minutes to store the containers on the porch and set the little cooler on the end of her counter next to the back door. That way she wouldn't have so far to carry the jugs, he said.

That wasn't all he said. By the time he was through, she had heard about his wife, his new baby, and all about the Little League team he coached.

"Would you like a sandwich?" asked Lita. "It's almost lunchtime."

"That'd be right nice, Mrs. Cordova. Thank you."

Over lunch, Lita learned quite a bit more than she needed to know about baseball and the silly parents who thought they knew everything there was to know about the game. She was glad to see Jim's truck pull away and have the house quiet again. She put some meat on to brown for burritos for supper and mentally listed and revised the things she needed to do this week.

By the time Benito came in, the burritos, refried beans, and salad were ready. He washed his down with two tall glasses of milk and was off to get some work done at the ranch before it got dark.

While the dishes soaked, Lita pored over her accounts. There was three thousand dollars left after funeral expenses for Tina. Since she owned the building that served as the church hall, she could donate the rent on the building in lieu of her pledge and use the rent she derived from Amy to go toward truck payments. She'd have to call the bank in the morning and ask how much she had in CDs.

Since Ben died, she'd dipped into the money that came in from Hugh for the ranch only once, and that was because Tina had needed tuition that last year. She tried to forget it was there, lest she be tempted to spend it. She needed to call that helpful gentleman at Morgan Stanley and ask him about her account there, too.

Every month she divided her rent money from Hugh and sent half to the bank for certificates of deposit and the rest to Morgan Stanley. John Simmons, yes, that was his name, had orders to treat her account as if it were his mother's and invest it as wisely as a serpent, or something biblical like that.

She made a note to herself to call Simmons and the bank tomorrow. As an afterthought, she added a note to call the art appraiser

Emilio had suggested before he took off. She really did need to know what she was worth.

Oh, and there were those gold coins that Ben had bought when the children were little and he settled a big case. The little sack was in the safety deposit box at the bank in Taos. Gold was down around thirty-five dollars an ounce then, and she'd been critical that he was throwing their money away, but now the ads on the Savage show said gold was up. She'd have to see if that was true.

Lita knew she should take a more active interest in her investments, but she and the children had gotten by, albeit painfully, on Ben's life insurance and Social Security. Everything that could be saved had been squirreled away. When the lease with Hugh was up, Benito was going to need more than he realized to make the ranch thrive.

She must remind Benito to be sure to sign up for one class a semester having to do with finances. That would be good insurance.

***

Sid Salazar, the prison guard, was allergic to chocolate and he hated licorice, so Petey received his care package from his sister almost as soon as it arrived.

Al Luna had just returned from a morning workout in the weight room. He was sitting on his cot wiping sweat off his neck when he heard Petey giggling. He looked up to see the young man leading an imaginary band with a limp licorice whip.

Petey heard Al growl, and grinned a wide grin that showed a mouthful of Oreos. Petey lifted his black whip and made an abracadabra gesture just like a real magician.

Al Luna started bellowing for a guard. After a while, one showed up, and after another hour, Al was able to call his lawyer.

When he finally reached Skettering's office, it was only to get a recorded message. He impatiently listened to his options, angrily punched number three, and shouted into the mouthpiece, "Skettering! This is Al Luna, you little shit! You call my boys and tell them to go see him! You hear me? Get my boys!" Slam went the receiver.

The guard checked to see if he'd broken the receiver after he was returned to his cell.

iii

While Mitch, Frank, and Luis were having their weekly meeting, down in the south valley, Tres Baca had cut classes so he could take care of Mrs. Benavidez' half-acre. He'd had a friend till the place yesterday. It was the best he could do on short notice.

He'd been here since before sunup. Now the straw almost covered the whole field and the marijuana that had been hidden in the bales was safely in his dad's trunk.

His dad had been at the hospital twenty-four/seven since Mano's heart attack.

It was as if his father couldn't think straight without his grandfather at the helm. When he made it back to the hospital, his dad was going to have to get it together enough to deliver the weed to the mule who would take it on to Oklahoma. Since he was driving his old man's car, his pop wouldn't have to switch the goods into another vehicle. When he left here, he'd call his mom's cell phone. When it vibrated in her purse, she'd get Junior out front so he and his dad could change places. He'd study at the hospital in a waiting room just across the hall from Mano's room, and then catch a ride home with his mom.

iii

Mitch was having fits as usual. Their entire case was sequestered at the Heart Hospital of New Mexico in room 408.

"At least we won't have to wonder where they are," said Frank. He had a date with Lieutenant Gordon tonight, and it was good to know he wouldn't have to go tearing off on some new hot lead in the Baca case.

Luis added, "Tres just called from Mano's place. He's been doing good-neighbor work for the Bacas and stopped to shower at Mano's before going to the hospital, so we know where he's been and what his plans are."

After a long discussion, it was decided to cut costs by not doing surveillance at the Bacas' as long as Mano was in the hospital.

"My department can't afford it," groused Frank.

Luis, whose department had been spending freely in this area, could think of six other ways that money needed to be spent. He nodded.

Cheapskate Mitch, always willing to let State, County, and City funds be spent while saving federal monies, just sat there looking pained, but wouldn't commit his own funds. The decision was reached by default. They would never know if they would regret it.

So the next day, no one was there to see the two men who knocked on the Bacas' door and snooped around the place. Neither Nate nor Jerry was there to watch them confer over the hood of their car before the short, skinny one went next door. In a few moments, he was back, and the Mercedes pulled out of the driveway and headed east.

Because no one had been watching at Mano's, the guard at the hospital was taken unawares by a short, skinny doctor and a huge companion, both dressed in scrubs and operating masks.

They walked right past him, turned, and before the guard knew what happened, they'd knocked him in the head. An orderly found him in a utility room later that day, trussed up like a Thanksgiving turkey with a wad of gauze in his mouth.

By the time Luis showed up at the hospital, Mano was doing much better, the guard had been questioned, and the head nurse had been able to give a pretty good description of Mano's callers.

She'd been walking past Mr. Baca's room when she heard voices. That patient wasn't supposed to have visitors! She barreled right into room 408 and cornered two strangers. They seemed ready to bolt, but she kept them there giving them her best what-for, and citing hospital regulations like a drill sergeant. Much chastened, the two men apologized and left. She'd chased after them, though, calling for security. The two men split up and disappeared.

When Luis introduced himself, Nurse Hadley looked at her watch to let him know she didn't have time for foolishness and said, "What do you need to know?"

Not "What do you want to know?" as if that would take up too much of her time.

"A description of the two men would be helpful."

She looked at him as if considering whether or not he was worthy of her observations before answering.

"The small one seemed in charge. He's about five seven or eight. He had on expensive cowboy boots so it was hard to tell. He has male pattern baldness and pulls his hair back tight into a braid that reaches just past his shoulder. He's beginning to gray. He must be in his early forties. Sunken face, high cheek bones, looked like he's been in detox a time or two. He had a stud in his left ear lobe."

"Nurse Hadley, what about the other man?"

"The one that was too big for the room? He's built like that actor who lives up in Santa Fe now. You know the good-sized one who's always a cop or detective."

"You mean Brian Dennehy?"

"Yes, that's the one." She knocked on the counter to her right, catching a nurse's attention, and handed him a stack of folders. "He's well-dressed in a flashy way."

"They weren't in hospital scrubs?"

"No, we found those in the shower in the patient's room. Sorry, but they've gone to housecleaning. You'd never find them with all the others."

"I'm sorry, too. Please describe what he had on."

"Gray silk blazer, with darker flecks, looked to me like shantung, and navy pants. I didn't see his shoes because he was on the far side of the bed. He has brown hair that looks as though he gets it styled. No cheap barber for him. He had on a big diamond pinkie ring."

"Anything else you can remember?"

She looked affronted for a moment before she grinned.

"Yeah, the one who looks like a cartoon rat, he had a tattoo on the inside of his right wrist. It was one of those flaming hearts. You know, the same kind as in those pictures of Jesus."

"Nationality?"

"They could have been Arabs, but I don't think so," Luis waited. "They were all spitting off rapid-fire Spanish when I heard them."

"So you don't know what they were talking about?"

"I've lived here too long not to pick up some of it. There was something about a bad deal."

Luis could have kissed her. Now he had something to go on. "Nurse Hadley, if it wouldn't take up too much of your time, would you mind if I dropped by tomorrow with a few pictures for you to look at?"

"I go on lunch break at one-thirty. I don't want you wasting my time on the ward. If you're in the cafeteria then, I'll see you." She shrugged and returned to her work.

Luis took the hint. "My treat tomorrow." Then, as an afterthought, he asked, "Where was the family during your run-in with the two men?"

"Mrs. Baca said she was watching her soap in the waiting room, and the son and his wife were in the coffee shop."

***

The next day, Luis was waiting in the hospital cafeteria when Nurse Hadley arrived. She waved at him to join her in the food line.

He found she wasn't much of a conversationalist off duty either. He selected soup, salad, and coffee. She, on the other hand, decided on the double cheese omelet, an order of fries, iced tea, and coconut cream pie. He made a bet with himself that she wasn't planning on cooking tonight.

She surprised him when they sat down. She warmed up and actually said a bit about herself, why she'd come to New Mexico (Army wife), and why she had stayed here (ex-Army wife). She had a daughter at UNM working on a master's in computer science.

When lunch was over, she took a quick glance through his photos, and Luis found himself wishing she worked for him.

She handed him the fourth page. "The one on the bottom row,

second from the left, is the big man. He doesn't look so well-groomed here, and he's lost maybe twenty pounds, but that's him." She found another picture. "This must have been before he got into drugs in a big way. And here's your Mr. Rat Face."

Sure enough, Raul Apodaca did look like a rat.

"How did you do that?" asked Luis. He'd never seen anyone so sure of themselves during the identification process.

"It's not so hard." She laughed at his quizzical expression. "I worked my way through college and nursing school at a plastic surgery clinic in southern California. You get used to seeing before-and-after accident shots, then the ones before and after surgery. You learn facial types and bone structure and how muscles sag. I'll bet you a Coke the big guy has had rhinoplasty."

"You're on, Nurse Hadley. I'll let you know if you win."

"You'll have to catch him first, and it's Ellen, when I'm not working."

"Thanks, Ellen, I think you've been a great help."

"I'd stay and chat, but work's waiting and I'm on a time clock." With that, she picked up her tray and strode to the conveyor belt where she dumped her plates and flatware. She took her tea with her as she moved on through the glass doors.

Luis took a few moments to go over his notes.

On his way to the car at the far end of the parking lot, a thought occurred to him and he broke out laughing; Nurse Hadley and Nurse Ratchet were both Ellen when they weren't working.

First thing Wednesday morning, Lita called the law office and asked Silvia to check on the legality of what Benito would call "finders keepers" and learned that in order for it to be legal, she'd need to put an ad in the classifieds in several papers for two weeks. Then if no one came forward, she could legally claim it or do with it as she saw fit.

Next, she called Leonard Salazar at the police station and said she had found something she thought might be of value but, being a widow, wondered if the police station's telephone could be used in the classified ad she needed to place in the newspapers. She was so afraid of those crazy people out there...

"Don't worry, Mrs. C. It would give me something to do here," said Lenny. "Tell you what, just bring your stuff by, and I'll send it off. That way, even the papers won't have your address. I'll keep you safe. I've been meaning to come by and see how you're doing. It's good to hear you're sounding busy. The family's been keeping you in our prayers."

"Bless you, Leonard. You are very clever! I've been doing okay. Thank you for this favor. Just please keep this conversation between the two of us."

"Won't even write it down, Señora. Don't you worry."

Lita sighed. "Thank you, and do give my best to your family."

It took quite a bit of research at the library in Taos to get the telephone numbers for the papers in Santa Fe, Albuquerque, Denver, and Amarillo. She would need to find out how much each ad would cost and then buy some money orders to pay for them. The pay phone at the library would work for this as long as she had the right change. She would then take down the ads and money orders to Lenny at the station. All she'd have to do was just wait for two weeks.

She knew she couldn't do anything until she had her car back with the money anyway, and that would be after the Fiesta.

On Thursday she'd soak beans, and cook them on Friday.

Oh, she could go ahead and put some Fels Naptha to soak. She needed to remember to use bottled water. Then everything would be ready!

iii

Everyone was in high spirits Saturday morning. Benito dropped off Lita, Glow, and the beans around eight at the food booth, and then went looking for Sweetie. Lita bought a cup of coffee and headed for the ticket booth. Glow pranced along beside her. It was going to be a warm, sunny day and if ticket sales by nine o'clock were any indication, the Fiesta would make money this year. The Barelas stopped by to buy more tickets and pet Glow. Wilma asked if the men who were looking for her had found her yet. They said Marion Pacheco had pointed her out.

"No" laughed Lita, "I'm sure easy to find. They won't be able to miss me." She gave no more thought to the exchange as more people were lining up for tickets

iii

The two men made their way out of the crowd on the plaza, meeting at their rental car. They drove slowly down the street, turning right at the old Dairy Queen and went down a back alley, bypassing the Fiesta as they made their way to the Cordova house. It only took a few minutes to tear the place apart, looking for money or deposit slips or a trail of some sort that would lead them to Al and Mano's haul. Furniture was tossed, drawers pulled out, mattresses and cushions slashed. The attic and basement were searched. Boxes were opened and books, papers, and the ravelings and treasures of several lives left in a jumble. Nada.

"Let's go," the big man said. As they moved swiftly through the sala, the little man kicked the cat hard enough to bounce Kitty Gato against the wall.

"Hey, man. Why you go and do that?"

"I hate sneaky critters! Cats. They give me the creeps," the little man shuddered. "You know how they're always looking at you like they think they're better or something."

***

Benito was the first to arrive home. He called Leonard Salazar. The police car was in front of her house when Lita arrived. She stood in the sala, shaking her head. What have I done? she thought. How is this going to end?

"Was the door locked, Mrs. C.?"

"Who in Los Santos locks their doors?"

"Do you know who would do this?"

"No." At least she didn't have a name or a face, did she? "What do you think they were looking for?"

"Whatever they were after wasn't here. Maybe we'll figure out what's missing when we get this mess sorted out. There isn't much of value except some of the art and the Indian pottery, and it looks like they're still here. We'll let you know if we find anything missing." Then she thought, Thank God the car's not here!

The questions seemed to go on forever. Lita kept volleying answers back as fast as they came. It was like those tennis matches on TV. She had always thought they were boring. Now she was worn out.

Lita didn't cry till later, when friends came to set the house to rights. Amy photographed each room and Mrs. Marujo had hobbled in on her walker and announced she would make a list of everything they found missing, broken, or damaged. When Benito and Virgie's husband, Mel, set the couch upright, they found Kitty Gato. He'd crawled under it to find a place to die.

"Benito, we'll bury him in that sunny spot in the garden he liked so much." She pulled the boy into her arms. "I'm so sorry, hijo. He was a wonderful old cat." It was then she lost it and sobs overtook her.

She thought she had herself under control, till that night. Before she went to bed, she opened the backdoor to let Kitty Gato in. Old habits were going to kill her! She covered her mouth so Benito wouldn't hear her moan and ran to her room. Glow tried to comfort her, but it was ineffective. Lita could feel the old cat jump on the bed as she was drifting off to sleep. That woke her and she started crying all over again. The cat had been Tina's best friend. They had slept together till Tina had gone off to school. Even lately, Kitty Gato still napped in Tina's room. Now both of them were gone. Her grief finally bested her and she woke more numb than alive to everything she knew.

By Monday afternoon, the women had repacked and labeled boxes, replaced books, and put pots and pans back in their places. Lita had ordered new mattresses, and an upholsterer was coming with fabric samples for the furniture. She was glad Ben had insisted on insurance. Looking at the ruined furnishings, Lita realized she had stepped blithely into a deadly game and she was going to have to be more careful than she had ever been before. She felt faint. Could she outwit mobsters? What were her chances? She didn't want to know how bad they were. She only knew she had to keep going.

***

Al Luna growled into the phone. "Skettering, you read the classifieds? You stupid piece of shit. You get my boys there! You tell them to use a fine-tooth comb. I want answers! Well, read the paper and find out!"

The next break-in made the news the next day. The little police station in Los Santos had been broken into. All the drawers and cabinets had been dumped on the floor. There were no suspects.

"Hello! Anybody home? Lita, are you here?" called Emilio from the front door.

Suddenly, Lita felt better. Her world was back in place.

"Come in! Come in! When did you get back? Tell me all about your trip."

"Late last night. I'll tell you later. This morning Sunny told me all about your excitement, and here I am. Are you all right?"

"Oh, that's all over. The only thing we lost of any importance was Kitty Gato."

Emilio put his arms around her and gave her a long hug. "I am sorry, little one." Then he suddenly let go. Looking at her directly, he asked, "Why would someone do this to you, amiga?"

"You tell me, Emilio!"

"Lita, you are a woman of mystery, with your hands in more pots than most people own! I'm glad to be back. Please trust me, if you need me."

That night, as Lita ran over the highlights of her day, she decided she liked being thought of as a "woman of mystery." It had been nice being hugged, also. She'd never realized how large Emilio's shoulders were. The car was safe in her own garage. Tomorrow would be another exciting day.

Lita couldn't sleep, so by three-thirty she was dropping money into the bubbling Fels Naptha water in the roaster.

She'd strung wire all around the basement and the electric roaster was on Ben's old work bench. Tables along the wall were covered with butcher paper. A towel was tacked over the window.

Wearing her new yellow Playtex gloves, she stirred the money with a long wooden spoon. In a while, she'd transfer the money into a tub of bottled water to rinse. She had buckets and pots under the bench to carry the rinse water up to the yard. On her way back down, she'd bring more bottled water.

She thought it was a rather "slick" operation and wondered if the CSI team would find anything wrong with it. She smiled. A woman of mystery!

She gave up trying to count the bills, all hundreds, except for the six banded stacks of fifties.

There were forty-six gold coins and twenty-three old coins mounted in little plastic cases. They had to be worth something more than their face value. Kip would take care of that. She'd written and told him she was sending him some reading material for Tina's cause. She wished she could see his face when he opened his package!

By nine, the wires were full of drying bills.

She carried up more water and took a break to eat some breakfast.

It was time to heat up the iron.

Ironing money in rubber gloves was trickier than she had imagined. She lay the bills out in rows on the butcher paper and skimmed the iron over them. Some needed Faultless Starch. This was going to take longer than she had thought. Maybe by next week it would be done.

At five, Lita was ready to drop. Her feet hurt. She hurt all over. She had been tense all day. She couldn't remember standing for such a long time. She fed Glow, made a sandwich and iced tea, propped up her feet to eat, and watch the evening news.

She was about to take another bite when a story came on about the owner of a funeral home in Newark, New Jersey, who'd been found crushed to death under a mountain of pinto beans with his wrists and ankles wrapped in duct tape. There was a picture of the crime scene. Lita could see a backhoe standing by, and yellow crime tape marking off a large parking area.

"Employees were surprised to find their parking places filled with beans this morning when they came to work," said the perky little blond reporter. "When the owner of the funeral home failed to appear, they grew worried and called the police."

"Jenny, what seems to be the motive behind this murder?"

"Kurt, it's just speculation at the moment, but it seems to be drug-related."

"Thank you, Jenny. Well, there you have it, folks. Stay tuned to WXTV for more on this story as it unfolds. This story seems to be more than just a hill of beans!"

After Mass the next morning, Lita was the last to step into the confessional.

"Bless me, Father, for I have sinned. I have caused someone to commit a mortal sin."

"And how did you do this, my child?"

"In acting on my faith, I have caused someone to commit murder."

"And where did this occur?"

"In New Jersey."

"And do you know who committed this crime?"

"No, Father."

"Did you know the person who was murdered?"

"No, Father."

The long and the short of it was that Lita was to say ten Hail Marys and pray for her active imagination.

She knew Emilio would think her disingenuous. Or was it duplicitous?

***

In Albuquerque, Frank Quintana called through the door, "Yo! Luis! Did you see the fax that came in this morning? Some guy in Newark was offed under a pile of pinto beans!"

"Get on the phone. We need more."

Lita spent every minute she could doing laundry, and after eighteen afternoons and most nights, she had the money washed, ironed, and boxed. Her hands were so swollen that her handwriting on the boxes' labels looked like that of a third-grader, but the letters were large and legible.

She hoped Kip could read the letter she had written. She had gone through Ben's files (he'd always kept copies at home, in case there was a fire at the office), and found a letter she could use as a model. She had requested his legal services as a fiduciary agent to discreetly donate the enclosed items to a memorial for Christina Maria Cordova. The memorial was to be sent to Catholic Charities in care of the Archdiocese of Santa Fe in Albuquerque, New Mexico. There was also a check for one hundred dollars as a retainer.

Lita shuffled to the phone when Virgie called to check on her.

"Lita, you okay? Jovita and I don't think you're looking so good. You need something?"

"Just sleep, Virgie. I'm just so tired."

"I got just the thing. The doctor down the hill gave me some pills, you remember, last year, when I couldn't get no sleep? Well, I saved some, for an emergency, you know."

"I don't know..."

"You look like one big emergency to us. You get in your PJs and I'll be right there. We can't have you getting sick on us. Jovita and I are busy with the goats, and you said you'd clean this week."

She took a pill while Virgie watched and then she went to bed. A little nap would do wonders.

A little nap wasn't near enough. She woke in a fog at six, fed Glow, and heated up some tortilla soup for supper.

She waited till dark to put the packages of money in the trunk, behind a sleeping bag and some potting soil. She would mail it tomorrow when she went to Albuquerque with Amy and Sunny, along with the dogs, who had appointments to be groomed.

After a warm bath, she turned on Michael Savage and set her alarm. They were to leave early.

The radio was still on when the alarm went off. I'm too old for this, thought Lita when they headed out of town at six.

Sunny was giggling in the backseat, and Glow and Tima were hopping and yipping as only happy dogs can. Then Sunny started prattling about what new clothes she needed. It was too much.

They stopped at the bakery on the right side of the highway for breakfast, the one before the plaza. The other two wolfed down huevos rancheros while Lita made do with coffee and an empanada.

She felt like she was going to be sick. Her head was spinning so from that stupid pill that she had to concentrate on Sunny's delight in the wooden mural where the sun was coming up in front of the mountains.

Two hours later, they dropped off the dogs and were in time to be at Weems Gallery on Montgomery when it opened. A laughing Mary Ann Weems met them at the door. Lita thought she had never seen such a long-legged smile. Amy was one of the jewelry artists Mary Ann Weems carried.

While Mary Ann and Amy discussed pricing and display space, Lita and Sunny toured the gallery, sucking on complimentary Tootsie Roll Pops. Besides the jewelry, there was pottery, sculpture, carvings, weaving, and every wall was full of pictures. Sunny laughed at some she called "Funky Ones."

Lita thought some were strange and some looked like they belonged in an office, they were so modern. She did admire some oils by Kathy Glidden, and Sarah Blumenschein's pastels were breathtaking. Steve Hanks did wonderful things with watercolors. She decided she liked those three artists best.

She looked at every price tag. Oh, my! Another way to look at it was that maybe her paintings might be worth something after all.

From the gallery, they drove to the mall. Amy and Sunny needed to find clothes that would fit and leave a bit of room to grow, while Lita ran her errands. They agreed to meet in time to grab an early supper in the food court before they picked up the dogs and headed home.

Lita checked her list before heading out of the busy parking lot. Her first stop was a wig shop on San Mateo. She chose a short gray wig because it had already been styled. The clerk was helpful and showed her how to adjust the elastic and rearrange Lita's bun higher on her head so it would look natural. Lita decided to leave the wig on, and paid in cash. She checked herself in the rearview mirror. She rather liked what she saw. Maybe she should cut her hair?

Her next stop was a Goodwill thrift shop. There she selected a nondescript outfit and a large pair of sunglasses. Again, she paid cash for her purchases.

She drove east a few blocks till she spotted a Wendy's and she pulled in.

She'd have to buy something. Ordering a small Coke, she drank half of it before going to the ladies' room to change her clothes.

Leaving Wendy's, she continued east until she found a UPS store.

She waited while a man had documents faxed and a woman mailed birthday packages to her grandchildren in Scotland. Why couldn't children live close, like we did when we were young, wondered Lita.

When it was her turn, she was glad to have the counter to lean on. She wasn't sure her knees were going to hold her up.

"Overnight or regular?"

"How long will that take?"

The clerk looked at the address. "Five, six days."

She was wondering if overnight would be too conspicuous and what might happen to the package being out who knows where, when she heard the cost differential.

"It doesn't need to be there tomorrow!"

"Okay. Now listen to this spiel. I'm more thorough than the U.S. Post Office. Is there anything flammable, edible, of an explosive nature, likely to die or give live birth in this package?"

Lita laughed. "No, it's mostly paper, with a wee bit of plastic and some metal."

"Too bad it's not all paper, 'book rate,' you know."

"Everything but the plastic can be read and there are stickers on them." She smiled.

He winked back. "Book rate it is."

Lita counted out her money and declined a confirmation.

She drove back west on Menaul, glad to have on the sunglasses. She should buy a pair of her own. She pulled into a gas station, spent twenty dollars for gas, and used the restroom to change back into her own clothes, remove the wig, and fix her hair.

Goodness, that wig was hot!

She went on down Menaul to Menaul School. She parked by Donaldson Hall and went in. It still smelled the same, and there were the same class pictures on the wall, only more. The office was busy, but a harried secretary gave her a pencil and paper.

She left a note that the wig, clothes, and glasses were for the drama department from an alum. She didn't sign the note.

Lita felt light-headed as she drove back east.

It was done, and she had done it! She was starving!

She made it back to the mall early, found a pair of summer-weight pajamas for herself on sale, and then found a special on men's underwear. Benito could use those.

She splurged at a kiosk and purchased her very own sunglasses. How chic she felt!

She chose a Chinese plate at the food court and then, when Amy and Sunny came, had a DQ Blizzard while they ate.

When had she eaten so much?

Since it was afternoon traffic, Amy offered to drive.

Lita was glad. She was getting tired.

The dogs smelled much better, especially Tima, who had recently discovered the goats, since Sunny now took her dog everywhere on her bike. Everyone quieted down on the trip home after Sunny had finished showing off every item in her bags.

Lita was grateful Amy was driving as she kept dozing off. When they reached Los Santos, Amy drove to her own home where they unloaded Sunny, Tima, and all their purchases.

Lita took off her new glasses and was surprised to find it was still early evening and not yet dark. When she pulled into her own drive, she was amazed by how quiet it was. That would only last till the weekend. Benito would be home and things would change. The wind chime tinkled by the front door.

When the house was burgled, Lita lost the name of the appraiser Emilio had given her. The person whose name Mary Ann Weems had provided was on an extended vacation, so Lita called an appraiser out of the phone book.

She scheduled an appointment with a Charles Godwin. His ad had looked discreet.

A few days later, a tall, good-looking man stood at her door wondering what he would find in this Godforsaken backwater. Who was this Estrellita Cordova?

He was surprised when a well-dressed woman opened the blue door of the ramshackle, sprawling, two-story adobe. You could tell a great deal about clients by the way they dressed. She wore slim black boots, summer-weight gray wool slacks, and a soft violet sweater with a cowl collar. She was holding a small dog that emitted a low growl. He looked up to her face and his estimation of his day shot up. Great bone structure and smooth skin. At least the company would be easy on the eyes.

"Mrs. Cordova, I'm Charles Godwin. You were expecting me."

"Do come in. Let me put Glow up." In a moment, she was back. "I hope your trip won't be a waste of our time."

Better, he mused, a well-educated, softly modulated voice. Then he looked around the room and, as he would later remember, was blown away.

He couldn't believe his eyes. His fingers itched. "Shall we begin?" he asked as he whipped out a camera and measuring tape. He reached into the satchel again and withdrew a leather-bound notebook with his initials embossed in gold. Always make a good impression.

There was only one new painting of the village, probably worth, oh, maybe eight hundred tops, but the rest, if they were real. Thank you, Lord! There turned out to be one good-sized Oscar Berringhaus, an early E.I. Crouse, another small but still valuable charming portrait by Critcher, four small scenes by Walter Ufur in his recognizable style and palette. He even took pictures of the backs of the paintings, which Lita thought strange. He wrote down the provenance of each one, as Lita remembered their histories.

"Before we go up to the ranch, there is one more small painting in my granddaughter's room. It was a gift from her maternal grandfather in Italy. I think it's dreadful."

Going into the room after Lita, Charles almost gasped at what he thought must be an early Modigliani. He looked closer. The shading was right and the long neck perfect.

"Mrs. Cordova, I think this is a valuable painting. I hope you will bring it to Santa Fe so it can be studied to make sure it is authentic."

"Gracious! Who would have ever thought it? Of course I will. Now, shall we go? The Baughmans are expecting us up at the ranch. Hugh is the nicest man. I don't want to keep him waiting."

She led him out the front door and locked it.

"A year ago I would never have thought of locking up."

He opened the passenger door for her and helped her in as if she were the Queen of England. He whistled as he glided around to his side. On the short ride, they chatted about the lovely little village, its age, and history. She and her grandson were heirs to all of it? Goodness. What a responsibility!

The ranch house was really a small, mostly well-kept hacienda. Inside, except for a few things belonging to Mr. Baughman, everything was an accumulation of generations of hard-working but prosperous people. The newest thing was maybe a three-by-five Helen Hardin hanging over the sideboard in the dining room. And what a sideboard! It looked to be Spanish and very old. It was probably brought out by wagon.

Lita led him to what she called a storage room and began dragging dust covers from huge gilt-framed oils. There were saints and more saints. There were romantic harbors and sailing ships. He knew some of the artists had been dead for four hundred years.

He did his best to document everything. Wooden bowls, pots, candlesticks, a French cradle, Lord, this was a museum that no one knew of, and the owner had no idea of its value.

If he could only get a few of these things into Clara's gallery, he could retire next month. "Mrs. Cordova, let me take you to dinner. It's the least I can do after you have given me such a pleasurable day."

"Thank you, Mr. Godwin that would be delightful. I'll have to stop at home first to feed my dog."

"Not a problem, as they say in Missouri." He smiled, "And please, call me Charles."

***

Emilio was backing out of Chuy's store when he saw Lita pass by in an all-too-familiar BMW. What was that urbane charlatan doing with Lita? He pulled on the wheel, changing direction, and followed them into Taos. He watched the sleek maroon car park across from the Taos Inn.

He pounded on his steering wheel and pulled into a no-parking space till they had crossed the street and gone in. He then drove past, and parked behind the yarn shop.

Emilio sat for a while considering the implications of the situation, got out and slammed the door, and slowly made his way to the Inn. He was so hot under the collar that he was glad of the cool interior.

Making his way to the bar, he chose a seat where he could look into the dining room and watch the couple read their menus. A waiter came back with a bottle of wine, holding it out to present the label. With a nod from the man, the waiter uncorked the bottle and poured a taste. The man sniffed.

Emilio snorted.

The man rolled the wine around in his goblet and took another sniff. He took a small taste, cocked his head, considered, took another sip, smiled and nodded his approval. When both their goblets were filled, he raised his goblet and made a toast.

Lita smiled and lowered her head.

Emilio ordered a Dos Equis and watched as the seduction unfolded. He nursed his beer but had to call for another. After dinner, the two lingered over brandy, talking, and the cad's hand was slowly inching across the tablecloth toward Lita's when Emilio had enough.

Making a beeline across the dining room, he called out, "Hey, you two. I didn't know you knew each other! What a little bitty world, no? Lita, how are you? How's it going, Charley? Found any more art to put in your wife's gallery? Lita, have you met Clara? Lovely woman!"

Perhaps his voice had been a little loud. There was silence. Seems everyone had heard. Everyone was looking.

Lita was mortified. Was this a scene from My Fair Lady, or what?

Emilio tried not to be embarrassed for them both.

Lita took a deep breath. "Thank you for the dinner, Mr. Godwin, and for coming to look at my collection. Emilio will take me home."

"I couldn't let you..."

"No," she held up a hand. "It's quite out of your way. Emilio, I'm ready." She stood and dropped her napkin in her plate.

Charles Godwin watched his early retirement and possible dalliance make her graceful exit. "Damn!"

Emilio didn't say anything until he had Lita safely in the truck. He wanted to tell her how proud he was of the way she had handled Charles. He wanted to tell her how lovely she looked.

He said, "I'm sorry. It's just that bastard has such a reputation. One woman after another and shady business dealings. I couldn't let him hurt you."

"Oh, Emilio, I'm such a foolish woman." She blew her nose. It wasn't pretty. "Letting a little charm and flattery slick my skids like that." She sighed and turned her head away. He thought he heard, "It's been so long."

"What am I to do now?" she asked

"Simple. You'll call tomorrow, early. He's never in then, and you say you have decided to go with another appraiser. Have him bill you for his time and give you all the negatives. If he used a digital camera he can hand you the memory card. He did take pictures, didn't he?"

"Lots."

"See, it will be easy. No problemo!"

She smiled. "That's what Charley said."

They drove home in silence, each one thinking their own thoughts. When they pulled up to her house, there were flowers by her front door.

"That man surely works fast," said Emilio.

"They're from Kip," said Lita as she silently read the note. "All's well. I'll never ask. Will call next week."

"Such a sweet young man," she murmured as she tore the card into tiny pieces.

When the balls of life and chance are racked and the shark takes careful aim, but his cue is weighted with pride and his anger gives too much force to his strike, the shot sends balls in wild directions, changing the game with unexpected consequences.

So it was with Dominic DeMarco, a man with connections, who grieved for the fruit of his loins, Ronnie. How he missed him. He knew in his bones that his son had been taken out by the Gamboa family, who had smothered his son under a hill of beans. He heard the message loud and clear: "You only do business with the Gamboas. How dare you let Ronnie branch out! You belong to us!" They were saying in no uncertain terms that he was to stop dealing with New Mexico. The fungi were to be his only supplier!

He called his family together, and it took them two months to come up with a plan to avenge the wrong that had been done to them. A devious plan to avoid a war between the families, and one that would draw the Feds. They would need to implicate and manufacture enough evidence to make it obvious that it had all been overseen by the cartel in Juarez.

They'd also need to do something to make the papers in New Mexico before the big event. What did they call it? "A red herring," that was it.

Men met in quiet bars in Manhattan, on pleasure boats on Lake Meade, in San Diego and Miami and in restaurants on The Hill in St. Louis. It would begin soon, but first, they would take care of New Mexico.

iii

"Really, Owen," said Miriam Wills to her husband over the Cobb salad, "I think your imagination is getting away with you. Last month you worried because Lita was checking out all those books on drug pushers and cartels, and I said she was just on a kick, just like you were when you were reading all those books about the Bilderberg group, one right after the other."

Owen "harrumphed" and reached for the pitcher of iced tea.

"I mean it, Owen. Don't worry about her. If she's checking out books on passive solar and church architecture, let her. That church up there is going to have to be rebuilt sometime. You did make that donation, didn't you? Be happy for her, sweetie. Let her dream."

"Well, as poor as Los Santos is, it'll be a cold day in Tunis before they get around to it. She'll be dreaming a long time."

"So it will take a while. Do you want more salad? We have blackberry cobbler for dessert."

***

Lita had charged her phone every night in anticipation of a call from Kip. She had it in her duster pocket tonight.

Jovita and Virgie were over to watch a new mystery and gossip when the phone chimed.

"Hello, Mrs. No Name!"

Lita motioned for the other two to keep watching and went into the kitchen.

"How is everything?"

"You wouldn't believe it," Kip answered. "I set up accounts in five different banks and I've seen the Bishop here. He's agreed to let me set memorial boxes in most of the churches as long as each church can make the deposits. Isn't that beautiful? Now we can make bigger donations. Whoever checks money deposited by a church? I've had to break some of the fifties to pay secretaries to make several deposits during their lunch hours and to introduce small bills. The secretaries bring me all the deposit slips. It's going to take us a while as each deposit has to be under five thousand."

"I hadn't thought of that."

"That's the beauty of the church deal; we can get it deposited much faster! Now, about those yellow things. I recommend we wait for now."

"Your call."

"Are you where you can sit down," asked Kip. "Are you sitting?"

"Go on." Lita held her breath.

"I've been to see a specialist about the plastic things. You know the word I want to use?"

She nodded and then remembered to say "Yes."

"Sweetheart, it seems that they are worth at least two-thirds of all the other things! It will take some time. Do you want me to try to sell them or go with a firm who specializes? They could get more, but they'd charge a commission."

Lita's head was spinning. She took a deep breath. "Put them away for now," she whispered, not wanting Kip to be involved any more than he had to be.

"Done. You're sure you want the checks sent to the Catholic Charities, Archdiocese of Santa Fe?"

"Yes, that's safest. Be sure it's specified for Los Santos under Tina's name."

"Right. I'd say I'm sorry to be doing this, but it is fun! You should be getting news by the end of August for the first part, half the yellow, no plastic."

"You are a godsend. I don't know how to thank you."

"Simple. Invite me to the consecration. Good night, Fairy Godmother. Sweet dreams."

Virgie cocked her head and winked. "Ooh, Lita, you got a boyfriend we don't know about? Going off to whisper where we can't hear like that has us thinking you got something going on." She and Jovita giggled.

"It was Kip Stokes," grinned Lita. "You remember him?"

"Who could forget Tina's novio! He's one hot stud muffin! What did he have to say?" asked Virgie.

"He's busy collecting money for a memorial for Tina. He's going to send it to Catholic Charities in Santa Fe."

Jovita chimed in. "That's one smart hombre. His mama didn't hatch no idiot. Now nobody's gonna be able to get to it through a lawsuit."

The women watched the rest of the show, wondering aloud during commercials if there would be enough to do something worthwhile, and how long it would be before they'd have a real church.

"Not in my lifetime. That's for sure," announced Jovita.

Lita wanted to tell, wanted to shout out her news, but she just smiled and said "Quién sabe?"

As she walked them to the door, Jovita struck her forehead. "Eeee! I forget everything! I saw Louise Ramirez at Chuy's this morning and she say her son's mother-in-law saw Father Mondragon come out of that new heart doctor's office in Taos yesterday. You think he might got a problem?"

"He has been slowing down."

"Lita, just 'cause he don't go as fast as you don't mean nada. Anyway, everybody know, we need to take good care of him."

A Little South of Los Santos, A Few Days Later

Lenny Salazar was making his way in the cruiser to Chuy's to get a diet Coke when he noticed a flock of birds having a free-for-all over by the new guard rail. Curiosity got the best of him and he pulled his vehicle around facing the morning sun. He ran over, shooing the birds aside. All of them left except a large magpie who was trying to pull something up, something shiny. Lenny noticed there was an area of new, freshly turned earth and gravel from the road work. No, this was more recent. Something was buried there.

He quickly returned to the cruiser and called it in. Lenny hated this spot. Right where Tina had flipped her car.

They radioed back to sit tight and wait for some honcho to drive all the way from Albuquerque. Lenny had plenty of time, so he went on to Chuy's for his Coke.

When he got back, the birds were at it again. He didn't want any more evidence disturbed, so he took his fishing rod out of the trunk, tied on a handkerchief, and kept swiping at the birds, staying as far away from the crime scene as he could.

His drink was long gone, his arms were getting tired, and he had to pee by the time a car, with a van close behind, pulled up. A tall, lanky guy about Larry's age, with really red hair held out his hand. "Hi. Nate Courtney from APD. What have you found here?"

Lenny switched the rod to his left hand and continued twitching it toward the birds and clasped a firm, cool grip.

"Leonard Salazar. I was on patrol and noticed the birds. I was curious, so I stopped. Walked over to what looks like a real shallow grave. Those birds sure do want that chain."

"It's always the birds," said Nate cryptically. Turning to the team suiting up and putting on booties over their shoes, he raised his voice and called out, "Well, I'll let you fellas do your thing. I don't want to disturb anything. Officer Salazar and I are going to get something to drink. You want something? Seven-Up, Pepsi, whatever? We'll be right back."

When they got into the car, Lenny said, "Thanks! I really got to go!"

They made it to the old trading post/grocery/postal substation just in time. On the way back, they chatted about the area, the people, and the break-in at the station.

Lenny was going to tell about the break-in at Lita's, but when they got back, the team was already waving them over.

They walked over to the hole in the ground. Lenny stepped back and thought he was going to be sick again. Jeeze Louise, he really didn't like this place!

"Look familiar?" asked Courtney.

Lenny forced himself to look again. The face had been wrapped in plastic and was badly beaten. There was tape over the mouth and the cheeks were puffed like a chipmunk, but still... The gold chains gave it away.

"Yeah, he was the guy who was in charge of the road crew that put up the guard rail this spring. I'd see him having lunch at Tessie's in town."

"Hold that thought," said Courtney as he hit speed dial on his phone.

"Hello, Luis, this is Nate. We've just found Junior Baca. He's been tortured. The van will bring his body to the morgue. I'm going to have lunch here. I hear they serve a mean gossip."

Turning to Lenny, Nate said "Officer Salazar, congratulations. You just joined our biggest drug case. We've had Mr. Baca's parents' house bugged for some time now, and we know pretty boy here hasn't been home for four days. First, his wife thought he'd found another girlfriend, but then she got worried. Guess she won't have to worry anymore."

"Hey, Nate, his mouth's full of frijoles, uncooked!" called out one of the team as he picked up his end of the stretcher.

They loaded the body in the van, shook hands, and were off with no more than a "Keep in touch if anything else should happen."

Nobody in Los Santos was going to believe this! Lenny turned and heaved over the guard rail.

The story made the late night news.

After Mass, Father Mondragon didn't feel so good and popped a nitroglycerin pill under his tongue while slipping into his side of the confessional.

Enefero Calderone had lost the rent money at the casino again.

Jerry Apodaca's jock itch had turned out to be more serious. How was he gonna tell his girlfriend?

Mrs. Hernandez was feeling guilty for threatening to move out after her drunken husband had tossed her dishes with the little pink roses out the back door, yelling he hated little pink flowers.

Sadie Lujan was going to get more than hugs and kisses if she didn't stop her fling with Archie Aragon. She better stop acting like her big sister or she, too, would have two bebés and be on welfare.

He was so sleepy...had he missed that first part? He could hear Lita Cordova sobbing, saying it was all her fault.

"Take a deep breath and explain again what's your fault."

"Haven't you been listening? The dead man..."

"You mean the one they found yesterday?" Everyone was buzzing about it this morning. "The one they say was in the drug business?"

"Yes," sniff.

"Listen to me. Just because he was found at Christina's descanso doesn't mean you had anything to do with it. You don't deal in drugs, do you?"

"No Father, but..."

"Do you take drugs?"

"Aspirin, Tylenol and...oh, Father..." sniff.

"See, you have nothing to worry about."

"But, Father."

"Did you know him?"

"No."

"Had you ever seen him?"

"I don't think so."

"What do you know about him?"

"Well, Tessie said he was a big tipper."

Father Mondragon shook his head. "Go home, say three Hail Marys, and go see a doctor. You have a problem. I think you should see someone."

He heard the door open and close. Poor Lita, she was under too much stress with Tina dying, Benito going off to school, and the land grant. God help her if she's going crazy.

Los Santos, Late June

Early morning mists had evaporated when Lita and her friends met to clean the old fellowship hall now being used as the church.

The women knelt and crossed themselves. "I feel stupid genuflecting here," puffed Jovita. "This still don't feel like church."

It didn't take as long to clean as the church used to, as there were no nooks and crannies, just folding metal chairs and the old altar on the tile floor.

Lita used a damp rag on the chairs, while Virgie washed the plate glass windows and Jovita mopped the floor.

"I sure hope when we get the new church we have floors like these ones. They clean up real quick," sang out Jovita as she threw the mop water out the back door.

"We don't want none of these windows, though," said Virgie, standing back and looking at her handiwork. "It takes too long to get the streaks out. It's a good thing these windows are on the west. Nobody's gonna notice them till the afternoon."

"And I vote for no more metal folding chairs. They make too much noise and the floor's hard to get off of when we kneel," chimed in Lita.

They had a pleasant time deciding on all the things the new church would have, like restrooms and closets and a heating system. Soon they were back out in the fresh air under a turquoise sky. Somewhere to the west, thunderheads were leaving diagonal sheets of rain across the desert and mesas. Arroyos would be filling up, rushing their flood waters towards the Rio Grande. It was July second and the annual monsoon had arrived.

Later this afternoon, Lita would watch the heavy cumulous clouds come in like ancient galleons in full sail, scudding along on warm thermals, their bottoms planed flat. Massive tops would be cream and white, tinged with pinks on their western edges. They would pile up against the mountains and the air would darken, then sizzle when the lightning started.

Lita had always loved those clouds. As a kid, she imagined using a butter paddle, scooping up bowls full of the thick fluff. It would taste of adventure and exotic spices and melt on her tongue like watermelon or homemade peach ice cream.

Since Tessie had closed the café to go to "that man's" funeral, they couldn't go for coffee, so they went to Jovita's and sat under the apricot trees and drank sun tea. Tessie wouldn't be back till late afternoon, so there wasn't anything new to gossip about. That left the goats. Lita decided her time would be better spent packing things for Benito.

She left early and walked home past the little fireworks stand which was trying to do business. She bet the Fourth of July celebrations would be canceled again this year and families would eat their chili dogs and drink their beers inside while the rain beat against tin roofs.

Sure enough, the fireworks display was canceled and the monsoon in Los Santos lasted into late August.

Except for the nightly news on the radio and television, the village was cocooned against the harsh realities of the world. The goings-on of drug dealers didn't make the news. Forest fires were much more important and much more dangerous. But Lita had decided not to confess any more to Father Mondragon. It didn't do any good. He didn't believe her.

Thursday was a big day.

Lita and Benito drove to Taos and bought a new truck for him to drive to college. They used some of Tina's life insurance money.

It was a small truck, bright red with a gray interior. Ben was on cloud eleven. It had a CD player.

When they were taking it for a second test drive, Lita told him she would make payments for the first semester as long as he made good grades, but if he got speeding tickets or a DWI, he was on his own. Also, if he ever got involved in drugs, he could kiss the ranch goodbye. She would sell it so fast his head would spin clean off.

It was a sober Ben Cordova who signed the papers for his truck.

Afterwards, they went to the Apple store and Lita bought herself an iPad. It was less than a computer, but it would do to keep in touch with her grandson.

***

Events were happening out there beyond the valley. Dominic DeMarco had seen to it.

Somehow, labels on a big shipment had been switched and the Saltillo tiles turned out to be just that, while the tequila delivered to Snooky's Liquors in Atlantic City turned out to be marijuana, kilos of it. Another time, guns were drawn and shots almost fired when the man from Jalisco delivered twice the shipment of cocaine that had been ordered and Gamboa's man had only half the payment. Luckily, only ugly threats were made.

After an anonymous tip and some cash left under a front door mat, a drug-sniffing Belgian Malinois in Miami led her handlers to a Gamboa underling and an illegal alien making a swap. One of the officers happened to mention something about Guatemala City. Both men were arrested.

Dominic DeMarco was pleased. He was pleased, and he was patient. He could wait to see if any more tweaking needed to be done.

***

During daily Masses the last week of August, Father Mondragon announced that the archbishop was coming on Sunday to make an announcement to the congregation. He was smiling. He hadn't done that in a long time. He was really feeling good. So good that he put his pills back in the drawer.

Lita was rather embarrassed by Sunday's Mass.

The Archbishop had said how generous the Catholic churches and the people of New York were, and that Los Santos should feel blessed by their generosity.

If he only knew!

She had cried along with most everyone. But Jesus, Mary, and Joseph, you'd have thought they were Pentecostals, not Catholics! All the whooping and hollering and dancing—well, it wasn't like any Mass she had ever attended.

Now she and Emilio had been asked to co-chair the building committee. Tessie was asked to serve by overseeing the kitchen plans, and Jovita would supervise the landscaping. Epie Vallejos, Jorge Sisneros, and Virgie were also asked to be on the committee.

Next week they would go to Albuquerque to look at churches and get some ideas before they met with the architects in Santa Fe that the church muckity-mucks wanted them to use.

This would be about the first building in the village that had been designed by a professional.

Kip really had been clever in his cover letter to the Archbishop, which he sent before the monies were wired to Santa Fe. He had stipulated that all the money was to be used to build a new church plant, for its upkeep, and anything else the parish in Los Santos needed to build to enhance the community and/or the welfare of the congregation. A copy of the letter had been sent to Father Mondragon.

Lita had just thought her part was done. God must not want her to have an idle moment.

Now here she was helping Benito get off. Emilio had stopped by after breakfast with a St. Christopher medal for the truck and stayed to help carry out bags and boxes.

He stayed, too, through a list of do's and don'ts, as well as a tearful "I will miss you, mí hijo."

Emilio moved in and shook the young man's hand, saying, "Ben, you are going to have a stupendous semester."

He steered Ben toward the truck. "Make the valley proud. Think of us and wish us well as we will be thinking of you. Now, you better vamoose before your abuela here starts crying again." He leaned into the open window and whispered loud enough for Lita to hear. "Remember, the state patrol just loves little red trucks."

Her boy winked at her and blew a kiss. "I'll call when I get there."

While the truck was still in sight, Emilio turned to her and said, "Now, how about a cup of leftover coffee and a story or two? I don't want you moping all day. Tell me about Glow."

⁂

Luis and his wife had finished breakfast. He was reading about the Lobos' proposed lineup for the opening game next week against Texas Tech when his wife said, "She must have been somebody special. I mean, just think, all that money given as a memorial."

"Hmm," replied Luis somewhere between the choices for tailbacks and tight ends.

"I hope they build a nice church," she murmured.

"Right," he replied, as if he knew exactly what she'd said. He'd better get to work. Mano had come home from the hospital yesterday. The police had to be alert to every move, to every clue. Something might happen.

Monterrey, Mexico, August

The Gamboa family sent their deal-maker, Carlo Fierro, to Monterrey, Mexico, to work with the Gulf Coast Cartel and mend fences. He was handsome, yet low-keyed. He possessed such a honeyed voice that men who'd done business with him swore that if he worked for Victoria's Secret and targeted pro athletes, every player would be wearing a push-up bra under their pads and jerseys.

Alberico Gamboa trusted Carlo's smooth negotiation skills. The business relationship with the cartel would improve.

Carlo was picked up by a gray limo at the Monterrey airport and taken to the Sheraton Ambassador Hotel. He was impressed when he walked into suite 862. It was decorated in soft creams and blues. The ceiling fan was on and the rooms were cool. After unpacking and a quick shower, he enjoyed a lobster dinner in the Vitrales Restaurant under the potted palms. The cream sauce was superb. He had a nightcap in the club lounge. There were calls to be made, so he called it an early night.

On the way back to his room, he stopped by a kiosk and picked up some brochures about the cathedral and the Museo Metropolitano. He'd make time to see them after his morning meeting.

After a surprisingly restless night, Carlo took a cold shower and shaved. As he slipped into his Italian linen jacket, his stomach rumbled. It must have been the lobster.

He looked into the mirror and was satisfied with the well-groomed man with warm brown eyes smiled back. He wished he felt as good on the inside.

The same limo took him to the meeting.

Once they were out of the city, the large car sped around one curve after another and at last came to the compound. The guard at the gate waved them through.

Instead of pulling up to the front door, the driver took him around to a side gate. That's putting me in my place, he thought.

Two armed men ushered him around to the pool area. There were long-legged beauties lounging in the sun, but Carlo had eyes only for the man sitting at a table under an umbrella, Felipe Cardenas.

He was eating a late breakfast. Without saying a word, he motioned for Carlo to take a seat. Felipe Cardenas kept his head down while he ate. The guards arranged themselves behind Carlo, and one of the pool girls sauntered over to a table laden with food, filled a plate, and brought it to Carlo. He nodded his thanks and looked down into his plate. His stomach lurched. Barely cooked eggs stared back at him. There were sides of beans covered with cilantro and chiles. A blob of something that looked like baby poop and smelled strongly of fish swam before his eyes. He smiled and lifted his fork, praying his stomach would stay put.

He belched. "Excuse me," he swallowed, covering his mouth.

The umbrella was tilted so that Cardenas was in the shade and Carlo was under the hot morning sun, which reflected off the water in the pool right into his face. The glare hurt his eyes. He could feel the sweat start to trickle under his shirt.

Carlo began his pitch, using his most honeyed tones and charming smiles. His presentation was punctuated with more belches, for which he excused himself, and farts he chose to ignore.

Cardenas kept eating. Carlo "The Deal Maker" Fierro was going nowhere fast.

Cardenas mumbled and ate while Carlo talked. He grunted a few times and poured himself more coffee. When Carlo came to a painful pause, "the man" took off his mirrored wraparounds and looked at his guest with cold, dead eyes. After a long, probing study, he held up his hand for silence.

He stood and made his longest speech. "I'm glad you came, Señor Fierro. It's good to know who longs to do business with us, no?"

He left Carlo to the guards, who ushered him out. When he passed by a piece of shapely pool dressing, Cardenas bent over her and said, "See that an appropriate gift is sent to the chef at the Vitrales."

Carlo had the limo driver stop along the side of the road so he could vomit his breakfast, his dinner, last week's lunch, and everything in between. He was shaking when he hurried across the cool lobby to the men's room.

Later, he went up to room 862 and showered. With a towel wrapped around his waist, he reached for his cell phone.

First, he called New York and left a message that he was going sightseeing and taking a flight to Guatemala to see the Mayan ruins before returning.

Next, he made a reservation for a flight the next morning to Puerto Barrios, Guatemala. He then checked his wallet for the number and punched the buttons for a Los Zetas contact. He would be met at the lounge in the airport.

While he dressed to stroll to the museum and cathedral, a woman in suite 864 punched the rewind button on a small tape recorder. She carefully removed her headset so as not to damage her hair. She stretched and took a long drag on her cigarette before calling in.

"He's going out for a walk now, and has reservations for a flight to Guatemala in the morning. Oh, tell Cardenas he has a meeting set up with Los Zetas." She smiled. Anyone who crossed Cardenas and did business with Los Zetas ever since 2010 was a dead man. The L.Z. had been the strong arm of the Gulf Coast Cartel, and before that, they had been members of the elite Mexican military special forces.

Carlo didn't get off the plane in Puerto Barrio. He missed the museum. He was on a late flight back to New York.

Mr. and Mrs. Alberico Gamboa had given a dinner party for some of the family in their penthouse. At the conclusion of the evening, Alberico walked some of their departing guests to his private elevator. He pressed the button and finished telling a joke.

The door opened. No one laughed. Someone screamed.

There was Carlo sitting in one of the lobby's wingback chairs. His head was in his lap and there was a banner across his chest which read, "Compliments of the Guatemalan Department of Tourism."

That story did make the nightly news. "Private Elevator Crime Scene... More at eleven."

Lita missed it. She was packing for Albuquerque.

Mrs. Pacheco agreed to loan the church building committee her old VW bus so long as they brought it home with a full tank of gas.

They left early and arrived in Old Town in time for an early lunch at La Placita.

The hostess lent them a phone book. As Virgie read out addresses, Emilio and Jorge marked them off on a city map. They discussed their route and decided that if any other churches looked interesting besides the Catholic ones, they would stop for a quick peek.

Lita gave everyone a notebook to help them remember things they liked and didn't.

They would start with churches in the South and North Valleys today, and do the churches in the Heights tomorrow. All of them had cameras to take pictures of things that really impressed them. They started across the plaza at San Felipe de Neri and then went south at a fast clip.

That night, an exhausted group sat around a table at El Pinto in the far North Valley. After supper, they settled back and rehashed the day.

They decided that Albuquerque must really have too much crime, so many of the churches seemed to have a problem with vandalism, and that a good Catholic businessman must have the corner on the terrazzo flooring market.

"Brr," said Virgie, shivering, "I felt like I was on a tomb tour!"

They teased Emilio for taking so many pictures at Santuario de San Martin of the hand-carved biblical story displayed in glass cases.

There were two churches they thought would look at home in Los Santos. One, in Corrales, had been turned into a theater and the other, Cristo del Valle, was Presbyterian. There they were impressed with the Trombe wall. They had learned that the wall would warm the sanctuary in under an hour. There was a fireplace with blowers to help with the heating.

Jovita liked the skylights.

Epie had taken pictures of their adobe wall.

They went on to discuss the next church.

They were all impressed with the baptismal font, a waterfall with running water at Our Lady of the Most Holy Rosary. Jovita was thrilled to see all the plants growing inside!

Epie and Jorge mapped out the next day's excursion, and everyone had more coffee.

Emilio made a call back to Los Santos and handed the phone to Lita.

She raised her brows and spoke quizzically into the phone, "Hello?"

"Oh, Lita. We're having so much fun!" squealed Sunny. "Thank you for letting Glow stay with us! She and Tima are having a blast! Wanna talk to Mom?"

Lita laughed. "No, sweetheart, you're enough, but give your mom a hug for being such a good sport. Thanks for taking such good care of Glow. Goodnight."

She handed the little phone back to Emilio. "Thank you," she smiled.

Ben would never have thought of calling about a dog.

"I didn't want you to worry. We need to be thinking about buildings," he said, winking.

After dinner, they drove back to the Days Inn where Father Mondragon had made their reservations.

While Jovita showered and Virgie went out for a smoke, Lita emailed Benito about the day and then made a list of what the committee had liked about each church.

They started early the next morning. The men were talking about the forest fires in Arizona which they'd seen on the morning news.

The churches that day were very different.

Lita liked a three-dimensional baptismal banner in pinks and grays at a Lutheran church that looked like a ship, and a harvest table in the narthex of a big Methodist church.

Emilio took lots of pictures of the carved wood at St. Charles Borromeo.

At lunch, Virgie griped that the kitchens she was seeing were mostly dark holes that Tessie wouldn't like, and that the rest of them were having more fun.

Epie said the Hoffmantown Church looked like a civic center, so they drove on by.

Jovita liked the landscaping at Faith Lutheran.

They all liked the chunky stained glass at Holy Ghost and their stations of the cross. They also liked the stations at Risen Savior.

Late afternoon winds were whipping around the dome at John XXIII. Emilio was excited about their cross and had everyone come and look at a triumphant Jesus leaping to heaven. He kept taking pictures, saying, "Every church should have one of these!"

Lita finally pulled him away to show him the skylight over the altar in the chapel. Everyone came along. Jorge and Jovita thought something like it would work well at home. They all took pictures.

It was almost five when they found Prince of Peace, which was larger than it looked from the outside. What they liked best there were the bancos in the narthex with the bright cushions. It made them feel welcome.

It was time to go back to the Days Inn and pick up their bags in the lobby.

As they were heading west on Paseo del Norte into a gorgeous sunset, Emilio said, "Look at those people carrying stuff into that church. I bet they'd let us in."

Jorge turned into a side road toward Sandia Presbyterian and Epie snorted. "How stupid, naming a church after a mountain!"

The youth group was setting up for a party. A man who called himself a night host welcomed them and took them on a tour.

The first thing they saw was the sunset coming through windows in a large gathering space. Going into the sanctuary, they were surprised to see the mountain glowing pink all along the east wall.

Jovita was drawn to the window to look longingly at a fountain within a walled garden.

"We have to have one of these," she commanded. "Look, that wall would protect almost everything."

They were amazed at the gym and its stage in the Family Life Center. Virgie couldn't help herself and to Lita's embarrassment, she went up and did a soft shoe number. They all clapped.

There were two kitchens and a coffee bar! In the children's area, there were murals on the walls and a computer room and a theater!

When it was time to go, they had to go looking for Jovita. She was sitting near the windows studying the fountain and its garden.

"Come sit," she ordered. "These are comfortable chairs. I wonder if they come with kneelers?"

After sitting in silence for a few moments, Epie said, "Let's eat in Santa Fe. I want a big enchilada and a whole basket of sopaipillas. I'm glad Jorge is driving, cuz I'm gonna have me a cold cerveza."

Since money was not a problem, the architects came up with a plan that met with everyone's approval.

Instead of a cruciform sanctuary, Emilio called theirs an angel apse.

It would be wider at the back, like a snow angel, with a fireplace on each side of the doors. Tall, narrow stained-glass windows were planned for each side of the nave.

Instead of horizontal transepts, theirs would be more like raised arms. The one to the left would have a place for the confessional and storage you wouldn't see from the nave. There would be plenty of room for musicians. The right transept would be a Lady's chapel with long windows on the right, looking out onto a garden, complete with a fountain, per Jovita. At the back of the chapel, acting as a low divider, would be the votive stand.

Lita was pleased that the choir would have a clerestory window on the nave side, which would fill the altar area with light.

To the left of the altar would be a small baptismal fountain, with flowing water, like Our Lady of the Most Holy Rosary in Albuquerque.

The ceiling would be of latillas and carved wood covering steel I-beams. There would be handsome carved corbels.

Lita and the rest of the committee were hoping to be able to find tin candelabras that matched the ones in the old church. Jorge offered to go to Juarez to find a tinsmith; if anyone could find a picture of the old ones, he'd take it as a pattern.

They had chosen to have a wide narthex with bancos and nichos for their old Santos on the inner wall and bancos and windows on the outer wall.

To the right of the narthex would be a wide hall, glassed on the side that swept around the garden and seen from the Lady's chapel, which would lead to classrooms, a kitchen, and restrooms with three stalls each! To the north of the classrooms would be a small gym with a little raised stage. Offices would be to the left of the narthex.

They had so much money left after the estimates were in, they went ahead with plans for six casitas and a doctor's office to be built to the north and west of the church itself.

As a surprise to the Valley, they bought a carillon bell system to ring out hymns and sound the hour.

The coins were still safe with Kip, so Lita felt secure in spending up to the limit they had. At night, though, she tossed in her sleep, worrying that the coins wouldn't sell, or worse, they'd be found to be stolen.

Everything might still fall apart!

The roof was to be copper, the walls rammed earth.

The women suggested Epie was too short-handed to make that many adobes, and besides, the rammed earth would go much faster. When Epie realized how big the project had become, he was secretly glad to be building only a wall.

The floors were to be of octagonal Saltillo tile set over a hybrid coil heating system.

Outside, Jovita had made sure there were water catchments in several places and French drains leading to them in the outer courtyard that would be paved with flagstone. There would be still another fountain with a bench around it in the entry court.

Jovita was already working with a landscape architect in Santa Fe and bringing plants home to harden over the winter.

Owen Wills was kept busy with all Jovita's interlibrary loans, and joined in the fun by bringing her books she would never have thought of asking for.

Emilio was busy making the altar for the Lady's chapel. He went to Albuquerque to visit with a fellow woodworker, Ernest Thompson, who was making the doors and altar furnishings. He'd promised to come by tonight for her approval of the plans. She wondered how late he would be. Should she cook him supper, or would just a dessert do?

While the building committee had been in Albuquerque, a bulldozer arrived and made quick work of taking down what was left of the old church. A grader came right behind and leveled the site.

On Sunday after Mass, everyone trooped across the plaza for a groundbreaking ceremony. Father Mondragon blessed the ground again, and all took turns using one of Epie's shovels to turn some earth. They were going to have a fine church.

For the next few weeks, the committee worked overtime making changes to the plan. Engineers came and put in stakes to mark the wide foundations for the thick walls.

Two days later, Lita and Emilio watched them pour the cement around the rebar.

"Now I know what they're doing, I'll go home and get some work done," said Lita. "It's not like I could tell if they were making a mistake."

Emilio agreed, saying, "Just wait till they get to the part that shows. It won't be long. The architects want the walls up and a roof on before it snows."

"They best hurry, then."

***

The Church in Los Santos wasn't the only organization engaged in tearing down and rebuilding.

The Gulf Coast Cartel was now locked out of New Jersey and places served by the Gamboa family. Upstart cartels were scrambling to make inroads into the area.

To stop their rivals, the Gulf Coast Cartel, instead of fighting on their home turf, decided it would be easier to have the Americanos do their dirty work. Enough blood had been spilled in Mexico.

They tipped off the DEA and Coast Guard, and drops being made by other cartels were stopped. Small, fast boats were boarded in US waters off Newport News, Miami, and Bay Head, New Jersey. Air drops into the Everglades and West Beach on Galveston Island were intercepted.

The Border Patrol and FBI were notified of shipments made from Tijuana. When enforcement agencies closed tunnels and apprehended teenage mules crossing the border for the opposition, it opened new business opportunities. From Tacoma, Washington, to Coeur d'Alene, Idaho, from Evanston, Illinois, to Enid, Oklahoma, old supply sources were drying up.

The Sinaloa and Tijuana cartels joined in to take their revenge.

After a few more bloodbaths in the streets of Mexico, tipoffs began arriving at the DEA offices on the East Coast. Customs personnel received explicit messages as to locations and times of drug transactions. Soon, the supply of drugs in the cities east of the Mississippi was as short as that in the West.

Prices rose on the street. Dealers everywhere hustled to find new suppliers and began turning on one another.

In Los Santos, Lita watched the news and shook her head. "What is the world coming to?"

She never dreamed she had anything to do with it.

iii

Mitch Sweeney was crowing at one of their meetings about a bust made at Jackson Hole. "Eighty kilos of marijuana and..."

Luis paid no attention to the amounts of meth and coke, while Mitch went on about how great the Bureau was, hardly mentioning the call that morning about the drugs coming in from Canada.

"What's up with you guys on the drug end? Anything new on the Bacas?" Mitch asked, as if APD were morons.

"That's a dead end at the moment," replied Luis. "Nate's on vacation and Mano is still recovering. I suppose they're still in mourning for Junior. Our best bet is backtracking. Hopefully, something will surface if we stir the pot again."

"Is that a pun?" Mitch purred in his condescending manner.

"No, just the facts," grimaced Luis as he jotted down a note to check with Nate and review all the Baca files yet again.

"What kept you from doing that yesterday?"

"Damn it, Mitch! We're covering a slew of unsolved robberies in the Northeast Heights, and if you paid attention to the local news, there was a double homicide on Solano last night!"

"Hey, no need to snap, sport."

"Cut the 'sport,' okay?"

Mitch raised his hands and pushed back from the table.

"Just touch base when you've had a chance to talk to Nate."

When the door closed behind Mitch, Frank, who had been quiet during the meeting, whistled and said, "I'm proud of you, boss."

The pneumatic rammers had been pounding all week, tamping down the earth between forms rising at the building site. Many people were complaining about headaches. It was a blessing when the workers stopped for lunch.

Amy timed her visit with Father Mondragon during this lull so she wouldn't have to shout. She hoped he could still hear after the noise of the morning.

They met at Tessie's.

"Father Mondragon, I have an idea that I hope you will approve of, and I want your support. I want to make a gift for the church of a new communion set, a chalice, and a paten. The problem is I don't have enough silver. Would it be possible to take up a collection of broken jewelry or whatever families might want to contribute? That way, they would all feel they were a part of the finished set."

"What a fine idea. It would be even better if you and your little girl were Catholics, but I'll make an announcement, and people can bring things to the church or call you to come get them."

"Thank you, Father. When I see how much I have to work with, I'll make some drawings and bring them to you for your approval. I'd like to know what you'd recommend for their design. Please tell me if there are any must-haves."

The rammers started up again. Plates and mugs rattled on the tabletops.

"Bueno!" shouted Father Mondragon over the noise as he covered his ears.

***

For the next few weeks, the silver trickled in. A broken spur belonging to a great-someone, conchos, bent spoons, bracelets and a belt buckle won by Epie's padre at a rodeo in Gallup. Amy was thinking that she might have to ask Emilio to produce a wooden plate and goblet that she could layer with a very thin coat of silver, when there was a knock at her door.

"Come in. Come in," she said to a worried-looking Jovita. The big woman stalked in, looked at the little pile of silver objects on the table, and blew out a deep breath. "That all you got for your project? Don't look like much to me."

"No, it does seem I'll have to modify my plans."

"You good at keeping secrets?"

"Guess I haven't told one since high school."

"And I guess that'll have to do." Jovita looked long and hard at Amy. "Come see me tomorrow morning, by yourself. Send Sunny to Emilio's or over to see Glow. I don't want no one else to know nada." With that, she stalked out the door, leaving the jeweler perplexed.

Jovita answered her door the next morning at Amy's first knock. She pulled the young woman in, and looked both up and down the road before shutting the door.

"Let's us have coffee first," whispered Jovita. They sat in the small kitchen amidst a riot of colorful plants and flowers, sipping in silence. Amy was counting up the various kinds of coffee cans Jovita was using to grow geraniums when the big woman put down her mug and ordered Amy to raise her right hand. "You promise me that anything and everything, the whole enchilada, of what I'm gonna tell you and what you gonna see won't ever be told or hinted at in any way, nowhere, no how?"

"I promise," whispered Amy, wondering what on earth she was going to be made privy to.

Jovita sighed and threw her braid over her shoulder. "Your project is an answer to years of praying. I got some things nobody should ever know about." She held up a rough hand and continued. "I know you been here long enough to hear what a sorry son of a skunkweed my ex was. What nobody knows is that he was different."

"I don't understand."

"You will. Follow me."

She led Amy down the back hall into a room stuffed with castoffs, chairs piled on chairs, lamps, and empty flowerpots. Bags of potting soil were stacked in front of a cracked mirror. Amy looked at all the cobwebs and felt like Pip in Great Expectations. Not that Jovita was anything like Mrs. Haversham, she thought as Jovita made her way to a trunk in the corner. Opening the dusty lid, she pulled out two large sacks.

They were still whispering. "I couldn't have done this if he were still alive." She reached into one of the sacks and pulled out a bundle wrapped in an old sheet.

"You open it. I can't touch it."

Amy slowly unwrapped a heavy tarnished menorah. It was almost black. "Go on. There's a cup that matches, and other candlesticks, all silver, and a funny horn with silly writing on it. There's silver on it, too."

Amy reverently unwrapped the ancient Kiddush cup and an equally ornate Seder plate. She carefully rewrapped them before undoing the old bath towel around the shofar. It was about twenty inches long, the silver black with the tarnish of age. While Amy was putting it back in its sack, Jovita unceremoniously plopped down the other bag.

"This here one has one of them roll-up books, but it has silver handles. And there's one of them little things that go on the door. My ex said he only wished I could put it up, but nobody had for years. Gracias Dios! I think my ex called it a mizzyu."

"It's a lovely mezuzah," mumbled Amy as she reached in and pulled out a pillowcase full of soft objects.

"Oh, never mind those. They're just old shawls and caps and cloth stuff. Can you believe my ex wanted me to put one on over my head on Friday nights and wave my hands and say some mumbo-jumbo? That was our first fight. Now, you can just burn them up and melt down this other stuff."

"Jovita! Do you know how valuable all these things are? They belong in a museum!"

"Chica, I can't give it to no museum! They'd want to know all about its history. I can't have no one knowin' how close I've been to this heathen stuff. They'd know I was married to a Marrano and they'd suppose I'm one, too!"

"How about me taking them to the History Museum in Santa Fe, saying they were left on my doorstep with a note saying that they are given to me to sell or melt down to make the church's communion set? Maybe they would buy them, or trade them for the silver we need. Would you let me do that?"

"Oowee, chica. You ask such a big thing."

"Tell you what, Jovita. You think on it, and if you decide I'm right and trustworthy, you can come and leave it by my door in the morning with that anonymous note. That way, I can honestly say I didn't see anyone bring it to my house and I won't be lying."

"You sure?"

"Cross my heart and hope to die."

"Know I'll haunt you if anybody finds out, 'cause I'll be dead of shame and I won't be no buena fantasma!"

"I love you, Jovita, and no one will know. I promise."

"Oh, I forgot. I got a little pointy thing. I hate to give it up. It's been just right to plant seeds with. Come take a look and see if you still want it." Jovita waddled out to her greenhouse with Amy right behind. She waited while the older woman pawed through what looked like junk with some string thrown in as Amy waited.

"Here it is. For a minute, I thought I might 'a left it out in the garden." She held up a grubby-looking object. "Let's clean it up and see what you have. I know it matches those handles."

They hurried back into the house and washed it off at the kitchen sink. Sure enough, the handle was silver attached to a thin arm ending with a delicately carved hand, pointing a finger. Amy thought the yod was ivory, but it was stained from so many years in the dirt, she couldn't be sure. She prayed the museum would be able to bleach it.

"Be sure to wrap it carefully. We don't want to break it now. I better go. I'll need to borrow Lita's car to take these to the museum. I'll tell her I need to go see about some silver. That will be true."

At the door, Amy kissed Jovita's leathery cheek. "Thank you for trusting me to make both our prayers happen."

The History Museum was amazed at the collection and said it was a wonderful find. The heavy silver was found to date from the fifteenth century, the shofar a bit later. The rest still had to be dated. Amy was invited to the director's office the following Friday. She could tell the director wanted the collection, but she didn't know how much. There was only one way to find out. She laid her cards on the table. "Sir, I'd love to be able to give you the entire lot, but it was given to me in order to have enough silver to complete my commission for the Eucharist set for the new church in Los Santos. I'll be happy to give you the cloth items, with their superb needlework. I'm sorry, but I cannot let the rest go without recompense." She swallowed. "If you can't buy them, I'll have to melt them down."

"Let me get back to you, Mrs. Jenkins," said the director.

Amy went home to wait. The next afternoon, the director called. The museum found a patron who was happy to make a donation of ten pounds of scrap silver in exchange for the entire collection of "rare crypto judeaca" as it would be described in a later publication.

Everyone was happy.

Amy could keep secrets.

She never told the museum where their bounty came from, and she never told Jovita that upon the death of the anonymous source, the history of the collection would be revealed to the History Museum of Santa Fe.

The drugs came in the bellies of two large shaggy dogs driven by a couple and their three little kids in a beat-up Volvo.

Tres met them at an Econo Lodge on West Central. He put the dogs in his dad's old pickup (thank goodness he didn't have to use his car anymore) and headed for the mortuary. He was enraged to see the changes taking place. There were men everywhere. He whipped out his cell phone and speed dialed home.

Mona's phone chimed as she was dressing. "Hello."

"Where's my loco tió?" screamed Tres.

"What are you talking about?"

"Your friggin' hermano!" he shouted.

"You watch your language!"

"Uncle Lorenzo! Mama, where is he?"

"What do you mean?"

"I mean he's not here! Inside there are painters and carpet layers and they're changing the sign out front!"

"Stay where you are. I'll call him at home. We'll get this straightened out."

"No way, Mama. I got two hairy dogs in Dad's truck. I'm coming home till you find him!"

"I don't want those smelly creatures in my house!" she hissed as she pulled up her pantyhose.

"Tough shit, Mama. You better hurry, 'cause we're on our way."

Mona dialed Lorenzo's home number and shut off the call when a recording said, "The number you have dialed is no longer in service. Please check..."

She hit speed dial for his cell phone. There was no answer.

She had to go looking to find Mr. Skettering's office number, and upon reaching the office, was put on hold. Her temperature rose. The jerk picked up after a Barry Manilow number and Neil Diamond's *"Song Sung Blue."*

"Hello, Mona. I'm glad you called. I wasn't sure whom to contact. We received a letter from your brother this morning saying he's sold his business. I called the bank and they said all transfers of money have taken place and they'll mail copies of the checks to me for Mano's records."

"Where is he?" yowled Mona.

"You don't know? He didn't leave a forwarding address in the letter he gave me. I thought you all would know all about it. I can tell you after Mano was paid off and with closing costs, Lorenzo didn't walk away with much."

"Too damn much, if you ask me!" she spat, and hung up on him.

When Tres got home, they put the dogs in the garage and left to go see Mano. He'd have to agree to new arrangements.

Mano told Tres in a whispery, weak voice that it was up to him get the heroin ready for shipment.

***

Tres ended up taking the dogs out to the West Mesa. He slit their throats and took the drugs from their warm body cavities. He figured it was only about eight pounds of heroin.

Mano had called two guys he knew, Manny Archuleta and his sidekick, Raul Apodaca, to deliver it to the DeMarcos in Newark. They picked up the heroin from Tres behind the Goodwill Store on Juan Tabo and headed out of town.

On their way to the East Coast, they were stopped for speeding. That led to their arrest on a number of charges, including possession of illegal substances, and carrying said substances across state lines. After looking further into the men's pasts, charges for murder and stealing a dump truck in New Jersey were added. When the Cops got a match on Mr. Archuleta's prints, they added charges from New Mexico, including assault and battery on a hospital employee while impersonating medical personnel.

***

When Nick got back from vacation, he and Luis spent one long, tedious afternoon in Luis' cluttered office going over everything old: old tapes, old newspapers, old film, old pictures, and old notes. Everything they had on the Bacas.

"If you ask me, I'd say this is getting old and cold," said Nick as he put one more item in the Los Santos pile.

"All but Los Santos...so many things were happening there: two break-ins, Christina Cordova's accident, Junior's body, and all that money from the churches in New York. Have we found out yet exactly how much that was?"

"Not yet. Nate, do you think you could go back up there and pump...what's his name? Officer Leonard—Lenny Salazar. That's it."

"Don't see why not."

"Come for supper tomorrow night when you get back and we can work on this some more. I'll get Frank working on the money from Catholic Charities. Just go and talk to as many people in Los Santos as you can."

***

"I'm thinking of going to Las Cruces for Christmas," said Lita to Emilio. It came out louder than she had intended. She had raised her voice to compete with the hum of the fans and both Heat-o-Later fireplaces going full blast below them. The heaters were curing the concrete that had been poured over the coils that had been visible until yesterday. Lita and Emilio were standing in the choir loft at the back of the sanctuary, one of the changes that had been made to the original plan. The fireplaces were located in the back wall of the big room. There was a banco across the back of the sanctuary and a fireplace in each corner.

"That will be good for you, not to be here. What's that going to do to Sweetie?"

"She'll die of a broken heart, I suppose. I'll ask Hugh, and maybe they can get away for a few days and join us, maybe in El Paso."

"Bueno. We can plan a big celebration for next year and I'll see that you're put in charge. Services won't be much across the street anyway. No matter how hard we try, Father M. and I can't make it feel like a church when you smell the coffee perking in the back of the room, and when everyone is looking out the windows to see who's not at Mass and wondering what they're doing when they drive by."

She laughed. It was true. Just last week, little Onofre Infante had called out, "Mira, Papa! There goes mi tío!"

Emilio grinned. "And everyone looked to see him driving by with Gloria Piño. See what I mean?"

"We can put a tall Christmas tree over there," Lita said, pointing to the left transept, "and the fellows can play from up here. It will be lovely."

"I can see it now. That will look magnificent." He paused. "You remember that soft turquoise-gray ceiling in that church behind Nob Hill in Albuquerque?" He put an arm around her shoulders and swept the other towards the choir. "How do you think it would look there?"

"The light from the clerestory would really make it pop, don't you think? 'Pop' seems to be the in word right now."

He squeezed her shoulder, teasing her. "Really, can't you see the morning light against that rough surface? It would look soft. It would glow."

Lita could see it. She could feel it, too. Gracious, it had been a long time since a man had touched her, simply sharing how grand it was to be alive and to be with you.

"Oh, it would. I like that idea! While we're at it, do you think that plaster technique where they mix marble dust into the plaster and then use car polishers to buff it smooth would look elegant here and in the narthex? Or would it be over the top?"

"I think, Lita, that you missed your calling. You should have been an interior decorator."

"That would have been fun, but how many of my neighbors would use my talents in their own homes? You've never even asked me to redo your place." She gave his ribs a gentle jab.

"Touché," he laughed. "Shall I walk you home?"

"How about I make you supper for your trouble? Would soup and sandwich do, or would you rather have a sandwich and soup? It's up to you."

"Hmmm, decisions are so hard to make. I'll leave it up to you. If you don't want to slave in the kitchen, I could take you out."

"We ate at Tessie's last week and you paid."

"It was my pleasure."

"Emilio, twice-a-week evening meetings to check on the progress of the building are going to add up, and there are the biweekly meetings when all the committee comes and we go to Tessie's afterwards for lunch."

"Ah, but everyone pays their own tab then."

When they reached Lita's, Glow was ready for attention. While Lita fixed them a quick supper, Emilio let the dog out and then played ball with her in the sala. From the kitchen, Lita kept hearing laughing and a ball bouncing this way and that.

There was a sudden silence.

Then she heard Emilio shout, "Praise God!"

She hurried into the sala in time to see Emilio exiting her bedroom with the dog, a ball, and a stupid grin.

"What is it?"

"I think I love you, you sneaky, clever, mysterious, wonderful woman!"

He plopped Glow on the sofa and took her in his arms. He laughed while he spun her around and gave her a big kiss on her forehead. "Do you realize I thought I was the only one?"

"What are you talking about?"

"I saw the picture when I went looking for the ball. I haven't voted for a Damnocrat since Kennedy! That's what I'm talking about!"

"So you know. Can we just think of it as a confession and keep it just between ourselves?"

"Who else could I tell? It's safe with me, lovely Lita. I don't want to be run out of town, either."

Soup and sandwiches never tasted so good. They sat too long talking about politics, Michael Savage, Michael Medved, and that poor Glenn Beck.

Lita snuggled under the covers that night, listening to the last of The Savage Nation. Her mind was in a whirl. Her world had changed. She wasn't alone. Emilio had kissed her!

Luis had six cases of Coca-Cola delivered to Nurse Hadley, along with a note thanking her for all her help. The big man had indeed had plastic surgery. It had been at taxpayers' expense, after a fight in the laundry room at the Barstow detention facilities in 1988.

Luis and Nate had a satisfying work session after a dinner of KFC. Luis' wife was at work, presenting an offer on a duplex, and their son was at an away soccer game.

***

Earlier, Nate had stopped at Tessie's for lunch and had dropped into the bookmobile on his way over to look at the progress on the church.

A Mr. Owen Wills, the librarian, remembered almost hitting a rude cyclist a few weeks before Junior's body was found. He described the bike and the purple helmet, which matched the picture of the cyclist who always zipped by the Baca place in the South Valley.

"We'll be able to bring him in," said Luis.

"Boss, there were two break-ins, not one," said Nate. "The first was at Mrs. Cordova's home. She's the grandmother of the girl who was killed last Christmas. I think the granddaughter is the one who is getting all that money given in her name for the church in Los Santos. The second break-in is the one Lenny told me about the day he found Junior's body, a week or so before Lenny's own office was tossed. Nothing seems to have been taken on either occasion."

"So?" asked Luis.

"So, I leaned a little on Lenny and he admitted that those classified ads were put in the papers in three states by the police station. Guess who footed the bill?"

"Mrs. Cordova."

"Bingo, boss!"

"Then New York sends money to Catholic Charities for a church in Los Santos."

"Coincidence, boss?"

"I think I need to go see Mrs. Cordova."

It was snowing when Nate left the Fernandez house. Luis' wife, Lydia, and son, whom she had apparently picked up from soccer, were pulling into the drive as he was pulling out. They waved as the garage door went up.

Nate wished he had someone waiting at home.

A few hours later, the phone on the Fernandez bedside table rang. It was three a.m.

"Fernandez," yawned Luis.

He listened and sat up, rubbing his face. A coed had been found in Tijeras Canyon. They'd found her body in the trunk of a car left at the turnoff for Cedar Crest on Highway 14.

"I'll be at the morgue in twenty—make that thirty minutes."

Luis jumped into his clothes and hurried out the door, only to have his sedan T-boned by a drunk on Candelaria. An ambulance took him to Presbyterian Hospital. He had broken ribs, a collapsed lung, a crushed pelvis, and other assorted internal injuries. The drunk who caused the accident went to the emergency room with a broken arm and a fake ID.

The hospital called Lydia Fernandez, who called the police station. Somebody else would have to go wherever Luis had been headed. Only nobody ever called somebody. Nate finally went after he'd heard about the accident.

Luis was in the hospital till December fifteenth. Nurse Ellen Hadley came to see him a few times, and he remembered her thanking him for the too many Cokes he'd sent for losing their plastic surgery bet.

The office brought work for him to do in the hospital, and when he was released, he worked from home for over a month. Frank or Nate would bring papers to sign and a little more work each day. Frank kept him abreast of station politics and his own infatuation with Beverly Gordon. Luis was glad it sounded like they were talking marriage. That would be one less thing to worry about. He knew Lt. Gordon's parents.

The police had located the cyclist, Ricky Travis, and had brought him to the Fernandez residence, as a person of interest, for questioning. They threatened to arrest him with conspiracy to commit a felony.

It was an empty threat, but it sounded real enough to Mr. Travis. It scared the bejeezus out of him as he sat on a kitchen chair, across from Luis' solemn face, with Nate and Frank standing over him.

Ricky saw his future crumble before him. He saw his wasted education and the student loans he'd still be responsible for repaying.

In his mind's eye, Karla's tear-streaked face looked at him accusingly.

How could he live in a cell without his bike?

He had trouble understanding, when Captain Fernandez said, "Mr. Travis, we are going to let you go on your own recognizance, but you must be aware that we can and will arrest you at any time. Do you understand, Mr. Travis?"

When the words sank in, Ricky wept. He hadn't cried since he'd watched his dad kick the crap out of his mom when he was eleven.

He was still sniveling when they put him in the squad car to take him back to his apartment.

Dolores Maldonado sat in the warden's office after her bimonthly visit with her brother. His face had been all bruised, and he had cowered on his side of the glass partition.

She had done all she could to protect him, doing what she had been told to do. Now it was time to try another approach.

The warden was taking notes and playing with the buttons on a recording device.

Out came her story: The two men, the threats, the baking and icky icing colors, the sorting of jelly beans and spice drops to get enough of just one color...

"So what was the code? Do you know, Miss Maldonado?"

When she nodded and shrugged, he continued, "Would you be willing to talk to the Albuquerque Police? They are the ones who arrested Mr. Luna, who's now in prison, and we think he has something to do with all this. I'll see what I can do to keep your brother safe."

"Thank you."

"You see, there's another type of color code associated with Peter. Men, the other prisoners, bring him bandanas of different colors when they go out with the road crews. I'll have APD contact you, okay? You'll be hearing from a Captain Fernandez or one of his officers."

"Thank you."

Nate Courtney came up to Dolores' apartment in Santa Fe to get a statement. The description of the men she gave matched those of Raul Apodaca and Manny Archuleta, Al Luna's henchmen.

Nate and Dolores both enjoyed their time together.

"Would you be free for dinner this weekend?" Nate found himself asking.

"That would be wonderful," she smiled.

Then Nate went to the prison out south of Santa Fe surrounded by chamisa and scrub. There, the warden told Nate the story he'd just heard from Dolores, and about the "gifts" Petey received from the other inmates working with the road crews. Nate wasn't surprised to learn Petey's cell was directly across from Alfred Luna's.

Luis is going to have fun with these puzzle pieces, thought Nate.

***

Once he had all the pieces it took Luis four days to solve the puzzle.

Going by Dolores' calendar and the dates from the prison warden as to when the road crews went out to keep the Land of Enchantment looking that way, one mile at a time, he was able to deduce that it all depended on the weather. In bad weather, Miss Maldonado got flowers. In good weather, the roads were festooned with bandanas.

The color black meant something bad. Al had seen the black code only once. That was before Junior Baca was killed and after Ricky Travis was seen around Los Santos. It happened about the time Mrs. Cordova had her house broken into.

Luis needed phone records from the prison, to determine if Al had anything to do with either event.

Just to double-check himself, he had called the National Weather Service. He now had a day-by-day listing of county weather sent to his office. It would cover the times between Big Al's incarceration and the present. Frank would bring it to him when it came in.

Being bed-bound was good for some things, but Luis sure would be glad not to have to rely on everyone else.

Three days later, Luis was feeling good about his hunches. Sure enough, when the weather allowed, the road crews were used to bring in the bandanas. When it rained or snowed or blew sand and dirt in from another state, Dolores was busy in her kitchen.

Luis was in his own kitchen leaning against the cabinet for support, trying to make lunch, when there was a familiar knock on the door.

"Come in, Nate," he yelled.

"Sir, we have a problem. I just got a call from the warden in Santa Fe. Petey Maldonado has been killed. They found him in the bathroom off the library. The cause seems to be prison water-boarding. He couldn't have had any information. It must'a taken two guys to hold him upside down. Do you suppose it was a warning to Dolores?"

Nate ran his hand through his red hair. Luis handed him a cup of coffee. He looked at the mug and then at his boss. Shaking his head, he said "We sure have gotten her in a bad situation."

"I'll call Mitch about getting her into a witness protection program. It's too late for her brother, but maybe Dolores would jump at the chance."

"How about me driving up to Santa Fe now and discussing the idea with her? We've kinda hit it off. Maybe she'd listen to me."

***

Owen Wills was busy packing a large shopping bag for Jovita—books that had come in on interlibrary loan. She was becoming quite serious about pH balances and soil amendments. Each bed or planting area for the new church would be specially prepared for the needs of the specimens she had selected.

Virgie, bless her heart, had given up romance novels and was reading old copies of interior design magazines and reading a book on the psychological impact of color to try and come up with a visual color theme that would please the entire committee and Father Mondragon.

What a job, he thought. From bodice rippers to this esoteric psychobabble, Virgie was having a metamorphosis.

Owen was flabbergasted when Lita put her books on the counter.

"Hello, Owen. I'm so tired of church stuff, the building program, and real problems. I don't have room in my head for anything real." She patted the books. "Maybe these will take my mind off reality for a while."

He looked at the authors. There were several Nora Roberts, a Danielle Steel, a Robyn Carr, and two Diana Gabaldons, *Outlander* and *Dragonfly in Amber*.

"I'm sure they will, Lita."

He was sure she was going to be taken to some places she had never been before. He needed to remember the titles for his wife, Miriam.

***

Benito flew home for Thanksgiving weekend. He and Lita were invited up to Hugh's. Ben couldn't wait to see Sweetie. At eighteen, three months seemed like an ice age. Lita was positive that Sweetie felt the same about him.

When they sat at the table and Hugh asked the blessing, Lita eyed the food. It wasn't like any Thanksgiving dinner she'd ever eaten. Sweetie had fixed it herself. There was a roasted chicken from Trader Joe's in Taos (Sweetie said she thought she should start small and work her way up to a turkey maybe next year).

The girl hadn't known to pour off the liquid from the can of sweet potatoes, and the marshmallows were floating on top. The crescent rolls were from the dairy case. Lita bet the Jell-O salad came from the same place.

The men smiled adoringly at Sweetie. The redhead blushed with pride at what she had been able to do. Lita remembered that feeling.

At least Sweetie had allowed Lita to bring the desserts, so they finished the meal with homemade pumpkin and pecan pies.

While the young ones did the dishes, Hugh and Lita sat in the cavernous sala by the fire and sipped their coffee.

He gestured in the direction of the kitchen, where they could hear giggling.

"I think it would be the most prudent course, Lita, if Sweetie and I declined your invitation to join you and Ben in El Paso over Christmas. We should take a trip of our own. Sweetie has never seen how they do Christmas in Europe. Hell, I don't know how they do it, either. Don't you reckon it would be smart to put a slow leak in that hot air balloon in there?"

She took a sip of coffee. "Hugh, have I ever told you how wise I think you are...and how glad I am that you have to take the blame for this separation?"

"We all do what we must," he intoned, "for the children, you know."

She chuckled. "And hope they don't hold it against us for the rest of our lives."

Father Mondragon sensed that Lita had been avoiding him since last spring. Was it because he had suggested there was something wrong with her? He had to admit she was pumping on all cylinders now. Yes, she had really picked up since the walls had risen.

He was just as proud of the new church as she was. Just think, they would always remember that he, Father John Xavier Mondragon, was the leader of this parish when they erected this beautiful church to the work of Jesus Christ. Praise the Lord!

He was a bit surprised when she called him at home that afternoon, and he was perplexed by her opening statement.

"Father, I feel the need to clear up something between us and thank you for being such a good sport about everything."

"You're welcome, I'm sure, but what are you talking about?"

"The church, of course."

"What about it?"

"Really, Father, I know you've always been critical of churches that have used drug money..."

"I certainly have."

"Then why didn't you say anything when I told you?"

"You never told me anything!"

"But I did from the first!"

"How so?"

"Remember, I told you I had found something of value and I asked if I could give it away, and you said yes?"

"You mean you found real money?"

"Of course, and then I kept telling you how guilty I felt when those men kept dying."

"You mean it was because you had stolen their money?"

"Don't put it that way, Father. I found it. I never stole it!"

"You are telling me...," his voice rose—and she would have been worried if she could have seen the pallor in his face—"that our church is being built with money that has bought and sold drugs?"

"Well, apparently, one way or another. I'm not sure which."

He started wheezing. "I must call someone."

"Must you?"

"Lita, I can't believe you kept this a secret."

"Father, you are being obtuse. I told you every step of the way. I even followed your directions on what to do with it."

His eyesight was going gray. He couldn't seem to fill his lungs.

"I must go," he wheezed.

Lita heard the line go dead.

He tried to dial the Archbishop, but dropped the phone. Pain shot down his arm. He was angry! Lita was the snake in his little Eden. He had always thought her a good, righteous woman, and here she was doing Satan's work all along!

His housekeeper found his body that evening when she came to heat up some supper for him. The poor man, God rest his soul, had been trying to call for help.

***

Lita felt even guiltier for Father Mondragon's passing than she had for all those other deaths she'd confessed. She cried herself to sleep with Glow licking her face.

The next morning, she awoke to the liberating realization that he had died taking all her secrets and sins with him and now he'd never be able to tell anyone! "Praise be to God."

Virgie thought he'd died because he was such a sour old thing.

Jovita thought that maybe he believed the new church would mean too much work for him, and he stepped aside for a younger priest the easiest way he knew how.

Tessie assumed he just wore out. Next to Lita, she'd cried the most.

Deacon Emilio thought...it must be time to move on.

Los Santos had only a memorial Mass for their priest. He was buried in Pueblo, Colorado, where his family had roots.

Luis spent days looking at photographs of the Bacas' Our Lady of Guadalupe. He had had an "aha" moment when he was able to put Ricky Travis at the scene on a particular date, on a specified road, near a mile marker...the one where they'd found Junior's body.

He didn't learn anything looking at the black-and-white pictures, but going to the colored photos, he could read the code. It was a simple color grid with red, yellow, and blue identifying the date, the road, and the mile marker respectively. For example, a red poppy next to the three purple iris stood for Wednesday. Any color or flower could be used for the day. It was the number of flowers that was important. A yellow rose followed by two pink tulips, four orange zinnias, and a red carnation would mean highway, road or farm road 241. Red was the first color, which stood for the date, so the color could be used again as a number. It made sense to have red stand for the number one as in the colors of the flag—red, white and blue, red comes first. Pink would come next to red on the color wheel and would be two, etc. Likewise, blue could be used as a number, as well as the flag for a mile marker.

Going back over the pictures by date, Luis could pinpoint places on the map. He had some of his junior officers out pinpointing descancos to the nearest corresponding mile marker.

The Bacas had been using the descanos as drop boxes for their payments or goods. Junior's death wasn't a part of the operation, but a message from someone.

"Hey, you guys," piped up Frank, when Luis had explained the code. "Remember that story we all laughed about last summer when that guy back East got buried under that pile of pinto beans? Then Junior had his face stuffed with them. Think they're connected?" asked Frank.

"Frank, I love your memory, but where the hell has it been the last seven months? You should try using it more often.

"After next month, the doctors tell me I'll be able to sit for a few hours at a time. Let's celebrate by going to Los Santos. I need to talk with Mrs. Cordova."

Luis rested in his recliner after his doctor's appointment. He wished he felt like working in his garden. His roses needed attention. He read an article about the drop in available drugs on the street, and was wondering if the feds would transfer some money into rehabilitation centers when his phone rang.

"Fernandez here."

"Boss, it's Nate. Where have you been?"

He started to answer, but Nate kept on talking. "Boss, there's big trouble. At the meeting with Mitch this morning, all hell broke loose! I wish you could have been there to fix things."

"Slow down, Nate. What are you talking about?"

"Jerry and I were there giving your report, and Jerry let it slip about Mrs., Cordova and her maybe ties to the case. Mitch hit the fan. He kept hollering how hard it was to work with dumb Mexicans. Then he really blew up, saying how all spicks stick together and he knew Estrellita Cordova was guilty as hell! He got on his cell right there and called a judge for a warrant for Mrs. Cordova's arrest! Then he called his office and told them to send two agents after the warrant and to pick her up - get this - for the murders of Christina Cordova and Manuel C. Baca, II, and for suspicion of drug trafficking!"

"Nate, get hold of Leonard Salazar in Los Santos and have him fax the accident report from when the girl died. And find out if Lita has a lawyer. Then get him or her to Albuquerque ASAP! Next, come get me. I still can't drive!"

"Yes, sir."

"Oh, and find the funeral home that did the service for Christina Cordova. Have them fax you a copy of her death certificate. That would be quickest. Find an autopsy report on Junior, too."

"I'm on it. See you as soon as I can make it."

"God! I hate that ignorant, prejudiced S.O.B.! Mitch, I'm coming after you!"

Luis was outside leaning on his front door when Nate arrived. He'd made a list of people to call. His list of phone numbers was in his office, or he'd have already called a few.

As they pulled out the drive, Nate reached in his pocket. "Jerry taped the meeting." He handed over the cassette. "He wanted you to know how well we'd given your report."

"Keep it, and make at least five copies. I think they'll come in handy." Luis smiled to himself, and added the Attorney General to his list. He was going to make life a living hell for Mitch Sweeney.

***

Two agents, a man and a woman, in flak jackets were at the door when Lita answered their knock.

"Estrellita Cordova?" the tall man asked. He stood straight and had short hair, like a military officer.

"Yes," she said. "May I help you?"

Both agents reached into their breast pockets and held up their credentials. "Mrs. Cordova, we have a warrant for your arrest for drug trafficking, and for the murders of Christina Cordova and Manuel Baca, II."

Lita gaped at them.

The woman agent began reading Lita her rights. It was the same one she heard every week on CSI! No matter what her rights were, she thought she'd faint right there in her own front door. Lita took a breath. At least they weren't drug dealers!

"Come in a moment. I need to call someone to come take care of my dog."

The agents exchanged glances. "You have the right to one call," the man said. "But first we'll need to handcuff you and do a search."

Lita was still staring at the bracelets around her wrists as the woman agent began to do a body search. She jumped when the woman's hands began moving over her body, looking for a weapon, she supposed. The agent found some hairpins and paperclips in one pocket and dog biscuits and a tissue in another. While she was doing that, the man took pictures of her calendar and address book. While the man searched the house, taking pictures, the woman let Lita use the phone, but stood right next to her while she dialed Emilio. Lita's knees gave way and the woman helped her into a chair. His answering machine came on. Thank goodness!

"Deacon Maestas, this is Lita Cordova. I find I will be gone for a while. Will you please come take care of Glow?" Her voice cracked when she said, "please." "It might be quite a while. The door will be unlocked. Thank you."

She turned to the agents. "Shall we go? Do I need my purse? It has my driver's license. Do I need a picture ID?"

"If you wish, but it will be taken from you when you're processed."

When they were all seated in the black SUV, Lita asked the young woman to go back in and unplug the coffee pot. "And, oh, the hose is running on my tomatoes in the backyard."

She sat as straight as she could in the backseat, praying as hard as she ever had, with an imaginary rosary slipping through her fingers. She was being blamed for Tina's death! How cruel! How ridiculous! She started praying again.

Lita opened her eyes and noticed they were on the south side of Santa Fe. She sighed, and supposed they thought she was horrible. She couldn't let them think that of her. "So, how long have you two lived in Albuquerque? Which church do you go to?"

By the time they reached the headquarters in Albuquerque, she knew that the young woman, Carol, was married and had a baby at home with her mother-in-law. Rowan, the man, played handball and had a four-year-old basset hound named Drool.

They were polite and walked on each side of her into the building. Rowan went to find a man named Sweeney. Carol took her downstairs where she was ushered into a room they called the Booking Office. There they filled out paperwork on her. That was bad enough, but then she was led behind a curtain where she had to take her clothes off and undergo a strip search! How humiliating! It felt degrading! Even her doctor in Taos never touched her in all those private places! She had to put on an orange outfit. Was it called a jumpsuit? They put the handcuffs back on her. She was fingerprinted and photographed. Carol was waiting to take her to Mr. Sweeney's office.

Mr. Sweeney was not as nice as Carol or Rowan.

He glared at her from across his desk. "Mrs. Cordova, I've had a call from a lawyer in Taos, a Floyd Patrick. Does he represent you?"

"Yes." Who had called Floyd? She didn't want him to know about this!

"He's on his way."

"Then we'd better wait on him, hadn't we?"

"Don't be flippant, lady!" God, she's a crafty bitch, thought Mitch. "After you have a chance to meet with him, we're going to have you take a lie detector test."

This wasn't going to be like going to confession at all! "I understand. Excuse me, Mr. Sweeney, could someone take me to the ladies' room? I think I'm going to be sick."

A female agent, older than Carol, leaned against the wall as Lita vomited, rinsed her mouth, and washed her hands and face. When she was through with her ablutions, the woman handed her a breath mint. Lita's eyes brimmed with tears. "Thank you," she whispered. They weren't all like Mr. Sweeney.

When she was taken back to that horrid man's office, he was on the phone and chewing his nails. Lita heard him say "Yes, ma'am. I'll get back to you. Thank you for calling, Governor."

He looked at her and sneered. "My, my, you do have friends in high places, don't you? While you've been gone, my phone's been ringing. Seems everyone knows you're here. Won't they be disappointed to learn you'll be living in a federal prison!"

A buzzer sounded. "That'll be your lawyer friend. Be quick about telling him your sob story, as if it'll do you any good. I have other things to do."

Floyd Patrick and Lita were put in a room with a coffee bar, a table and five chairs. Floyd put his briefcase on the table and headed for the coffee. "Do you want a cup before we start?"

She shook her head.

"Lita, what in the hell is going on?" He poured a cup, tasted it, and made a face. He set the cup aside.

"I'm not sure. I don't want to talk about it...Floyd, get me out of here, please!"

"Lita, I know you didn't have anything to do with Tina's death. What about the man, this Manuel C Baca, II? How can they think you're mixed up in dealing drugs?"

"What am I going to do?"

"Nothing! Lita, you're not going to do anything. You are not going to say anything to anyone. Is that clear?"

"Floyd, they want me to take a lie detector test."

"Not in my lifetime! We are going back in there and say you're ready to go to the Bernalillo County Detention Center where you will stay until we can get you before a judge and get you bailed out. We'll take it from there, one step at a time."

"How much is that going to cost?"

"Between one murder count and the drug charges you're looking at, well, at least a hundred thousand."

"I don't have that kind of money!"

"Yes, you do, in the Grant account. It'll about wipe you out, though. Don't worry about money now. Just think about getting out of here. I'm going to your house. There have to be some things that will prove you weren't anywhere close when this Baca character was killed. Do you remember when that was?"

"I can't remember my own name right now."

"Okay, I'll see what I can come up with. I probably won't see you until you see the judge to set your bond. I'll be there with the DA. I hear he's a good guy. It'll probably be tonight."

The next few hours were a nightmare in high speed. Lita finally sat in a cell, by herself. Handcuffs removed, she sat on her bunk rubbing her wrists, worrying about how she could come up with the money Floyd thought she needed. How much time would she be given to gather that amount? What if Floyd was wrong and it was more, or what if there wasn't that much in the Grant account? Her head kept spinning. How soon would they come to tell her when she would see the judge? She had to know what financial abyss she faced!

Somewhere, she heard an argument. Someone screamed. Guards ran by. She was relieved to be alone. She hoped Emilio had checked his messages. She didn't want to think of Glow being all by herself, without food and water or company.

It was much later when a guard came by and told her that all dockets were full for the evening court. She should settle in for the night.

She tried stretching out on the bunk, listening to the strange sounds around her. The lights were dimmed and the noise dropped in volume, but not enough.

Lita kept praying. She missed Glow. She missed Michael Savage. She must have slept. When she opened her eyes, the lights were back on and the noises were there. She wanted to shower in her own bathroom. She ate breakfast with the other inmates and was returned to her cell.

She learned to wait.

***

Captain Luis Fernandez had been busy. He'd been in touch with Lita's lawyer, Floyd Patrick. Floyd had brought down Lita's calendar, appointment book, and a bunch of pictures taken in various churches in Albuquerque. Lita was in some of them. He also brought a receipt from a Days Inn in Albuquerque. The dates from the motel matched the time of death on Junior's autopsy report. Luis made copies of everything, for himself, for the DA and for the judge. He added a copy of the tape of Mitch's ravings to each folder. The folder included two autopsy reports on Tina, as well as a copy of the accident report.

Luis quickly made his way to the DA's office. The two men had worked well together over the years and had grown to respect and trust each other.

"Paul, I want you to listen to a tape with me," he said as soon as he was through the door.

"Sure, Luis, but make it quick. I have documents to get to Judge Romero's chambers before a bail hearing this afternoon, and you know how he likes to know what's up before the perp and his lawyers are standing in front of him."

Luis nodded and pressed the play button. They listened in silence as Mitch Sweeney's voice filled the room.

The DA whistled.

"Will you see that Judge Romero gets a copy of this tape? There are other documents here, too, gathered by the defendant's lawyer and other parties."

A secretary knocked on the door. His Honor, Judge Claudio Romero, was waiting in his chambers.

"Thanks," said Luis. "I owe you one."

"Yes, you do, other party." They both laughed.

***

Judge Romero looked down at Lita as she stood between Floyd Patrick and the DA. The charges had been read. "We are here today to determine the amount of bail to be set for you, if you merit bail at all. I have spent the last hours reading over evidence in this case. I would like to begin by saying that the two charges of murder are baseless. Both charges are to be dropped. As for the charges brought against you for interstate trafficking of illegal substances, I would like to speak with you in my chambers before I hand down judgment."

Lita in her orange suit and handcuffs, her lawyer, and the DA, trooped into the judge's chambers.

"Sit down. Sit down. Gentlemen, I want to hear an account of exactly what Mrs. Cordova has been doing with her time, and why the FBI believes she's in business with drug dealers. Mrs. Cordova?"

"Go on," said Floyd. The DA nodded.

Lita was hesitant in front of these men. What would they think of her? Had she done everything right, or was she guilty for something she wasn't aware of? "It all started a year ago last Christmas..."

It took over an hour to tell her story and answer their questions. She never really said how much money she had sent to New York, or mentioned that some of it was gold and rare coins, but only that Catholic Charities had received almost ten million dollars. The men were stunned. The judge shook his head. The DA coughed. Floyd said, "Christ, you think you have money problems now! Lita, that's four million in taxes you're going to owe!"

"Why? I never banked it. I did what the law said I needed to do. I never said to the lawyer in New York exactly what I was sending him. Uncle Sam can't prove that I ever had it in my possession!"

Floyd bit his lips. "Lita, the law doesn't work that way."

Lita started to cry.

Judge Romero coughed, getting everyone's attention. "We need to get back in the courtroom so I can rule on Mrs. Cordova's bail."

Lita was so upset about owing the government four million dollars that she barely heard the Honorable Judge Claudio Romero say, "I find this case not prosecutable in my court. The accused is not involved in this case. Therefore, all charges are dismissed, and Mrs. Cordova is free to go." The gavel descended with a decisive blow.

Floyd hugged her and the DA shook her hand. She turned in time to see the back of Mr. Sweeney as he left the court.

"I'll take you home as soon as you've changed. I'll be in the lobby of the jail."

***

Having her own clothes on made Lita feel almost human. She'd signed for them, and they let her change behind the same curtain she'd been behind yesterday, or was it last year? Someone showed her the way to the lobby. Floyd wasn't there. She took a seat and waited, feeling abused and dirty. She wanted a bath. She wanted it to be last week, last year. Instead, she sat there trying to be invisible. She watched people passing by and tried to guess their destinations.

She closed her eyes and tried to imagine where she was going to come up with four million dollars. She doubted that if she were able to sell the entire land grant, which she couldn't, she would come close to that amount.

"Mrs. Cordova? My name is Nate Courtney. I'm with the Albuquerque Police Department. Our office has contacted Mr. Patrick, who is on his way back to Taos. We asked to escort you home. He'd appreciate a call from you tomorrow."

Lita took his proffered arm and walked dumbly out into a late afternoon sunshine and freedom.

When they were both buckled in, Nate reached into the backseat of the patrol car and handed her a warm sack. "I thought you might be hungry. Sadie's makes a great stuffed sopaipilla." He blushed to the roots of his red hair. "There's iced tea in there, too."

"Thank you," she said, wiping her eyes.

They drove in silence while Lita ate. After a while, the young officer said, "I'm sorry about what the F.B.I. put you through. Mitch, er, Mr. Sweeney, sometimes goes off on a wild goose chase...gets ahead of himself, you know. He gets frustrated and tries to take it out on someone else. His office is under a lot of pressure, you know. They are in charge of this interstate drug investigation and things aren't going well for them."

"This wild goose almost got cooked," she said. "I suppose it was you who contacted Floyd Patrick and had my granddaughter's autopsy and accident reports sent to him?"

"Yes, ma'am. Those things and a few others. Why don't you put your head back and try to rest. You're worn out."

Lita sat back and closed her eyes, but her brain was still working. So, Floyd wanted her to call. Well, he could wait a bit. She'd have to keep him on because of the land grant. Lawyers who specialized in those were rare birds in New Mexico. She yawned. Still she wanted a lawyer to take care of her personal business, and that was no business of Floyd Patrick! Then, for a while, she forgot to think.

When they reached Los Santos, Nate had to wake her up to get directions.

Lita said, "Don't take me home. Take me to my deacon's house. I need to get Glow, my dog." She pointed to the left and he turned the corner.

Nate opened the car door for her and helped her out. He waited till the porch light came on and a good-sized man came to the door. He supposed it was the deacon. The fellow had a wiggly little dog in his arms.

Lita turned and waved good-bye to Officer Courtney and went in. Glow vaulted from Emilio's arms into hers. Lita was hardly aware of Glow licking her face. She and Emilio stared at each other.

"Hello," he said.

"You've been working. You have blue paint on your cheek."

"It's cerulean."

"Oh."

"Lita, where have you been? Why was a policeman bringing you home?"

"It's a long story, Emilio. Do you have time for a pot of coffee, or better, a glass of wine?"

"You sit right there." He pointed to a comfortable leather chair. "I don't want you out of my sight. I've got a bottle of cabernet here somewhere."

"You find it and I'll wash up."

When she was seated, he brought in their wine and sat on the ottoman across from her. "I'm all ears and waiting," he said. "By the way, that dog is spoiled."

She took a sip of wine and ran her fingers through Glow's coat. Soon, the story was tumbling out, like water down a mountain stream.

Emilio would laugh and nod, or frown and sometimes ask a question. So it went. Three glasses of wine and a snack later, she came to a close, saying, "A woman of mystery does strange things. What time is it?"

He looked at his watch. "Twenty till two. Let me take you to your abode." He stood and held out his hand. When she took it and rose, he enfolded her in his arms. "We were all so worried. Lita, I was so afraid." He rocked her back and forth as if she were Sunny's age. "Mi amiga, do you realize how strong you have become? I am proud of you, but still I worry. Tell me you will be more careful."

She tilted back her head and smiled into his eyes. She felt so tipsy, sleepy, and safe.

It was warm for a March New Mexico morning. The sun had already melted a light dusting of snow on the sloping copper roof of the new church.

Nate, who was driving, whistled and they all gaped at the structure.

"Let's stop and take a tour," said Luis. "We have time." His hips were aching from the car ride. The three made their way slowly toward the site.

A man came out of the construction trailer and intercepted them. When they showed their badges, he shook their hands, put them in hard hats, and took them on a tour.

"It ain't as if'n the roof's gonna fall in, but sure as shoot'n, if you all didn't have these on, the inspector would show up. Things'd slow down, and we're being paid big bucks to see this job gets done on time. At this point, hats are just for show. We're down to the icing on the cake, mostly inside stuff. Nothing dangerous."

There were several men working on the Stations of the Cross, applying large, handmade tiles to the walls. Each intricately glazed tile was about eighteen inches square. They were being cemented to the rough base coat before the plaster was applied.

Two more men were almost finished installing stained glass windows. Each one was about four feet wide and went from two feet off the floor to within a foot of the ceiling, Nate figured about twenty-five feet. It was heavy, chunky stained glass.

One of the installers told them it was called faceted glass, made in Blanko, West Virginia, where they poured two-inch-thick slabs of glass in five-by-eight forms. Glass cutters cut the desired shapes, and hammers were used to chip clamshell flakes away, leaving glass that would shift and change with the light. The glass had then been placed in the patterns, and granules and epoxy had been poured between the glass. Then it had cured. Because of the size of the window, they had been constructed on site.

"I'll be happy to see those babies up and out of the way. We've all held our breath every time we had to walk by them. They ought to be finished day after tomorrow. Then we'll put on the plaster, buff it, scrub the floors, and go over everything with a fine-tooth comb. There's some ladies on the building committee who are demanding Taj Mahal quality."

"How much do you suppose all this has cost?" asked Nate when the three went back outside.

"According to the Archbishop's office, about six and a half million so far."

"You're pulling my leg!" squawked Frank. "Up here?"

Luis hobbled towards the car. "If you look around on that side, you'll see a clinic and some casitas. Those'll add to the cost.

"Frank, I want you and Nate to walk over to Tessie's Café and have lunch. Nate here tells me she's a good cook and has some great posters. I'm going to try out my driving skills on the quarter mile up to Mrs. Cordova's. I'll come back and pick you up."

Lita was surprised to see a man leaning on a cane at her door when she answered the knock. Glow, who seemed to be a good judge of character, wagged her tail.

"Hello, Mrs. Cordova, I'm Sgt. Luis Fernandez with the Albuquerque Police Department. I realize I'm out of my jurisdiction, but may I come in? I think you may be able to clear up some things for us. I'd like to apologize for the mix-up with the FBI a few weeks ago."

Lita opened the door. "What an interesting way of saying, 'you're under arrest, again.' Do come in."

He smiled. "Not under arrest at all, unless you murdered Manuel Baca, II."

"Gracious, no! Won't you sit? Wasn't that just awful? I will say it kept Tessie the center of attention for a while. She even went to the funeral."

"We know."

"Oh, then you must know everything?"

"Only the sequence, I'm afraid."

"I'm not sure where I fit in as far as the order goes, but I'll tell you what happened and when. Then you may ask your questions. Would that be all right?"

"Yes, ma'am."

"We have our Fiesta here in Los Santos in May. I cook beans every year. The house smells just awful. This year, as I was walking home from Chuy's, the general store, I noticed my granddaughter's descanso was crooked. That's the roadside cross we put up to honor her, you know."

"Yes, ma'am."

"I went to straighten it, the descanso, lost my balance in the soft dirt and fell. That's when I found the money. I fell right into it."

"How much?"

"Well, some of the little coins haven't been sold yet."

"To date then?"

"Some people in New York City may have really been generous."

He looked at her. "Ahem."

"Ten million, so far."

"Tell me what happened to the money."

"I hid it till I could figure that out, but not at home! Then I asked Father Mondragon if I could give away what I had found. He said yes, but that I'd better check, so I did. First, I had Silvia, at my husband's law office, look up the law. Next I called Lenny Salazar. I hope that boy won't get in any trouble for helping me. I asked him about putting an ad in the classifieds. He was such a sweetheart and took care of everything. If anyone had lost something and could identify it, it would have been returned. They only had to call the Sheriff's office."

"That's when your home and the station were broken into?"

"The station. The house was done during the Fiesta, in May. They killed my cat."

"So no one came forward to claim the money?"

"No," she smiled. "So I washed and ironed the bills. I had to use starch on the really limp ones."

Luis was trying to keep a straight face.

"I wore my new rubber gloves so as not to leave prints. I went through several pair, the ironing, you see. Then I took it to Albuquerque and mailed it, book rate, because you could read it. I shipped it to New York City, to a friend. There it was deposited in banks for the building fund in Christina's memory. But it takes forever to give that much money under the radar.

"To make things go more quickly, mission boxes were put into the churches in Manhattan. Someone at the church would take the box to the bank weekly. That way, huge sums could be donated and the churches would get credit for large mission gifts. I don't know how much money was given by New York church members, besides the other money stuffed in. I tell you, Sergeant, it was just like elections here in New Mexico!

"Anyway, the churches deposited their contributions, and then everything was shipped to Catholic Charities in Christina's name for a new church here. Would you like to see a copy of the letter?"

"Yes, and then I have a question. Did it ever occur to you, that first day, that it might be drug money?"

"Oh, yes, after that first moment, which was wonderful, I tell you. Yes, deep down I knew, but you don't know how badly we needed a new church. And Christina, bless her, had promised everyone a new roof on Christmas Eve. I'm sure you heard about that? What can I say? I felt like I was having a religious experience and that my granddaughter had kept her promise."

"Mrs. Cordova, it is truly a beautiful church."

"Yes, and when Jovita Esquivel puts in the gardens and flower beds this spring, it will be wonderful."

Luis studied the small woman before rising. He thought, Holy cow! This prim little lady has carried out a huge heist, followed every rule of both church and state, donated all the money to charity, and walked away clean!

"Sir, I did keep the bank bags. The ones that the coins came in. Do you want them? I had to rip the seams since I didn't have keys to the locks. I keep them in the car."

"Please. You know, if you haven't sold the coins yet, they could be traced to the buyer. It just might lead us to the person who killed Mr. Baca."

"Who would the money belong to then? Would it be returned to Christina's Fund? We have plans for that money."

"I believe the coins would still be yours, or the funds. No one came forward to claim it, did they?"

"No," she smiled. "I'll give you the number of my lawyer in New York. You can talk to him."

Bubbling Crock-Pots and roaster ovens filled Lita's kitchen. It was Fiesta time again. The community had decided to wait till now to dedicate the church. Tessie had commandeered the new kitchen for a celebration meal and all the electrical outlets were being used for other dishes, so Lita found herself cooking beans again. Was she going to be stuck doing beans like Emilio was stuck with church work?

It had been hard on Emilio, Lita thought. Giving long hours as an artisan to the building project on top of the homilies, visitations, and all that was expected of a deacon. It was too much. He looked tired.

A traveling priest, Father Paul, came in once a week to hear confessions and to bless the bread and wine, but all the rest seemed to fall on Emilio.

Emilio looked the part, she thought, as she added more garlic and chile pepper to the beans. He was tall and strong, with those wide shoulders and smile lines, so kind. That's what Peter must have looked like when he heard, "Come follow me." Would he become their priest as the bishop was urging? She hoped not; he'd have to leave and go to seminary.

She should hurry. Virgie's husband, Mel, had promised to pick up her food at ten to take to the church. It was almost that now.

***

The church was glorious that afternoon. People had come from everywhere to celebrate. Even Captain Fernandez was there with a group of people from Albuquerque.

"Mrs. Cordova, may I introduce my wife, Lydia. And these are my men, Nate Courtney and Frank Quintana, and their novias, Dolores Maldonado and Beverly Gordon."

"Thank you for coming. Hello again, Officer Courtney. It's nice to see you under different circumstances."

"That it is. It's a beautiful church."

"I'm glad you like it."

"Breathtaking!" said Miss Maldonado.

"Isn't it?"

"Last but not least, this is Mitchell Sweeney, of the FBI office in Albuquerque."

Lita swallowed. "It's good of you to come help us celebrate."

"I came to apologize for bringing you in on what you might consider trumped-up charges and to see if I could get you to come work for me. I need a criminal mind to help catch the bad guys when I return to Washington."

Luis changed his glare to an icy smile. "Agent Sweeney is taking a desk job next week. Quite a demotion, wouldn't you say, Mitch?"

There was a frozen silence.

Lydia gasped.

Nate blushed.

Lita laughed lightly. "Maybe another time, but I'll take that as a compliment. If you'll excuse me, I see someone I must speak to."

She spotted Benito and Sweetie. They had both gotten away from school. Ben, she knew, had taken his finals early. She had no idea how Sweetie had managed to get away.

Hugh waved from behind them. He made a great acompañante. Kip was with the group, having arrived two days earlier. He'd brought the empty plastic cases and enlarged photographs of each coin for identification. Perhaps he could give them to Captain Fernandez today and save him and Lita a trip to Albuquerque. Luis and Kip had come to an understanding that if the coins were turned over to the authorities, the church could claim them, but both men agreed Lita needed them to pay taxes on the money when it was in her possession. Kip told her that Captain Fernandez had reminded him that justice was blind. Lita had been worried sick, thinking she had to come up with all that money! Perhaps everything would work out.

Kip had arrived two days ago and this was his third visit to the church. He was still finding new things to comment on. He could take care of business later.

Jovita was thrilled that people were interested in her gardens. She was holding forth, in her new black dress, about the dogwood she was trying to grow in the garden between the Lady's chapel and the hallway leading to the kitchen and multipurpose room.

Lita passed by on her way to see if she could help in the kitchen where Tessie and her daughters reigned. They shooed her out when Virgie came running up, rearranging her pink silk scarf that had slipped again.

"Lita!" called Virgie as she pushed her glasses back in place.

"What is it?"

"Have you been to the Lady's chapel?"

"Not yet. Why? Is there something wrong?"

"No, nothing, but Emilio finally brought the Santo for the altar! You need to see it!"

Lita made her way back down the hall and into the narthex, admiring the old Santos who looked down from their scattered nichos.

"Hola," she smiled and hugged and shook hands as she passed into the sanctuary where she genuflected toward the altar. The Archbishop would use Amy's new communion set there in a little while. People were beginning to find their places for the ceremony and the bells were ringing. She didn't have much time.

She turned into the Lady's chapel and admired the blue-green faceted glass at the top and bottom of the windows. She could see the Santo's blue robes – no, cerulean – and moved closer. Where were her glasses?

Her hands went to her mouth. Tears filled her eyes.

Emilio had used the skills he had acquired in Germany, and now she was looking at the face of her Christina, dressed in the robes of the Virgin Mary.

"Do you think it's in bad taste to have used her as a model?"

Lita turned at the sound of his voice.

"Emilio, she is lovely! Stories will be told about her for years. You have made her into a legend. Thank you. What else can I say?" One tear ran down her cheek.

"The chances are you'll think of something. She was made for you."

Acknowledgments

I want to thank my husband, Dewey Johnson, for being patient with me over the time it took to tell this story.

Thanks also to Sandra Scofield and other teachers at the University of Iowa Summer Writing Festival. They have so much to share with wannabe writers. I hope I have not disappointed them.

What would storytellers do without listeners and readers to edit and critique their work? Thank you, Sally Borgerson, Mary Seal and Yetta Tropp. You are dear to me.

Many people helped me with facts I did not know: Jan Vessel, Yvonne Lopez, John Phillips, Joe Cunningham, Dennis Burt, Jim Cramer (author of *Become a Thinking Fly Tier*), and the nice man at Ford who knew that 1986 was the last year that a separate key was used for the ignition of the Mustang.

Thanks to New Mexico for allowing me to watch your people and note their idiosyncrasies and learn how deeply they care for one another. Thank you for teaching me to dance in the rain.

Special thanks and love to Janet Thompson for her support and for believing in this project. Both she and Humano Productions LLC helped poke, prod, and pray *Stolen Miracles* into existence.

My love and gratitude to each of you.

Have you ever visited in New Mexico? Did the author capture any of your experiences? What impressed you? What are the vistas? The colors? The foods? Would you go back?

Think about the title for a moment. How many miracles do you think were stolen? Which ones were they? Which was your favorite deed of questionable intent?

Most of the major characters in this book are 'past their prime.' How many other novels can you think of that have similar (age? personality? etc.) Who are the leading characters? What, if anything, do they have in common?

There are many female characters. Which character do you identify with?

New Mexico is described by geologists as high desert. Have you ever tried growing anything in a "high desert" area? What are the difficulties? Does Jovita impress you with her gardening abilities? She seems to make everything thrive. Why do you think she was unable to make her marriage work?

All small towns are different. Those in New Mexico include as many, if not more herbivores than people. Both are bound in a close-knit community. Is this concept of community foreign to you?

Estrellita Maria c'de Roybal y Cordova is quite a mouthful. What does this name mean? Do you think it is a reflection of her character or vice versa? What part does a name play in who one becomes?

Lita is land rich. Is her concept of husbanding her 'wealth' a smart approach to go through life or has it limited her?

After making her momentous decision about what to do with the money, Lita finds herself explaining things in half truths. Have you ever found this a convenient way to handle a sticky situation? How did it work out?

Emilio's abeulas (grandmothers) called Lita "a votress." Do you think they were correct?

Where did Emilio's abeulas (grandmothers) come from?

Do you remember your first love? Have you ever wondered about the might-have-beens? Why do you think Emilio and Lita have never become an item? Is there hope for them?

Memorials on highways are governed by state laws. Have you notices descansos along highways in your communities? What do you think or feel when you see one?

There is much to laugh about in this story. Is this book merely humorous, or is there a more serious message?

What role does the wind play in the story?

Does your community have a Lita? Jovita? Virgie? How do they cause and implement change?

Lita's family has lived in the same place in America for over 400 years. She would object to being referred to as a "Latina." How does she compare to people in your community who speak Spanish? How would you identify and describe Lita?

If this story were on television, who would play the leading characters? What prequels or sequels would you most enjoy knowing about?

Was the ending satisfying? Why?

CPSIA information can be obtained at www.ICGtesting.com
Printed in the USA
LVOW13s2359210314

378476LV00004B/284/P

9 780865 346581